AT SOME POINT, DOMINGO'S LATE-NIGHT RELAXATION WAS INTERRUPTED BY . . .

Well, that was the million-dollar question, wasn't it?

Someone came inside. There was, Ray guessed, an argument. While Domingo's back was turned, the other person snatched up the nearest heavy object and bashed Domingo over the head with it. Still holding the lighter, he—or she, no telling yet, although the person was probably at least as tall as Domingo and strong enough to kill with a single blow—wiped his fingerprints off it. He wrote the word "quantum" on the wall, presumably using a tool and not his finger, since he was obviously careful not to leave fingerprints anywhere else, and then he took his leave.

The killer had not, at a glance, left any signposts pointing to his identity. Unless the mystery word was somehow one. If so, it was as vague a signpost as Ray could imagine.

Ray had not been at this job for as long as his colleagues, but he understood the fundamental principles underlying it. Everyone left traces of themselves on people with whom they came in contact. Maybe it was the orange hairs, maybe the bits of plant fiber, maybe fingerprints he had not yet located, but somewhere in this house was the key—the signpost Ray needed.

He would keep looking until he found it.

Original novels in the CSI series:

CSI: Crime Scene Investigation
Double Dealer
Sin City
Cold Burn
Body of Evidence
Grave Matters
Binding Ties
Killing Game
Snake Eyes
In Extremis
Nevada Rose
Headhunter
Brass in Pocket
The Killing Jar
Blood Quantum
Serial (graphic novel)

CSI: Miami
Florida Getaway
Heat Wave
Cult Following
Riptide
Harm for the Holidays: Misgivings
Harm for the Holidays: Heart Attack
Cut & Run
Right to Die

CSI: NY
Dead of Winter
Blood on the Sun
Deluge
Four Walls

CSI:

CRIME SCENE INVESTIGATION™

BLOOD QUANTUM
a novel

Jeff Mariotte

Based on the hit CBS series "CSI: Crime Scene
Investigation" produced by CBS PRODUCTIONS,
a business unit of CBS Broadcasting Inc.

Executive Producers: Jerry Bruckheimer,
Carol Mendelsohn, Anthony E. Zuiker,
Ann Donahue, Naren Shankar, Cynthia Chvatal,
William Petersen, Jonathan Littman

Series created by: Anthony E. Zuiker

POCKET **STAR** BOOKS
New York   London   Toronto   Sydney

Pocket Star Books
A Division of Simon & Schuster, Inc.
1230 Avenue of the Americas
New York, NY 10020

First Pocket Star Books paperback edition March 2010

POCKET STAR BOOKS and colophon are registered trademarks of Simon & Schuster, Inc.

For information about special discounts for bulk purchases, please contact Simon & Schuster Special Sales at 1-866-506-1949 or business@simonandschuster.com.

The Simon & Schuster Speakers Bureau can bring authors to your live event. For more information or to book an event, contact the Simon & Schuster Speakers Bureau at 1-866-248-3049 or visit our website at www.simonspeakers.com.

Cover design by David Stevenson

Manufactured in the United States of America

10 9 8 7 6 5 4 3 2 1

ISBN 978-1-4391-6078-7
ISBN 978-1-4391-6927-8 (ebook)

Acknowledgments

My sincere gratitude goes out to all the hardworking people behind *CSI*, to Maryann, to Ed, to Dianne Larson, to Howard and Katie, to the Crime Lab Project, and to authors Jeff Edwards, Jan Burke, and Dr. D. P. Lyle, MD.

This one's for Anita, who knows all about science.

1

IT ALL HAPPENED SO fast.

That was what people always said about this sort of thing, as if their minds couldn't quite keep up with the rocket-propelled pace of events. That wasn't how Drake McCann felt about it, though. To him, it had happened at the speed of life, no faster and certainly no more slowly.

He had been kicking back in his suite on the Cameron estate, watching some late-night TV with Kathleen Slides, the family's live-in housekeeper. They were friendly, nothing more complicated than that. Both were single, but he knew he wasn't her type. If he had a type, he had never figured out what it was, despite years of trial and error. And although he had dated fellow employees a couple of times, it always seemed to go bad. Someone made a mistake, and the whole situation ended up in Mrs. Cameron's lap, and she gave one of those stern lectures she was so good at, talking to the help as if they were wayward toddlers, and then fired one of them. So far, he had been lucky and had not been the primary target of her wrath, but last time it had been close, and McCann had decided not to take that chance again. The world was full of women who didn't work for his employer

Kathleen was a petite blonde who wasn't hard on the eyes, they had some laughs together, and they both enjoyed watching celebrities plug their wares on the tube after Mrs. Cameron had dismissed them and the day's work was done. That was good enough for now. He didn't need romance, and he enjoyed her company, and she seemed comfortable in his. Safe all the way around.

McCann was in charge of security for the estate, so even though he had a man on duty, when the front gate opened up, red lights flashed on instrument panels in his living room and bedroom. No visitors were expected that night, so he flicked on a monitor and selected the camera trained down the driveway toward the gate.

He was reaching for his phone when the call came in.

"I see him," McCann said.

"Know him?" Lyle Armstrong asked.

"Never seen him before." The monitor showed a white male who looked homeless at best and maybe deranged on top of it. His clothes were filthy, pants with the knees blown out and the hems ragged from being walked on, a shirt that might once have been white underneath a corduroy blazer that looked as if it had been wrapped around a truck tire and driven on for a hundred miles of hard road. The guy could have been wearing the jacket at the time. His hair was long and wild, ditto his thick brown beard. McCann could make out some facial scars from there, over the small monitor. The man's eyes glinted with madness, and he had an uneven gait, not quite a limp but almost. His hands were empty, but they kept bunching into tight fists, then relaxing.

"I'm in the control room. Want me to—"

McCann cut off the question. "You stay on the cameras, Lyle. And call the police. I'll intercept him."

He turned away from the monitor and nearly ran into Kathleen, who had come up behind him and was staring at the screen. "Who do you think that is?" she asked.

"No idea."

"But he came through the gate, right?"

The gate had still been swinging shut when the image first appeared on McCann's monitor. "Yeah. He must have got the code from someone, or he just got lucky. Either way, he's not supposed to be here."

Because Kathleen had been over, McCann was still dressed in a polo shirt and khaki pants. He pulled on a windbreaker against the cool of the April night, slipped on some loafers, and took a .38 revolver from his gun cabinet. It was loaded—he didn't keep unloaded weapons in the cabinet—but just the same, he checked to make sure.

"Be careful," she said.

"This is what I do," he reminded her. "Anyway,

that guy's not going to be a problem. His kind never is. Probably just off his meds."

"Should I go to my room?"

"You can stay here if you want. I'll be back in a few. Let me know if Letterman says anything funny."

With the .38 in his hand and his hand in the windbreaker pocket, he went out, locking the suite's front door behind him. He had a private entrance, off the back of the main house. A paved walkway led around the west side of the building, down along the tennis court, then wound through a rose garden and over to the driveway. McCann took it at a near jog, wanting to get in front of the guy before he got close to the house. Helena Cameron had enough problems these days. The last thing she needed was to worry about intruders.

When McCann emerged from the roses, the stranger was still a good way down the flood-lit drive. His limp made his progress slow and ungainly, almost as if he had to remind his left leg to keep up with the right at every step. He was looking down at the ground and muttering something McCann couldn't make out.

"That's far enough, pal," McCann said. "Let's just stop right there."

The guy snapped his head up and glared at McCann. He could have been anywhere from twenty-five to forty-five; hard living and desert sun had creased and leathered his skin. Eyes that had looked a little crazy on the monitor a few minutes ago burned with rage. As far as McCann could tell, that rage was directed at him.

The guy shouted something. McCann couldn't make out the words, so garbled they might have been in a foreign language, but the tone was of barely restrained fury.

"I said hold it right there," McCann ordered. He showed the gun.

The guy took it in at a glance and spat out more unintelligible words, but he didn't stop or slow. He was stoned, drunk, mentally ill, or all three at once. McCann wasn't quite sure he was speaking English or that he understood it when it was spoken to him. He suspected that what came across as anger probably wasn't really, that the man just couldn't control his emotions or project them the way sane people did. But he couldn't afford to count on that hunch. He had to play it as safe as he could and assume the intruder was every bit the threat he appeared to be.

"Freeze," McCann said. He pointed the gun at the guy's midsection. "You've gone far enough. The police are on the way."

The man kept coming. A wave of stench engulfed McCann, the sour reek of clothing gone too long without washing, of a body that hadn't bathed in some time. His feet spread for balance, McCann held up his left hand, palm out, the universal signal for *stop right there*.

But this guy didn't clue in. He took another awkward step forward, then another. The smell of him closed around McCann's throat like the fingers of a strong hand. "I won't warn you again."

The guy said something else, his words so slurred that McCann couldn't make them out, and he shoved his right hand deep into the pocket of his shabby blazer. In the unrelenting wash of the flood-lights, the shape in that pocket looked threatening.

As promised, McCann didn't bother with another warning. His job was to protect Mrs. Cameron and her property. Since he didn't hear sirens yet, and Willy hadn't arrived to provide backup, he squeezed the trigger, and the .38 in his hand boomed.

The shot tore into the man's left side. He staggered back, pulling his right hand out of the pocket with something clutched in it. McCann fired once more, twitching the barrel just a little. The second shot hit the man dead center, and he crumpled and went down.

McCann let him lie there for a few moments, until he stopped moving. There was, in fact, something clutched in the man's fist, but it wasn't a weapon after all. It was a slip of paper.

McCann heard sirens now. He crouched beside the guy, used the barrel of his gun to nudge the hand enough to see what the paper was. It was maybe five inches square, torn from something else, maybe a menu. Most of it was covered in penciled writing, every bit as unreadable as the man's spoken words had been impossible to decipher. But on top of the pencil were other words, written with black ink in what looked like a woman's hand. A couple of words stood out, and some numbers, and Mc-Cann realized he was looking at directions to the estate and the combination code for the front gate.

Someone had *sent* him there.

He pocketed his weapon and backed away, taking deep breaths once he got past the nimbus of stink surrounding the dead man. The cops would be there in seconds, and he didn't want to be crouching there with a gun in his hand when they came. The shooting was justified, but guns made people nervous.

Especially cops. Especially when there was a dead man involved.

Lights angled up the drive, headlights and blue and red rooftop flashers. McCann raised his arms above his head and waited.

"Nice place," Greg Sanders observed.

"Vegas royalty," Catherine Willows said. She was driving a Las Vegas Police Department Yukon up a winding driveway in Seven Hills, south of the city. The property had been landscaped to within an inch of its life. "You can't touch this neighborhood for less than a couple million."

"And this estate really belonged to Bix Cameron?"

"The one and only." Bix Cameron had been a casino tycoon, one of the city's prime builders back in the 1950s. Catherine's father, Sam Braun, had known him, and she had met Bix once or twice. She remembered a tall, fit man with close-cropped silver hair and a friendly twinkle in his eye, who always clasped her father's hands with both of his, then went down on one knee to greet her father's daughter.

"What's it been, like ten years since he went missing?"

"Around that." Greg was fascinated by the city's criminal history, and Bix Cameron's disappearance—what everyone assumed to be his murder—

fit into that, even though, in life, Bix had been believed to be on the straight and narrow. Still, in those days, one could hardly build a casino without cutting the mob in, and Bix had built several. The assumption, when he had disappeared a decade ago, was that he had wound up crosswise with one of those criminal elements. Greg could have talked about the old-time gangsters for days if Catherine had let him. But the Cameron home loomed before them, looking like a palatial Italian villa, with walls of a pale mustard color and an undulating terra-cotta tiled roof, and Catherine wanted to focus on the job at hand. She had seen pictures of similar homes clinging to the hills around Lake Como. Lights blazed throughout this one, casting a glow down on the long driveway and the hundreds of roses arrayed on broad steps flanking the house. She brought the vehicle to a halt in front of a strip of yellow crime-scene tape, beside a couple of patrol cars and an EMS van.

She turned off the engine and stepped out. The fragrance of the rose garden hit her first, the April days warm enough to bring out the blooms, and though the nights were still cool enough for her light leather jacket, they no longer dipped below freezing.

Two steps farther up the drive, the smell of spilled blood and an unbathed human's dying moments replaced it. She preferred the roses, but not enough to quit her job and take up landscaping.

Greg stopped beside her, a camera in his hands. On the ground inside the yellow tape was a man, his arms outspread, legs together and slightly folded.

A pool of blood darkened the pavement beneath him. "Guess we found our vic," she said.

"I guess we did. And so did the chalk fairy."

Catherine looked again and saw a thin white line inscribed around the body. "Great."

They had passed one uniformed officer at the gate, there to keep the press out and allow official vehicles in, and signed in on his crime-scene log. Another one approached them now. "You the CSIs?"

"I'm Supervisor Willows," Catherine answered. "This is CSI Sanders."

"Cool." The uni addressed Catherine. His name was Vernon, according to the tag on his chest. He was African-American, mid-twenties, a weight lifter judging from the way his arms and chest swelled against his clothing. "Detective Vega wanted me to send you up to the command post when you arrived." He tilted his head up the driveway. She saw people milling around near the house. "He's there with the witnesses and the perpetrator."

"We already have a suspect?" Catherine asked.

"Security man for the family. Claims it was a righteous kill."

"I don't think that's his decision to make, but it would make our lives easier." She glanced at Greg. "You want to start taking pictures while I meet the suspect?"

"You got it."

Catherine went around the taped-off scene and up the hill, carrying the steel box containing her crime-scene kit. The command post was nothing more than a blank stretch of pavement beside the

house, established to give the various cops someplace to congregate that wouldn't compromise the
crime scene. Staggered around were a couple of obvious civilians, recognizable by the shell-shocked
look in their eyes, with uniformed cops either talking softly to them or just standing by, keeping them
separated. As always seemed to happen these days,
there were cops standing around talking quietly into
cell phones. She wondered who they were all talking to. Girlfriends? Reporters? Bookies? It was anybody's guess.

Sam Vega, solid and dark, stood with a burly,
red-faced man in a windbreaker and jeans and
another man, short, balding, and bespectacled,
who could only be a lawyer. He wore a thousand-
dollar suit and Bruno Magli shoes with a professional shine on them, and he had an imperious
air about him, as if despite his physical stature, he
was used to looking down at other people from on
high—metaphorically speaking, at least. But when
he wanted to, Sam could glower like nobody's business, and the lawyer almost seemed to be wilting in
his presence.

"Catherine," Sam said, breaking into a smile at her
approach. "Glad you're here. This is Drake McCann,
head of security for the Cameron estate. He used to
be on the job, back in Detroit. Marvin Coatsworth
here is Helena Cameron's attorney. Mr. Coatsworth,
Mr. McCann, Supervisor Willows is the crime lab's
night-shift supervisor. She'll be in charge of the
crime-scene investigation."

"Supervisor," Coatsworth said, shaking her hand
with such brisk efficiency that Catherine wondered

if he billed by the millisecond. He hadn't paid for that suit by being generous with his time.

"Good to meet you," McCann said. He offered his hand and a smile. Catherine happily took both; genuine courtesy from a shooting suspect was a rarity. She had met plenty of murderers, and for the most part, they were human scum, not people she would want to shake hands with. This man wasn't like that. "Wish the circumstances were different."

"I'm sure. Can you tell me what happened? I know you've already told Sam."

McCann looked to Vega, but the detective encouraged him to tell the story again in his own words. Coatsworth nodded his approval, and McCann launched into his tale. By now, he had surely told it enough times to winnow it down to the bare bones. "Guy came in the front gate. Apparently, he had the combination code written down on a piece of paper. But take a look at him—he's a real case, let me tell you. Homeless at best, maybe mentally ill. Probably. He came at me angry, shouting something I couldn't understand, and ignored all my commands to stop. Finally, he reached in his pocket. I thought I saw the outline of a weapon, and after warning him, I fired twice. Put him down, and that's that."

"We've already got the weapon," Sam added. "It's a registered thirty-eight revolver."

"You mind if I swab you for gunshot residue?" Catherine asked.

"I already told you I shot him."

"It's a formality." The truth was, she had seen too many cases in which one person tried to take the rap for someone else. A GSR test would show whether or not he had fired a gun. His prints on the weapon would connect him to that particular gun, and ballistic analysis of the barrel and the markings on the round would link the gun to the bullets inside the dead man. Even in a case that might have been a legitimately defensive killing, she wanted to make sure the dots were connected.

She spotted Coatsworth nodding again, out of the corner of her eye. For a lawyer, he hadn't said much. Maybe he billed by the word, too, and was trying to give Mrs. Cameron a deal. Then again, she was reputedly one of the richest women in Las Vegas, so maybe he just didn't have anything to say at the moment.

"Fine, whatever," McCann said.

Catherine took a couple of cotton swab sticks from her kit. "You shoot with your right?"

"Yeah." McCann held that hand out.

"Were you wearing gloves?"

"No gloves."

She ran the swab across the back of his index finger, his thumb, and the web connecting the two, then capped that swab and did the same on his left hand. Lead, antimony, and barium were generally deposited on the hand, and sometimes on clothes, by the blowback that occurred when a weapon was fired. Revolvers tended to leak more of those materials than other weapons, and less than an hour had passed since the shooting, so the test should be fairly conclusive. All three substances also occurred in nature and could come from other sources, so the test wasn't absolutely positive, but it was a strong indicator.

Few things were a hundred percent definitive in criminal investigations. The best she could hope for was to develop a preponderance of evidence showing one person's guilt, and that's what she meant to do. The fact that McCann had already confessed to the shooting, and the additional fact that he might never even be charged for it, didn't change that.

"Thank you," she said, putting the swabs carefully back into the kit. She glanced down the driveway, to where Greg was taking pictures of the body. "Do we know who the deceased is?"

"Yeah," McCann said. "He's a skell. A nutbag. Did you get a whiff of him? Look at that guy. I hate to say he got what he deserved, but—"

"Then don't," Catherine interrupted. "When I look at him, all I see is a John Doe who caught one more bad break in what was probably a long series of them. Everybody deserves his own name—we need to find his out and give it back to him."

"Maybe he just wanted a look at how the other half lives, " Sam suggested.

"Yeah," Catherine said. "But instead he found out how *his* half dies."

2

"Were you the first on the scene?" Greg asked.

The uni named Vernon was young, round-cheeked, and sturdy, with an all-business air that seemed contradicted by his casual way of speaking. "Yes, sir, me and my partner. We were in the area when we got the 420 call. Another car came in right behind us, though."

"Where are your partner and the other cops?"

"Gebhart's the one you saw down at the front gate. He's my partner. The other ones are staffing the command post."

"Who touched the body?"

Vernon's gaze swept across the paramedics sitting in their van, as if they had nowhere better to be. Even CSIs had the occasional—*very* occasional—quiet shift, so anything was possible. "Shooter claims he didn't touch him. These guys showed up a couple of minutes after us. Gebhart checked the stiff's pulse, two fingers on the neck, so you'll find his prints. He told EMS that the guy was dead, but they wanted to check it out themselves. I told them not to move the body, but they might have shifted it some."

Greg jotted down a note in a spiral notebook he carried. "They should know better. Who drew the chalk outline?"

"Gebhart did that."

"Is he a rookie?"

"Pretty much, yeah. Couple months on patrol, not many homicides."

"But you know better?"

"I was talking to the suspect, Mr. McCann. When I turned around again, Gebhart's there drawing the outline. I told him to stop, but he was pretty much already done."

"If this goes to court, those crime-scene photos I just took will be inadmissible," Greg pointed out. "The chalk outline shows that the body's been tampered with."

"Sorry about that," Gebhart said. "But Mr. Mc-Cann confessed, right? He's head of security here, he told us. I don't see the state filing charges here, do you?"

"It's not my job to know what the state might do. Or yours. It's our job to control the scene and to investigate it."

Vernon's eyes were downcast. "I know, I screwed up."

"Let's hope it doesn't become a problem."

Greg had taken plenty of photos, showing the approaches from the gate and from the house, photos of the body where it lay—in spite of the chalk outline that he knew would render those photos inadmissible—photos of McCann, and wide shots of the entire scene from every angle. Some of them would never be presented as evidence but would help in reconstructing the scene if necessary and would nudge the memory of the detectives running the investigation. The pictures of the body were still good for that, if nothing else. But he wished that cops who rode patrol had never watched TV shows or movies, because they picked up a lot of bad ideas. He'd heard about a cop who had jumped into his cruiser and tried to drive, letting the wind close his car door, because he had seen it done in a *Starsky and Hutch* episode on DVD. He had ended up falling out of the vehicle and watching from the ground as it plowed into a garbage truck.

His photos finished, Greg had put the camera away and made a simple sketch of the crime scene in his notebook, showing the placement of the body, the driveway, and the house, noting landmarks such as the rose garden and the property wall. He hadn't had a chance to speak directly to McCann, but Vernon showed him where McCann had claimed to be standing, giving him a quick rundown of the security man's story as he did, and Greg marked that location down with a note reminding himself that it was unconfirmed. He agreed with Vernon that McCann would probably never spend a day in court over this—a licensed security guard shooting an apparently homeless intruder—but that conclusion would have been more cut and dried had the intruder had a weapon. So far, he had seen no evidence to indicate that he did.

Then he turned his fuller attention to the body. The square area defined by the crime-scene tape was mostly empty—no shell casings, no cigarette butts, little of the stray bits of matter that crime-scene investigators had to collect and try to account for, even though most of the time they turned out not to be even remotely associated with the crime. That wasn't something they could know in advance, though, so they bagged and tagged all of it and did the hard part of weeding it out later. This area, though, appeared to have been regularly maintained by what Greg assumed was a full-time staff of groundskeepers, so the pavement was clean and dry except right around the body itself, where blood glinted wetly in the floodlights.

Vernon showed him the route that he, Gebhart, and the EMTs had used to get close to the dead man, and Greg used the same path. Near the body, the smells of the dead man's soiled clothing and his profound body odor were stifling, joined as they were by the metallic tang of blood and the sour-sweet smell of death. Standing as close as he could, Greg noted the details of the man's appearance. He was a Caucasian man, with matted brown hair and a beard shot through with a few strands of silver. He was about five-nine or -ten, maybe a hundred and eighty pounds. A bit of a belly but not much of one. Homeless people generally didn't have to worry about keeping their weight down, and what food they could afford was usually high in empty calories, low in nutritional value. Greg would have been astonished if the dead man wasn't homeless.

He peeled back an eyelid, revealing a bloodshot

brown eye. His shirt was torn and bloodstained in two spots, both entry wounds. Greg was sure that if he turned the man over, he would find exit wounds on his back, unless both rounds had stayed inside him. He hadn't seen any bullets or indications of where the rounds had ended up, but once he determined that they had passed through the man—as the amount of blood pooled beneath him indicated—he would have to widen the crime-scene perimeter and look for those.

Greg couldn't get a good read on the man's age, because of the effect of constant exposure to the Nevada sun. The man's mouth was open a little, and his teeth were in terrible shape. Closer examination might reveal some fillings or other dental work, which could help identify him, but those would have been done in his younger days, since he had clearly not been to a dentist in recent years.

Officer Vernon watched from outside the tape line. "Anybody check him for ID?" Greg asked.

"No, sir, not yet."

"Okay, thanks." That was something, at least. It was hard to go through a dead body's pockets without shifting the body around. Now that he had documented the scene as well as possible, he could take that chance.

He started with the jacket pockets. By the time he reached the pants, he had pulled out dozens of scraps of paper, most of them written on and scribbled over so many times that nothing on them was legible at a glance. He was just starting on the pants pockets when another vehicle pulled up, the coroner's van. David Phillips shut off the headlights and got out, pushing his black-framed glasses up on his nose. "Sorry I'm late," he said. "I was on another call."

"No problem," Greg said. "I'm just looking for some ID."

"All that paper and no wallet?"

"Not yet. None of it's money, either. Looks like this guy was big on taking notes, though."

"I guess."

"Hey, David, can you get my camera out of the Yukon? I thought I was done, but I want to take some pictures of all these paper scraps."

David nodded and went to the SUV. When he returned with the camera, Greg showed him the path to follow to the body. "I can take over now, if you want," David said.

"I'm done with him," Greg said. "He's all yours." He took the camera and snapped some photographs of the papers he had removed from the man's pockets. Those and a stub of pencil were all he had found. The John Doe hadn't been carrying so much as a nickel, much less a handy driver's license or passport. Had the night air not been absolutely still, Greg would have worried about wind snatching the scraps away. Had it not been April in Las Vegas, he might have worried about rain. Those were both major concerns with outdoor crime scenes; neither seemed likely to be an issue tonight.

"Thanks," David said. "At a glance, I'd say we know the cause of death. That second shot must have gone straight to the heart. Nice big pool of blood, too."

"Nice," Greg replied.

"From a forensic perspective, I mean." David knelt by the body and drew up the shirt a little so he could see the dead man's back. "Some lividity present," he said. Blood—that which hadn't flowed out through the exit wounds—had been drawn down by gravity and darkened the skin on the side that faced the ground. David touched the dark area, and the skin paled. "Still blanching."

"The security guy here admits to the shooting," Greg said. "Says it happened around midnight."

David glanced at his wristwatch. "One forty-two now. Seems about right. I'll take his temperature."

Greg didn't feel compelled to watch that procedure. He started walking the scene, using a strip pattern—almost like mowing a lawn, starting at one end and walking to the far end, then moving over a step and returning in the direction he had just come from. There were various patterns that could be used, but some were better suited to multiple investigators, and since Catherine seemed to have been waylaid at the command post, he was on his own.

Anyway, he had already determined that there wasn't much to be found. In the bright floodlights, he would have noticed the glint of shell casings. A thought occurred to him, and he called Officer Vernon over. "Do you know what kind of gun the security guard used?"

"I think it was a Colt," Vernon said.

"Automatic? Revolver?"

"Sorry, sir. Thirty-eight revolver."

"Okay, thanks." No shell casings, then—they would stay in the cylinder until they were emptied out. Judging from the story as he had heard it, he

wouldn't expect to find much trace evidence anyway. According to Vernon, McCann and the dead
man had never actually come into physical contact.
You didn't have to get very close to shoot a man in
the heart with a .38. The Locard Exchange Principle
could still come into play—one of McCann's fingerprints could be on one of the bullets that had killed
the man, for instance, and if McCann had come
close to the body, even after the shooting, he might
have traces of the man's blood on his shoes. But
he had the feeling, right out of the gate, that this
wasn't a case that would turn on hair or fiber evidence or a mysterious fluid or anything like that.

No, it was probably every bit as straightforward
as it appeared to be.

In a way, that would be a relief. These days, it
seemed every case he worked was more complicated than the last. Juries were becoming more sophisticated, too, more aware of what crime-scene
investigation could accomplish, and the more they
knew about it, the more they wanted to see. Greg
had heard of open-and-shut cases—a liquor-store
robbery, for one, in which the perpetrator had
been caught two blocks away downing the six-pack
he had taken along with forty-two bucks from the
till—in which the jury complained to the judge that
there was no DNA evidence presented, and without DNA, how could they know for certain that the
defendant was guilty? Never mind the surveillance
video, the eyewitnesses, and the fingerprint evidence, juries these days wanted science.

So if this turned out to be a justifiable homicide,
an honest man protecting his employer and her

property from danger, that would be just dandy. Not every case had to test his forensic skills and challenge his imagination.

Or so he wanted to believe.

"I should get back down there and help Greg," Catherine said. She had finished swabbing McCann's hands, and she had taken and bagged his windbreaker, in case there was GSR on the sleeves, and his shoes, in case he had stepped in blood. In his socks and short sleeves, he looked like someone caught off guard by a fire alarm.

"Greg's fine," Sam Vega said quietly. "There are more people here I'd like you to meet."

"You're the detective."

"I know that. But I also know you have a good eye for detail, and I don't want to miss anything."

The grunt work was the stuff that had drawn her to forensic science to begin with—collecting and analyzing evidence, employing the cold hard facts of the physical world to put criminals in jail and let the innocent go free. But Sam's point was valid, and in truth, she was more than a little curious about the other folks the police had cooling their heels outside this luxurious home.

Sam led her to a wrought-iron table, painted white, where two men sat waiting for the police to talk to them. A sleepy-eyed uniformed cop stood watch over them, biting on the ends of his mustache hairs as if that was the only thing keeping him awake. Sam went through the introductions, presenting Catherine to Craig Stilton and Dustin Gottlieb.

"I'm Mrs. Cameron's financial adviser," Stilton said. Everything about him was round—his pale, mostly bald head, his tortoiseshell glasses and the cheeks propping them up, his physique. "Well, the whole family's, really."

"But why are you here tonight?" Catherine asked. "The family's finances aren't involved in the shooting in any way, are they?"

"Of course not," Dustin Gottlieb said before Stilton could answer.

"I was still here when it happened," Stilton said. "I had been working with Helena on some financial matters until late in the evening. When we finished, we were relaxing with a drink. There's a guest room in the house that has, I'm afraid, turned into my home away from home, so I was just getting ready to bid her good night and turn in when all the ruckus started. It was terrible, the shooting and the sirens and all of it. Just awful."

"Where's Mrs. Cameron now?" Catherine asked.

Dustin Gottlieb was built like a tennis pro, with long legs, broad shoulders, and a lean torso. He was tanned, with short dark hair cropped close to his scalp and a friendly, open face. "Ms. Willows, I'm Mrs. Cameron's estate manager. I don't know how much you know about the many stresses on Mrs. Cameron these days . . ."

"Fill me in."

"Well, heavens. She and Daria have both been very ill. The reason Mr. Stilton was here working with her is that she doesn't expect to live much longer, and she wants to know that everything is squared away before she dies."

Stilton shook his head sadly, but he didn't deny Gottlieb's words.

"And Daria," Gottlieb continued, "her daughter, has gone missing. A couple of days now. We're just frantic over it."

Now that he mentioned it, Catherine remembered hearing something about the young woman's disappearance. Day shift had the case, though, and she had been plenty busy with her own workload, so she hadn't paid much attention to the details. It was hard enough to track her own shift's cases without filling her head with work that didn't immediately concern her. "I'm sorry."

"You know how it is in this city. The police never believe someone is truly missing until years have gone by. Until then, they assume the person is a runaway or having an affair or something."

"There's a large transient population here," Catherine agreed. "People come and go a lot. They don't always leave forwarding addresses."

"Not Daria Cameron. She's a smart young lady, accomplished. She grew up here. She wouldn't just leave voluntarily, and even if she did, she wouldn't do so without telling Helena where she was going. Not after what happened to her father and brother. I wasn't with the family then, but I've heard she was just literally destroyed by that. She would never do the same thing to her mother. And especially given the state of Helena's health—neither of them is well, in fact."

"What's the matter with them?" Catherine asked.

"I can't tell you that."

"Why not?"

"Not only is it a personal matter, but the fact is that there is no diagnosis as of yet. All I can say is that they're not in good health. And if nothing else, I believe that would prevent Daria from abandoning her mother."

Catherine could have refuted that argument but didn't see the point in it. Sometimes people went away to die. Sometimes encroaching death brought old family arguments, long since buried, out into the open and set them off again. She would let day shift worry about trying to convince the family and staff of those things—that wasn't what she had come for.

Gottlieb stuffed his hands into his pockets. "So when I heard there had been a shooting on the grounds, I didn't want Mrs. Cameron to know about it. Maybe tomorrow, in the light of day. But not tonight. She's too weak, and her physical and emotional states are too precarious to have to worry about something like that. I interrupted her drink with Mr. Stilton, gave her a pill, and sent her to bed."

"A pill."

"A sleeping pill. Prescription. There are no drug addicts in this house, if that's what you're thinking. But she's not well, and Dr. Boullet provides her with the medication that she needs."

"I wasn't implying anything, Mr. Gottlieb, and I'm sorry if I sounded as if I was. It's just that if she was having a drink—"

"Mrs. Cameron drinks only sparkling water at night, nothing alcoholic. I apologize if I jumped to conclusions, Ms. Willows. I guess all of our nerves are more than a little frayed. Daria's disappearance—particularly in the light of Mr. Cameron and Troy vanishing, ten years ago last month . . . it's all a bit too much. Just entirely too much."

"I'm sure."

Marvin Coatsworth stepped up behind Sam Vega and tapped him on the arm. "Detective Vega, are we quite through for tonight? I'd like to allow Mr. Mc-Cann to retire. He's been through an emotional occurrence."

"Not just yet, Mr. Coatsworth, but soon, all right? My crime-scene people will be here for a while, and the coroner's assistant has just arrived, so it'll still be a while before the John Doe is removed from the driveway. But I'll be able to cut these people loose soon enough, I think."

"Sooner rather than later, please." Coatsworth spun around and returned to McCann's side. If there was any love between Coatsworth and Stilton, Catherine hadn't noticed it. The air had been almost glacial when the two men were in close proximity to each other.

Sam pulled Catherine aside. "The very rich," he said. "Just like you and me, except that they're not, right?"

"I don't think I'd want to be like them, but if they wanted to pay some of my bills, that would be okay."

"Did you sense anything from any of them?"

"Other than the fact that the people working for Mrs. Cameron don't like each other very much? Nothing that seems to have any bearing on the case, at least at first glance."

"There are two eyewitnesses, as well: Lyle Armstrong, a security officer who was monitoring the whole thing from the security command room inside the main house, and Kathleen Slides, a housekeeper who was watching on a video monitor inside McCann's suite."

"Two witnesses, one step removed, and there's also surveillance video?"

"That's right."

"Why haven't we all gone home?"

"Hey, I agree with you—I think this is just what it appears to be. But the intruder didn't have a gun. Daria Cameron is missing, and there hasn't been a ransom demand or really any clue whatsoever where she's gone. Dustin Gottlieb seems like a perfectly nice guy, but apparently, he was fired a couple of months ago, then rehired three weeks ago. Some of the other members of the household staff seem a little resentful of that. This place is more than a little on edge, and I want to cover all our bases as to what went down before we call it a justified kill and let McCann walk."

"Well, we need to find out who the dead man is first. Find out where he got a piece of paper with the address and the front gate's combination code on it.

"When we know those answers, I'm sure the rest will fall into place."

"We're already on it, Sam. I don't know about falling into place. In my experience, crimes seldom do that when you want them to. But maybe this one's the exception. Let's hope."

"Oh, I'm hoping," Sam said. "Believe me, I'm hoping like crazy."

3

QUANTUM.

The word was written on a smooth white wall in foot-high red letters. The medium of choice appeared to match the substance spread around the living room, most of it close to the dead body that was the reason Ray Langston and Nick Stokes had joined police captain Jim Brass in the house. If the word hadn't been scrawled in blood, it was a good imitation.

"Quantum?" Nick said, apparently noting that Ray's attention was drawn to the wall. There were several reasons for that. Ray had been a doctor once, specializing in forensic pathology, and since then, he had been a university professor. At Gil Grissom's invitation—shortly before Grissom left the crime lab—Ray had become a Level One CSI. He had found that there was a significant difference between examining the victim of violent crime in the controlled environment of a hospital or a university lab and seeing it in its native habitat—on the streets, in nature, or, as in this case, on the floor of a relatively clean and high-end Las Vegas home. Ray didn't object to studying a body as closely as was necessary to do the job, but he still liked to ease up to it. Looking at the overall scene first helped him do that.

Second, it wasn't every day that he saw a word written in blood. The way he'd heard it, in what seemed like a dozen bad crime stories, it was the victim himself who wrote his killer's name in blood. But this victim was sprawled on the floor, and the word was five feet up on the wall. It didn't seem likely that the dead man had managed to stand up—especially once enough blood had flowed to give him something to write with—and if he had, why write that word? Was the killer named Quantum? Ray had encountered some strange names, but he'd never heard of anyone with that one.

So it was the word on the wall, rather than the body on the floor, that started his mind spinning first. The body was the important thing, and he knew he would have to turn his attention to it momentarily. The deceased was the reason they were there. A human being's life had been snuffed out, most likely at the hands of another, and they would have to search for the who, the why, the wherefore, to make sure the guilty were punished and the victims avenged to the extent the law demanded. In the most recent part of Ray's career arc, questions of life and death, crime and punishment, had been academic ones. No longer. Now they were specific and real, and the consequences were huge.

For the moment, though, he was most curious about who had written *QUANTUM* on the wall and even more curious about why. "Quantum," he repeated, aware that an uncomfortable length of time had passed since Nick had said it.

"Anybody have a guess what that's all about?" Nick asked.

"Not a clue," Jim Brass said. His voice was a low growl, like a bear just awakening from hibernation. "I was hoping maybe it was something you learned in CSI school."

Ray had to glance at the cop to ascertain that he was joking. Brass's sense of humor was as dry as a Nevada autumn, and Ray hadn't known him long enough always to be certain when it was being employed. Brass looked like a serious guy, sturdy enough to stand up to a hurricane, with a short, no-nonsense haircut and a face that could go from solemn to unexpectedly sunny in the space of a heartbeat.

"If it was, I was absent that day," Ray said.

"And I must have skipped school," Nick added.

Brass folded his arms over his chest and glared at the wall, as if warning it to give up its secrets or face his wrath. "Well, if you come up with anything, let me know, because I'm stumped."

"What do we know about the vic?" Nick asked, returning everybody's attention to the most important topic of the moment.

"His name's Robert Domingo," Brass said. "He owns this house. He also owns another one on the Grey Rock Paiute Reservation, where he's the tribal chairman."

"He's the chairman, and yet he lives off the reservation?" Ray asked. "Is that normal?"

"I don't know," Brass said. "I only know it's the case here, because when I found out who he was, I ran a background check. He's an important man in the Grey Rock tribe."

Nick nodded his head. He was wearing a dark blue ball cap with "Forensics" printed on the front in yellow letters. "No kidding . . . that's like being the president, right? Top of the heap."

Ray sniffed the air, trying to isolate the smells. Blood, death, and cigar. Cigar odor permeated the room—the draperies, the black rug covering part of the expensive tile floor, maybe even the paint on the walls. There had been one smoked recently—a butt rested in an ashtray on an end table—but Ray got the feeling Domingo was a man who liked a cigar or two a day, every day.

Finally, Ray let his gaze drift back to the body and linger there. Robert Domingo was facedown on the slate-gray tiles. He was wearing a black silk shirt, black pants, a sleek black leather belt, and black socks. A pair of black leather wingtips was parked beside the door, as if Domingo habitually removed them there when he came in. There was blood all around the body, and in the middle of that blood was a gold cigarette lighter with a chunky base, the kind that sits on a table instead of going into a pocket or a purse. The gold was flecked with blood.

The back of Domingo's skull was caved in, probably not coincidentally by an object the approximate size and shape of the gold lighter.

"Cause of death looks pretty straightforward," Nick said, crouching for a closer look at the wound.

Ray agreed. "That lighter."

"That's my guess."

"I gave you the victim's identity," Brass said. "And you're probably right, I think we'll find that the COD is blunt-force trauma caused by a blow to the head by that cigarette lighter. Didn't help him, anyway, that's for sure. But I know how you crime-lab types love a mystery . . . so I guess that's what the 'Quantum' is there for."

Ray adjusted his glasses and looked at the captain. "What, figuring out *who* hit Mr. Domingo with the lighter isn't mystery enough?"

"Just trying to make sure you're intellectually challenged, Professor."

"I appreciate the consideration, but don't put yourself out on my account."

Nick straightened up again. He was handsome, square-jawed, broad-shouldered. Looking at him now, Ray could still detect traces of the Texas high-school football star he had once been. "You know what?" Nick asked. "And before you say that I'm stereotyping, you're right, I am. But it just occurs to me that this is the home of a Native American tribal chairman, and you'd never know it from the décor."

He was right. The furniture was sleek and modern, the art on the walls contemporary and most of it as meaningless to Ray as motel art. A flat-screen TV almost as wide as a barn door dominated the room. The whole place could have been an upscale hotel or a model house, for that matter, for as much of Domingo's personality as it revealed. There didn't even seem to be a family photograph around that Ray could see.

Or maybe it did reveal something after all. Ray just wasn't sure precisely what that might be. That Robert Domingo was a colorless man, who lived a sterile existence? Maybe. Or that he was hiding out here, seeking an escape from the untamed hues of real life? At any rate, Domingo seemed fond of black and white; even the abstract paintings he had chosen were mostly black, white, and shades of gray. They looked to Ray as if an artist had dripped paint chosen from a very limited palette onto canvases and then left them out in the rain, but he wasn't there to pass judgment on the deceased's taste in art or his other decorative choices.

The stereotype would have been native blankets and baskets and pots scattered around, maybe a spear or a bow on a wall. Maybe even *kachinas* and carved coyotes, to take it to the absurd extreme. Ray wasn't surprised that some Native Americans would choose to pass over those traditional trappings, to adopt a different style. But he wondered how the people living on the Grey Rock Reservation felt about their chairman having a luxurious home off-reservation, a home that showed no traces of the chairman's heritage. If they even knew about it.

"What do you know about the Grey Rock Paiutes, Jim?" he asked.

"Not a hell of a lot," Brass admitted. "Their reservation is one of the closest to Las Vegas—I believe some of its holdings actually fall within city-limit lines, although, of course, those limits are carved out by the tribe's sovereign territory. Lots of poverty on the reservation, which is unfortunately not unique to this tribe. For decades, they had a gas station and smoke shop on the interstate outside of town. In the past ten or fifteen years, though, they've expanded their commercial ventures to include a casino, a hotel and spa, a golf course, and I think more that I can't remember just now. So they're bringing in some cash, but apparently, it hasn't flowed out to all the members yet."

"How long has Mr. Domingo been chairman?"

"Quite a while, I think, but I'd have to check."

"I'm just curious."

"Of course."

They stood looking at Domingo's body for another minute, Ray wondering how angry someone would have to be to do so much damage with a cigarette lighter. *That's a pretty up-close and personal way to do someone in,* he thought. *And a weapon of convenience, not one that someone who had come here planning murder would have used.*

"Ready to get to it?" Nick asked.

"Of course, Nick. Let's go."

"I'll leave you two to do your thing," Brass said, starting toward the front door. "There'll be a uniform outside, and the coroner's people should be here soon. Let me know if you turn up anything interesting."

"You got it," Nick said. "Ray, you want to take the inside while I take out?"

"That works for me," Ray agreed. "Let me get my kit."

Nick walked slowly around the house, training his flashlight on the ground near the doors and windows and then on the doors and windows themselves. He was searching for tool marks, footprints, or anything that might have been dropped near the house, checking each to see if someone had entered through anything except the front door. That door had been left standing wide open, lights blazing inside, which had attracted the attention of a neighbor taking his incontinent briard on a two a.m. stroll. The neighbor had never known Domingo to leave his door open like that, and having been the victim himself of a still-unsolved break-in six months before, he had rushed home and called 911 immediately. Responding officers had knocked, entered, and found Domingo dead in his living room.

The first thing Brass had pointed out to them when Nick and Ray arrived was Domingo's black Cadillac Escalade parked in the driveway in front of a three-car garage. The passenger-side window had been smashed, chips of glass strewn all about the seat and floor, and the brick that had presumably done the smashing still sat on the passenger seat. Nick knew he would have to process the car as its own crime scene, but he wanted to do the walk-around first. Even if he found something out there, he could still process the house's exterior and the vehicle in the time it would take Ray to do the living room. Ray was undeniably thorough, but he was still working on being fast.

The house's landscaping was pure water-wise desert xeriscaping, bare dirt and fine gravel, broken up here and there by a cactus or succulent. It made sense environmentally, and it was a lot easier to search than someplace with a lot of thick grass or bushes. Near a French door at the back of the house, Nick found a series of footprints, really not much more than scuff marks in the gravel. He wasn't sure he would be able to get a good tread impression from them, but at least he could get a sense of the size. He photographed them, using an oblique light source and including a ruler in the shots for scale, then measured a couple. Eight and a half. A man's shoe print, he believed, based on the width, but a smallish foot. And of course, a woman could wear a man's shoe. He hadn't measured Domingo's feet, but the shiny black shoes left sitting by the front door would be boats compared with these.

He stood back and looked at the scuff marks, trying to make sense of them. Someone had apparently come around from the front of the house, approached the back door, and stood there for a bit, moving around a little, side to side, stepping forward and then back. Presumably, the person had gone inside, because there weren't visible tracks leading back the other way. There was soil in a doormat in front of the door, which Nick would have to check out. It probably matched the soil of the yard, as there were no dirty tracks on the inside floor. So he had watched and waited from out there, maybe until Domingo came home in that SUV with the busted window, gone in the back, killed the chairman, and then escaped out the front door, leaving it standing wide open? Made sense. If the killer had a vehicle out on the street, once he had bludgeoned Domingo and written that word on the wall in blood, he would want to make a quick getaway.

Nick turned and looked away from the house, in

case the killer had come from that direction instead of the street. Domingo's property angled down to a solid eight-foot adobe wall. On the other side of that appeared to be open desert; Nick could make out a wash with some scraggly desert trees in it, and then on the other side, the land rose again into a series of low hills. Anyone coming that way would have had to do a lot of hiking, then climb that wall. It could be done, but it wouldn't lend itself to a quick getaway. It was more likely that someone drove up, parked outside, then used the darkness and desert landscaping to sneak around to the back of the house. Later, he would look in both directions for footprints matching the ones he had already found.

Examining the brass doorknob, Nick didn't see any obvious fingerprints—patent impressions, visible to the naked eye. He would dust it, though, looking for unseen, or latent, impressions. The door was closed now, so if this person had gone inside, he probably had to open it and then closed it behind himself—or herself; he still couldn't afford to make that call. Before he did that, however, he took a closer look at the shoe prints. There wasn't enough detail to them to make plaster-casting worthwhile. He would double-check in front, on the driveway, the sidewalk, and the street, to see if the shoes had carried some dirt around and made latent prints on the concrete. Failing that, these would be of interest, could maybe buttress a case, but would not clinch any convictions by themselves.

So far, he had a lot of not much at all. He hoped Ray was doing better inside the house.

* * *

"Brass."

"Jim, it's Ray."

"What is it, Professor?"

Ray cradled the phone between his ear and his shoulder while he turned over the piece of paper he held in his hands. He had already photographed the room, the body, and the probable weapon from every conceivable angle, then walked around recording his impressions verbally, before even touching the body. "I might have something for you."

"That's fast."

"Maybe we should have looked in Chairman Domingo's pockets before you left."

Brass chuckled. "Maybe so. What've you got?"

"I know where Robert Domingo spent his evening."

"Not sitting at home scrapbooking, I take it."

"Hardly." Ray studied the fine print on the credit-card receipt. "Do you know a place called Fracas?"

"It's this week's trendy nightclub," Brass said. "Loud music, skimpy clothing, watered-down drinks, bad lighting. Just like a lot of other trendy clubs. There's always a new one coming down the pike."

"I gather it's an expensive club. According to this credit-card receipt, Domingo spent eleven hundred dollars there tonight, of which a hundred and fifty was a tip. He cashed out at twelve-fifteen."

Brass gave a low whistle. "That would buy a couple bottles of Taittinger."

"I'm still just getting started processing him," Ray said. "I should get back to it but wanted to let you know that."

"Thanks, Ray. I'll check into it."

Ray ended the call and dropped the phone back into his jacket pocket. He bagged the receipt and wrote the pertinent details on the plastic, then added it to the trove he was developing. Domingo's pockets had contained keys, a wallet, the Fracas receipt, a couple of Mont Blanc pens, and a partial roll of mints.

On Domingo's clothing, Ray found a couple of short orange hairs—they stood out like neon against the shiny black of his silk shirt—and three pieces of some dry plant fiber he couldn't identify. He bagged those, too.

"How's it going, Ray?" Nick asked, coming back in through the open front door.

"It's going." He filled Nick in on what he had found so far. Nick told him he found footprints at a back door, leading by a roundabout route out to the street a couple hundred feet from the house, but no finger-ridge impressions on the doorknobs and no signs of entry at any other doors or windows. Then he left Ray to his work and went back out to process the Escalade with the broken window.

Ray took samples of the blood on the floor, the blood on the lighter, and the blood on the wall. It was probably all the same blood, but until it was tested, that was no certainty. He didn't want to dust the lighter for prints here, although he had become much more proficient at the process than he had been when he'd started on the job. But he saw no patent prints, even in the blood, and he wondered if the lighter had been wiped and then dropped into the pooling blood, instead of having been dropped immediately after it struck Domingo. There didn't seem to be any good way to transport the thing to the lab without further smearing the blood, and he finally decided to set it aside until he was finished, hoping the blood would have dried on the metal, then carry it in a paper bag.

He had been surprised at first to learn that damp or wet items were put into paper bags rather than plastic. But once it was explained that in the more airtight confines of a plastic bag, moisture could cause bacterial growth or molds that would then contaminate precisely what the investigator was trying to preserve, he understood why. Paper wasn't airtight, and that was exactly the point. Even if the blood on the lighter seemed dry to the touch by the time he was ready to go, he would bag it in paper, just in case.

With the body as closely examined as he could manage in that setting—soon the coroner's crew would arrive to take custody of it, and they would do the more detailed examination back at the morgue—he shifted his attention back to the rest of the room. There was a black leather sofa, with highly polished black steel end tables flanking it. On the right-hand table were a couple of business magazines and an ashtray with a cigar butt in it. The furniture was reasonably clean, but a thin layer of dust coated the table, and a dust-free spot showed where the lighter probably ordinarily rested. Next to the magazines was a cut-glass tumbler with about an eighth of an inch of some pale amber liquid left inside. Ray sniffed the glass. Scotch, watery. There had probably been ice cubes in it when he started drinking it. Condensation had made a ring in the tabletop dust. He would collect the liquid and get it to the tox lab to check for poison.

So Domingo spent his evening at a nightclub, leaving there a little after midnight, having racked up an eleven-hundred-dollar bill. He came home. At some point, somebody—maybe he himself—smashed the window of his SUV. Where was that—at the club? In the parking lot? On the way home? Or right there, where it was parked in front of the garage? At any rate, Domingo probably knew about it. They would have to check his phone records to see if he called in a criminal complaint.

Once he got home, he took off his shoes, sat on the couch, smoked a cigar, and drank some scotch on the rocks. Maybe he flipped through the magazines. He kept his house clean, even leaving his shoes by the door so he didn't track anything on the floors. He was, by all available evidence, a fairly meticulous guy.

But at some point, his late-night relaxation was interrupted by . . . well, that was the million-dollar question, wasn't it? *Someone* came inside. There was, Ray guessed, an argument. While Domingo's back was turned, the other person snatched up the nearest heavy object and bashed Domingo over the head with it. Still holding the lighter, he—or she, no telling yet, although the person was probably at least as tall as Domingo and strong enough to kill with a single blow—wiped his fingerprints off it. He wrote the word *QUANTUM* on the wall, presumably using a tool and not his finger, since he was obviously careful not to leave fingerprints anywhere else, and then he took his leave.

The killer had not, at a glance, left any signposts pointing to his identity. Unless the mystery word was somehow one. If so, it was as vague a signpost as Ray could imagine.

Ray had not been at the job for as long as his colleagues, but he understood the fundamental principles underlying it. All people left traces of themselves on those with whom they came in contact. Maybe it was the orange hairs, maybe the bits of plant fiber, maybe fingerprints he had not yet located, but somewhere in this house was the key, the signpost Ray needed.

He would keep looking until he found it.

He knew when he took the job that it wouldn't be easy. The hours, Grissom had promised, were terrible, and the pay was lousy. *Gil was true to his word*, Ray thought with a wry grin.

But the rewards—well, they were beyond measure. So far, Ray had found it absolutely worthwhile, in every conceivable way.

4

FRACAS WAS STILL OPEN when Brass got there. *Doesn't anyone in Las Vegas ever sleep?* he wondered. *Besides me?* He knew cops who moonlighted as security at places like this, sometimes making more money in a single late-night shift than they did in a week in uniform. He couldn't begrudge a working person the extra dough, but he hoped his life never depended on the shooting ability of a police officer who'd had only eight hours of sleep in the last seventy-two.

The parking lot wasn't as full as it would have been earlier in the evening—well, morning—but there were still vehicles scattered about, and the valet parking area held its share of BMWs, Mercedes-Benzes, and Jaguars and even a few American luxury cars, Caddys and Lincolns, mostly of the SUV variety. The valets wore black shirts, maroon bow ties, white and gold vests, and black pants with maroon stripes up the side—kind of an old-fashioned look, half-mobster, maybe, but at least it made a statement.

The building looked smallish from the parking lot, a concrete-block rectangle with the name in red neon letters on the wall. But small neon. Discreet, if such an adjective could ever be applied to red neon. Just inside the door—no rope line to handle, not this time of night—stood a human-shaped mountain with a bald head and thick-framed black plastic glasses. Not a cop; Brass doubted if the uniform existed that could have fit the man. The specs were a nice touch, giving the bouncer a kind of egghead quality, but from the size of his shoulders and mitts, you wouldn't want to cross him. Behind him was a second door, and Brass could feel bass notes from behind it rattling his teeth.

Brass was reaching for his jacket, to draw it back and badge the guy, when the bouncer smiled and said, " 'Morning, Detective."

"It's that obvious?"

"You might as well wear a uniform. To be fair, I've been doing this a long time."

"Glad I could still maybe fool a newbie," Brass said.

"Maybe. If he had vision problems."

Brass paused next to the big man. "You know Robert Domingo?"

The bouncer shrugged. "You'd have to ask inside. I don't know names."

"You don't know names?"

"Why would I? I let people in the door. Sometimes I throw them out. I don't need to know their names to do either one."

"But you expect me to believe that if some sweet blonde with a tight butt and a short skirt gave you the eye and then asked you to call her after you got off your shift, you wouldn't want to know her name?"

"Detective, this is Las Vegas, and we're the flavor of the month. I don't need to know her name, because someone else just like her will be along in ten minutes."

Brass nodded sagely. "That's a tough life you have."

The guy shrugged once more. "Someone's gotta live it. Might as well be me."

"You mind?" Brass asked, gesturing toward the inner door.

"Be my guest. Enjoy yourself."

"It's not that kind of visit."

The music smacked into Brass like a falling wall when he went inside. The lights were low, and around the perimeter of the place were large booths that were almost completely lost in shadow. Anything could have been going on in those. Brass decided not to try to see through the shadow, because he didn't want to have to have Vice raid the place—not unless he couldn't get the cooperation he wanted from the management. Dim colored lights flitted rapidly across the floor, as if operated by someone in the midst of a seizure, picking up people dancing to a loud, pulsating beat. Most of the dancers were moving languidly, and he figured that by this point in the festivities, the ones still on their feet were either completely smashed on booze and/or drugs of some kind. Even the Ecstasy users were starting to crash.

He worked his way across the edge of the floor, between the dancers and the booths. At the back of the room, which was far larger inside than it had appeared from the parking lot, a bartender worked at a tall, sleek metallic bar. Behind him were glass shelves, lit from underneath to throw colorful reflections on the mirrored surface backing it. The bartender was short and lithe, wearing a dark shirt with three buttons open and the sleeves rolled back over his forearms, and he moved with economical precision. He looked as if he had been doing this job for a hundred years, although he couldn't have been older than thirty.

He greeted Brass with a friendly grin. "What's shakin', boss?"

Brass badged him. "You probably knew that already, though."

"Had a feeling," the guy said. He was toweling off glasses he had already washed.

"Apparently, I give off a vibe."

"Lots of people do. Some are worse than others. At least you don't give off a creepy vibe or a sicko one."

"You get a lot of those in here?"

"Get all kinds in here. I've worked at some other places in town, too. Lot of nice people in Vegas, lot of decent tourists, and then there are those people that you just know you're gonna see turn up on one of those true-crime shows."

"I meet my share of those," Brass admitted. So far, except for the music and the possibly unsavory activity that could have been taking place in those dark booths, he liked the place. Or he liked the people working there, which basically came down to the same thing. Every joint played the same music and served the same drinks; it was the people who created an atmosphere that was either welcoming or off-putting. These folks seemed as if they'd be entertaining to hang out with for an hour or two.

"What can I get you?" the bartender asked.

"Just a tall cool glass of information."

The bartender put down his towel, placed his hands on the back edge of the bar, and leaned forward a little so Brass wouldn't have to shout over the music. "Yeah? What do you need?"

"Robert Domingo. You know him?"

"He comes in sometimes."

"How well do you know him?"

"Well enough not to expect to retire on his tips."

"That's probably handy information to have."

"It is when you live on tips."

"He was here tonight," Brass said. He didn't phrase it as a question, but the bartender answered anyway.

"Yeah, he was in earlier. For a while."

"Ran up a big tab."

"I guess, yeah. Big for some people. Not for others."

"Seemed like he tipped all right."

"The dollar amount was decent," the bartender said. "But it was almost exactly fifteen percent."

"But that's standard, right?"

"You don't retire on standard. In this town, one high roller who has a good night can give you a good month. But a few guys like Domingo can make you have to choose between rent and groceries."

"At least he didn't stiff you."

The bartender grinned again. "There's that."

"So who did he spend this money on?"

"He bought some bottles of champagne. A couple rounds for everyone at the bar, although he bought those when there weren't a lot of people at the bar. He took a booth for a while, and people sat with him as long as he was buying. That kind hang around every club—they can sniff out who's spreading the booze around, and they'll be your best friend until you close out your tab. It doesn't take long to rack up a thousand-dollar tab if you have expensive tastes."

"And he did?"

"Always."

"He's a regular, I take it?"

"Like I said, he comes in sometimes. And he may not be a great tipper, but he also might not appreciate me talking about his personal habits with the cops."

"I think he's beyond caring about that."

The bartender's face went dark. "No shit? What happened?"

"He might not appreciate me talking about his personal situation with a bartender."

"I gotcha," the man said.

"Point is, he isn't going to be a good tipper or a bad tipper anymore. So feel free to talk about him as much as you want."

"Okay, what else do you want to know?"

"Anybody in particular who spent time with him tonight who comes to mind? Did he get into any altercations, disagreements? Anybody threaten him?"

"No and no. He was Mr. Happy tonight. All smiles and big laughs and 'Pour my friends another drink!' He had plenty of friends tonight, let me tell you."

"As long as he was buying."

"He was buying almost up until he left. I guess at the end, the last forty minutes or so, the last champagne bottle ran out and the crowd dissipated. Then it was just him and this one girl."

"Who was she?"

"I didn't know her."

"Did he leave with her?"

"I wasn't really paying attention. But now that you mention it, I think he did. You think she . . . ?" The bartender made a slicing motion across his throat.

"You never know," Brass replied.

"Dude, that's messed up."

"It's not considered the ideal way to end a pleasant evening."

"Not at all."

"Can you describe the girl?"

"Pretty. Black hair, dark eyes. She wore black, I think."

"Lot of that going around."

"Yeah, it's kind of the uniform. I guess I can't describe her that well, but you can see the video if you want."

"There's video?"

"Seven cameras."

Brass liked the sound of that. "Show me."

The bartender picked up a phone. "I need someone to cover me here for a minute," he said. He spoke briefly into the receiver, then hung up. "Just a sec."

"So you have no idea who this girl might have been?" Brass asked while they waited.

"Not a clue. She looked Native American to me. Straight hair, darker skin. But I'm no expert. I can tell you one thing."

"What's that?"

"Man, was she a hottie. I never saw her before, but I wouldn't mind seeing her again."

5

CONRAD ECKLIE WAS AN extremely ambitious guy.

Catherine didn't have a problem with ambition. She had plenty of that herself. But she wasn't in his league, not in that regard.

When she had first known him, he was a day-shift supervisor at the Las Vegas Police Department Crime Lab, the counterpart to the job she held now as night-shift supervisor. She didn't know if he would move up from there or not, although she suspected he had his eyes on the commissioner's job. A guy like him, driven, she wouldn't put a run for the mayor's office past him one of these days, even if the lab was hardly a common stepping-stone to that position.

Gil Grissom hadn't used his supervisor's job as a rung on any career ladder. He had become night-shift supervisor and stayed in the position until he left. But there had been extenuating circum-stances in his departure, most notably an unfinished relationship with former CSI Sara Sidle, which had driven Gil out of the lab and out of Las Vegas. Catherine didn't expect to leave the city, and as long as she lived there, she had to work, at least until she had put in enough years to get full retirement bennies. So there might come a day, she reasoned, when she would try to follow Ecklie's career path. At least to some extent. She'd had enough headaches in her life, especially as the single mother of a teenage daughter, to know she didn't ever want to be the mayor of Las Vegas. *Talk about headaches . . .*

So she accepted Ecklie at face value. That didn't mean she liked the guy. She just didn't judge his ambitions, the way Gil sometimes had.

No, any problem she had with Conrad Ecklie was because she often found him judgmental and sometimes brusque, even rude when it didn't seem to serve his goals but just allowed him to feel superior to those he barked at. And if his promotion out of the lab into the position of undersheriff still rankled sometimes, that was because the position was open only because its previous holder, Jeffrey McKeen, had murdered her friend and fellow CSI Warrick Brown. Warrick's death certainly wasn't Ecklie's fault; the whole affair just left a bad taste in her mouth, and there was something unseemly about benefiting from it, even by default.

Gil had often thought that Ecklie put his career ahead of his work. He hadn't complained about it much, because that wasn't the kind of man Gil was. But Catherine could read between the lines with Gil, and she knew how he felt. Still, Ecklie had been a damn good CSI once upon a time—even Gil admitted that—and Catherine liked to try to keep that in mind when she had to deal with him.

Especially when, as in this case, he was doing everything in his power to remind her who called the shots.

"People upstairs are very concerned about this case, Catherine," he said. "And you know as well as I do, when those people take an interest in a case, things can go ugly fast. If the crap rains down on me over this, you can expect showers coming down on you."

"Trust me, Conrad, I'm taking this very seriously."

"It's not simply a matter of serious," he said. He had called Catherine into his office, the better to impress her with how much bigger it was than hers. She could have had a big one if she had wanted—still not undersheriff big, but upon his departure, Gil's office had become available, and she was its presumed next occupant. But she hadn't felt right about taking it, was comfortable where she was, so the big space was now being shared by Nick and Greg and Gil's irradiated fetal pig. "It's a matter of keeping in mind the prominence of the Cameron family in Nevada politics."

"They're not in politics anymore," she said, knowing even as the words escaped her lips that it was the wrong thing to say. *Politics* didn't always refer to elected office.

"Helena Cameron is past her prime," Ecklie admitted. "But she has lived a long time, and she has a lot of friends. Her dead husband had a lot of friends. Some of those friends still inhabit the mayor's office and Carson City."

Nevada was a curious case, Catherine knew. The bulk of the money and political juice was in the southern tip, the knife blade around Las Vegas that stabbed down between California and Arizona. But the state capital was north in Carson City, almost all the way to Reno, and the governor and legislature still liked to believe they ran the show. By mentioning both places, Ecklie was covering all his bets.

"I understand."

"Bix was a popular guy here," Ecklie continued.

"I know. My father knew him."

"Everybody knew Bix Cameron. There are shoeshine guys working in casinos who still tell stories about him. The thing is, his wife is popular, too. Maybe it's mostly reflected popularity, still shining off him, but that doesn't matter. She's been through enough. Nobody wants to see her hurt."

"Hurting her is the last thing I want to do." Catherine knew what Helena Cameron had gone through, and Ecklie understood she knew, so he didn't elaborate. When Helena's husband and son had disappeared, a small amount of cocaine was found in Bix's abandoned car. It was widely believed that Bix had mob connections, however much he had tried to keep his businesses clean, and that the disappearances were mob-related. In those days in Las Vegas, only the mob dealt cocaine, so that clinched it for most people. Their bodies were believed to have been buried in the desert or else worked into the foundation of one of the huge newer casinos.

"That's good." Ecklie's smile wasn't a thing of great beauty, but it seemed sincere this time. "I'm glad to hear it. So whatever happened between her security guy, what's his name?"

"McCann."

"Yeah, him. Between McCann and this homeless guy, whatever went down there, Helena should be kept at arm's length."

"Got it."

"A very, very long arm."

"The long arm of the law," Catherine said.

"That's not the original meaning of the phrase, but it'll do for now."

"Understood, Conrad. You want me to keep her clear of it."

"Exactly."

Catherine hated what she had to say next. *But "had to" means what it means,* she thought. "Unless the evidence points at her."

Ecklie gave her a scowl. She imagined that particular expression had terrified a lot of suspects over the years. She almost felt like confessing to a crime just to get him to turn it off. "Catherine . . ."

"Conrad, the evidence leads where it leads. You know that. You also know I can't ignore what it tells me."

He sighed and wiped his high forehead with his hand. He looked a lot more human than he had a few seconds before. "I know."

"But I'll do what I can, within reason, to keep her clear of any fallout."

"That's the best I can ask, Catherine. Thanks."

From Ecklie's office, Catherine went down to the morgue to check on the autopsy of the man Drake

McCann had shot. She didn't like referring to him as a "homeless guy" or even as John Doe. She wanted to put a real name to him, and the sooner she could do so, the better she would like it. Some cops preferred to use John Doe because it allowed them not to humanize the victims they had to deal with. It was, she thought, a defensive thing. A homicide detective could deal with dozens of deceased individuals in the course of a year, and it could be easier if they were just vics or DBs or John Does rather than Bills and Suzys and Toms.

But the crime lab and the morgue were the last people in line. If they didn't restore identities to these people, no one would. Sometimes that was as important to her as finding out who killed them in the first place.

"Good morning, Catherine," Doc Robbins said when she walked in. The morgue, as always, was bracingly cold, but his mood seemed as sunny as ever.

"Doctor," she said. "How's it going?"

He waved a scalpel at her. "I was just about to make the coronal mastoid incision," he said, as cheerfully as if he was discussing going to a play. "You want to glove up and assist?"

Catherine was hard to shock. After so many years as a CSI, she had seen just about everything. But that didn't mean she went out of her way to see the gory bits. She crossed her arms over her chest and cocked her hip. "I'll observe from over here, thanks."

"Suit yourself, Madam." Doc Robbins leaned on his crutches, bending forward to get a good view of the top of the John Doe's head, and made a clean, practiced slice from ear to ear. He set the scalpel down carefully on a tray and peeled the man's scalp back, exposing his cranium. "No fractures to the cranium," he said. "Check that—no *recent* fractures."

"You mean there's an old one?"

"That there is. Left parietal bone."

"From . . . ?"

The coroner held up one bloody gloved hand. "Patience, Catherine. All in due time."

She knew better than to expect Albert Robbins to rush an autopsy, for her or anybody else. "Sorry."

Doc Robbins continued his examination at his typical steady pace, checking the interior of the scalp for any damage. "No contusions or lacerations to the scalp," he said. "Old scarring above the old fracture."

"That makes sense."

"Yes, it does. So how's your night going, Cath?"

"I've had better."

"So has this gentleman."

Catherine knew that was true. "What's his overall condition?" she asked.

"The usual, pretty much. The correlation between poor health and homelessness is a complicated one. Issues of mental or physical health can drive people into homelessness, and once homeless, people are at risk for a great many diseases and conditions, so it's a vicious circle. HIV is more prevalent among the homeless than in the general population, as are communicable diseases such as influenza and tuberculosis. Most homeless deaths are from heart disease and cancer, just as they are for the rest of us, but there are additional complications involved in treating the homeless. Various sorts of substance abuse are common as well. In this gentleman's case, his arteries are in pretty bad shape, and he's got some melanoma, no doubt the result of too much exposure to the sun. His teeth are a mess. But even with that old head injury, it looks as if he would have lived a good while longer if he hadn't been shot."

Doc Robbins took out a bone saw. Catherine didn't like the whirring noise or the sharp smell of burning bone, but then she had never liked having cavities filled, either. In the end, the sensations were pretty similar, except that she didn't have a dentist's hands digging around in her open mouth or the strange numbing of the novocaine.

For the benefit of the recording made of all autopsies, the coroner described what he was doing and seeing as he went. Every now and then, he looked up and caught Catherine's eye, and she knew which of his comments were meant for her.

"He's probably lucky he was shot," he said.

"Lucky in what way?"

"Most homeless people are never autopsied. Like much else in our society, autopsies tend to be performed on those who are better off—more men than women, more whites than blacks or Hispanics, and so on. And since somewhere around a third of all official causes of death are incorrect—"

"You're kidding," Catherine interrupted. "A third?"

"At least. Many CODs are guesswork or are based on faulty or incomplete data. Sometimes they're simply made up for one reason or another. Overwhelming caseloads, lack of resources, general incompetence—a lot of factors come into play.

Anyway, given the number of bodies that are never identified, this gentleman is fortunate that he's getting an autopsy that will determine his actual cause of death and lucky that he died in this jurisdiction so that every attempt will be made to figure out who he is and to locate his next of kin."

"That's job one," Catherine said. "Somewhere, someone cares about him."

Doc Robbins nodded his agreement, then bent to the body. "I'm removing the calvarium," he said. As he spoke, he did so, and he held up the skull's upper dome so Catherine could see it. "Intact, undamaged." He bent over again and took a deep whiff of the exposed brain. "He passes the smell test."

Sometimes odors that wafted out as soon as the brain was revealed could give a coroner important clues to the cause of death. In this case, they didn't, or Robbins would have said so. Everybody assumed the COD was the two bullets McCann had put into the man's chest, but none of them was paid to make assumptions. Doc Robbins would get some tissue into toxicology as well, to find out if there was any chemical component to the man's death.

"This is interesting, however," he said.

"What is?"

Doc Robbins picked up tongs and reached into the dead man's skull, digging around with some effort and finally gripping something, and brought it out. "Appears to be a forty-five to me," he said. "But I'm no ballistics expert."

"We'll check it out," Catherine said.

"I know you will." He dropped the slug into a clean stainless-steel bowl.

"How long has that been inside him?" she asked.

"That I don't know, Catherine. But it's been there for a while. There's an abundance of scar tissue built up around it, holding it in place between skull and brain."

"It was pressing against his brain?" Catherine asked, thinking she already knew the answer.

She could tell by the intent gaze he threw her that he understood what she was driving at. "Yes," he said. "And I'll have to investigate further, but it's entirely possible that there was some brain damage as a result."

"The shooter said he was acting crazy. Mentally unbalanced."

"That's not quite how I'd phrase it. But yes, it could be that this old bullet wound affected his personality, his behavior, to the point where the layman would have called him crazy."

"That," Catherine said, "might explain a lot."

"It would answer some questions, wouldn't it?" Doc Robbins said. "But then again, it seems to raise a lot more . . ."

Back in the lab, Catherine found Greg Sanders in the layout room with the dead man's clothing. Greg had dozens of small pieces of paper spread out on the large tabletop, as if a heavy snow had fallen. A snowfall with huge flakes and one that was already as gray and dirty as if it had been plowed and sprayed with exhaust for a week. Every bit of paper looked as if it had been written on and rewritten on and written on again over that.

"To-do lists?" Catherine asked. "These were all

in his pockets? He must have crinkled when he walked."

"They were pretty stuffed. And I don't know what it all is yet," Greg admitted. "Most of it I can't read. Maybe the guy was a doctor, judging from his handwriting."

Catherine looked more closely at the scraps. Greg was right—the man's handwriting, if it was his, was cramped, the letters tiny, and with all of the writing over other writing, layer upon layer, it was all essentially illegible.

"We'll get QD on it," she said. If anyone could make sense of these notes, or whatever they were, the experts in Questioned Documents could. "I have a feeling if the dead could talk, this guy would have some fascinating stories to tell."

"If the dead could talk," Mandy Webster said, having paused at the open door, "it would be the beginning of the zombie uprising, and we'd all be in big trouble."

Catherine looked over her shoulder at the fingerprint tech. "Looking for something to do?"

"Greg thought maybe I should check some of his paper scraps for fingerprints."

"I figure the John Doe's are most likely to be on them," Greg said. "But even if all we could find were someone else's, maybe that would still help us figure out who he is."

"Have at it, then," Catherine said, gesturing toward the bits strewn across the table. "There are plenty to choose from."

"I did find one note that's intriguing," Greg said while Mandy picked up a few of the scraps with gloved hands and carried them away. "I mean, maybe they're all intriguing, but I kind of doubt it, except in the most abstract sociological way. But this one is different." He pointed to a sheet of paper larger than most of the rest, although it had been folded and crumpled down to the same small size as the other bits.

"Does that mean you can read it?"

"Some of it. The pieces of paper are mostly scraps of whatever the guy had available to write on. The margin of a newspaper, the back of an envelope, a cash-register receipt, whatever. Apparently, he had a lot of thoughts he wanted to get down on paper. But this one he carried around for a long time, and at least at one point, it was a contract."

Catherine was surprised by this revelation. "A contract? What do you mean?"

"I might be using that term a little loosely," Greg said. "It's sort of a rental agreement. I can't read the names on it, because they've been written over too many times. But the gist of it is that whoever signed it down at the bottom is agreeing to abide by the rules of some tent city."

Another surprise. "There are a few tent cities around, and I've heard the population has been swelling as more and more homes have been fore-closed. Does it say which one?"

"It doesn't have a name—at least, not that I can see. But there's an address at the top, way out on Green Valley Parkway."

"I've seen that place, way out at the edge of the desert."

"Not quite as close to the edge as it used to be,"

Greg pointed out. "Las Vegas has spread into the desert, even there. But yeah, that's the place. It's been there for years."

"That's right, it's nothing new. Is there a date on the agreement?"

Greg bent closer and peered at the unfolded, scribbled-over sheet of paper. "May 2004," he said. "Guy's been there for a long time. If he still lives there."

"If. Let's get this stuff into QD, Greg, and then you can go find out."

6

STILL CONVINCED THAT THE heavy gold lighter was the murder weapon, Ray decided to check it for fingerprints after all. It could be inspected more thoroughly back at the lab, of course, put into a fuming chamber where cyanoacrylate or crystal iodine vapors could reveal latent impressions. He thought about spraying it with ninhydrin, which was an easy process, but it could take a long time to work. The gold was a surface that would show prints well, and he thought that if he could lift some, maybe he could close this case in a hurry.

He set the lighter on a thin sheet of plastic, on top of a table, and dusted it with a gray aluminum powder, which showed up well on the highly polished gold. After the powder settled, he examined it closely with a magnifying glass. All he found were smudges, though, with not nearly enough ridge lines to offer anything close to a positive identification. After turning off the overhead light, he beamed an ultraviolet light at it to see if that would reveal anything he had missed.

No luck. Whoever had clobbered Robert Domingo had held on to the lighter long enough to wipe it down, before dropping it into the pool of Domingo's blood. Not even Domingo's prints remained on it, which they should have if he had used the thing to light the cigar he had smoked that evening.

Ray was disappointed but not disheartened. If the murderer had wiped the lighter, then whatever he had wiped it with would have some of Domingo's blood on it, maybe even some hair or bits of scalp. It would have taken a serious blow to kill Domingo, and the lighter was heavy, but there would have had to have been some muscle behind it, too. A blow like that would leave some trace on the weapon. And if the weapon had been wiped, then that trace would have transferred. Maybe he used a shirt, maybe a handkerchief or even a washcloth or towel taken from Domingo's house. Whatever he had used, Ray had not found it in the house, so the killer had taken it away.

When they found it, they would have a piece of nearly undeniable evidence to take to court. For an investigator with an appropriately open mind, even a lack of clues could be a clue.

He thought of another possible way to find prints on the lighter if fuming failed . . . although, like the fuming, it would have to be done at the lab. The oils and salts on a human hand could corrode metal, even with a brief touch, and that corrosion could be detected by applying extreme heat or an electrical charge to the metal object. Ray couldn't do it there, but Mandy might well be able to get something off the lighter yet.

The longer he spent in Domingo's house, the more Ray was convinced that the murder had not been premeditated. Someone had come there with Domingo or had come to the house after Domingo had come home from the nightclub. Domingo had let the person in, since there was no forced entry. They had talked, argued probably. And in the heat of emotion, the killer had picked up the lighter and caved in Domingo's skull.

He or she—but probably he, as the nature of the crime and the strength that would have been necessary to do such damage with the lighter indicated—had the presence of mind to wipe the lighter down, then dropped it in the blood. He might then have wiped the doorknob and anything else he had touched, as well. Ray would check those for prints next.

It all made for an interesting puzzle, though. Who would be emotional enough to be so swept up in the moment that he would bludgeon someone to death but then cool enough to remember to eliminate any traces of his visit? Most murder victims knew their killers, and the reasons for those murders involved money or love or some other strong emotion. This one looked to be the same in that regard. But most of those killers weren't clever enough to cover their tracks completely, no matter how hard they tried. They left prints, fluids, fibers. They left articles that belonged to them. Murderers, like criminals of every stripe, usually weren't the smartest people. Ray couldn't keep track of how many cases he had heard of in which crooks essentially fingered themselves by doing things such as writing hold-up notes on their own deposit slips and passing them over the counter to a bank teller. In the case of murderers, especially of acquaintances or family members, sometimes they were so consumed by guilt that they simply turned themselves in. Often, they called the police on the spot, confessing to their crimes.

This one hadn't, and Ray had a feeling that he or she wasn't about to do so.

No, they would have to figure this one out the old-fashioned way, one piece of evidence at a time, amassing enough to make an airtight case.

Doorknobs next. Ray got busy.

Nick was collecting fingerprints off the plastic part of the Escalade's dashboard, on the passenger side, when a dark blue or black dust-caked pickup truck stopped at the end of the driveway. The fingerprints had shown up easily with titanium white powder, and he lifted them with tape, which he then closed over the attached acetate sheet. Beautiful prints, they would be easy to scan and compare with the AFIS database.

He heard the truck first, then looked in the Escalade's rearview mirror and saw the occupants getting out. A truck driving up to the house of a murder victim so early in the morning was noteworthy, to say the least. Nick put down the acetate and got out of the SUV, walking around to the Escalade's rear.

Two young men with long dark hair, shoulder-length in one case, stood at the end of the driveway, watching him. They met his gaze with aggressive stares. The one with longer hair was slender and wore a black T-shirt and jeans. The other was a bigger guy, barrel-chested and with a gut billowing his black, heavy-metal-logo T-shirt. His shorts were calf-length, black, and baggy, with what seemed like dozens of random zippers and straps on them. His arms were sleeved with monochromatic tattoos. Both looked Native American, with dark complexions, hair black and straight, slightly Asiatic facial structure. "Something I can do for you?" Nick asked.

"We lookin' for Chairman Domingo," the smaller one said. "Who the hell are you?"

Nick showed his badge. "I'm CSI Stokes, with the Las Vegas Crime Lab. Who are you?"

"Crime Lab?" the big guy echoed.

"That's right."

"Where's Robert?" the smaller one asked.

He had called him Chairman Domingo a moment ago, Nick noted. Was he trying to play up their familiarity now that he knew the police were involved? Or had the surprise of Nick's response elicited a more honest view of their relationship?

Nick watched the slender guy's face when he said, "He's dead."

The guy was good, Nick had to give him that. The shock registered in his eyes, which opened wider, but only for an instant, and in a sudden intake of breath. His spine straightened briefly, too, as if his muscles had tensed up all at once. But none of it lasted longer than a moment, and then he was back to normal, poker-faced, in that same aggressive stance.

The heavier guy wasn't as polished. Even though Nick had been watching the smaller one, he heard the other guy's gasp.

"That sucks," the smaller one said. "Let's go, dude."

"Wait," Nick said. "Since you know the guy, I'd like to ask you a few questions. Maybe you can help us find out who did it."

"Screw that, we got us some ass to kick," the slender one said. The two rushed back to the dark pickup and jumped in. The engine roared to life, and they screeched off into the waning night. Nick was able to catch the first four characters of the license-plate number—a tribal plate, he noted—in the first gray light of dawn, and he wrote them down on a notepad. It wasn't much, but the guys had reacted as if Domingo's death was a surprise, if not entirely unexpected, and a turn of events that demanded action. Reprisal, probably. They didn't come across as suspects at all, but they might become suspects in a separate crime if they took the law into their own hands. He could call in the plate, try to make sure they didn't get into any trouble, but unless they actually committed a crime, they weren't his business. If nothing else, maybe they would lead the police to a suspect. Either way, he had to stay there and keep working, to make sure that when they did narrow down a suspect, they could close the case.

* * *

Ray stood by the window, looking into Robert Domingo's manicured backyard. Dawn was breaking over the valley, and in the soft light of morning, the yard looked peaceful, a good place for contemplation.

Ray was doing some contemplating of his own, thinking about "Quantum," that word written in blood (but with some sort of tool, not a finger, unfortunately). Ray figured the person who wrote it had used something like a stick or maybe a spoon. He hadn't found it in the house, but it was something else that would have traces of Domingo's blood on it and could help tie the killer to the scene. When they did locate it, they'd be one step closer to a conviction.

The dictionary definitions, as he understood them, were that a quantum was an amount, or else a small, indivisible unit, of energy. Quantum physics, quantum mechanics . . . the word was commonplace on the WLVU campus these days, at least in the math and science departments. But Robert Domingo was a businessman and a tribal leader, not, as far as Ray knew, a physicist or a mathematician. So it still didn't make any sense in this context.

Ray wondered if there was some other meaning of which he was unaware, something to do with tribal issues or with one of the various businesses that Domingo oversaw in his role as chairman. Brass had named a few of those enterprises but suggested that there might be more. Ray thought that perhaps his next step should be to find out more about the victim, in hopes of closing in on what "Quantum" meant and who might have wished Domingo harm.

Ray knew a couple of Native American experts at the university, scholars who were much better versed in such things than he was. He was an educated guy, good in his specialty, and with a wide grounding of knowledge in other areas. But the important thing was that he knew enough to know what he didn't know—the amateur's mistake was to believe he knew it all and didn't need to turn to anyone for help. Ray had always turned to others for help understanding things or finding out facts he didn't know, and had learned that most people enjoyed talking about their areas of expertise. They tended to study and work in fields they were interested in, and sometimes the opportunity to show off to outsiders—especially with information that would appear arcane, although other professionals would consider it common knowledge—was all but irresistible.

The hour was early yet, but he could head over there when he had finished up, see if the word rang any bells for his friends. His shift might be ending soon, but one of the first things he had learned about this job was that it didn't hew to any specific schedule. When you had a hot case, you ran with it. If you had any integrity at all, you went home only when there was nothing going on, no clues to follow up on, no statements to take, no bodies waiting for justice to be done.

The sun inched higher in the sky, and Ray knew that he was in for a very long day.

7

"NOTHING." DETECTIVE JOE SPITZER spread his hands apart, as if to let the air between them indicate just how much nothingness he meant. "I got zip. *Nada.*"

"But the Cameron family is very prominent in town," Catherine said. They were in a diner on Flamingo, not a place Catherine would have picked for breakfast, but apparently Spitzer ate there almost every day and hadn't died of food poisoning yet. He had named the meeting place, and she went along with it. "Daria Cameron couldn't have just vanished from the face of the earth. Somebody somewhere knows something about it."

"Far as I know, she was abducted by aliens." Spitzer had ordered three eggs, over easy, with sides of hash browns, bacon, and sausage. When his plate arrived, he had looked at it, looked at Catherine, and said, "Gotta toughen up the arteries, that's what I say. Mine are damn near invulnerable at this point." He had splashed Tabasco sauce on the eggs and ketchup on the potatoes. Now he was mopping grease off his plate with toast and shoving it into his mouth. He swallowed before he spoke again, a small mercy that Catherine appreciated. "Kind of a habit with this family, seems to me."

"Aliens are a habit?" The waitress lit briefly, re-filled Catherine's coffee, and bustled off to help some other customer. The place was busy, buzzing with conversation and the clink of china and flat-ware, shouts between waitstaff and chefs, and the sizzle of the grill.

"Disappearing is a habit."

"You think Daria had mob ties?"

The detective shook his head. He was rail-thin, and considering how loaded his plate had been at the start, she didn't know how he stayed that way. Catherine had gone with a muffin and a cup of cof-fee and didn't think she would finish the muffin. "I wouldn't say that there's no organized crime in Las Vegas at all," he said, spearing a runaway bit of po-tato. "But it's decreased in importance and power, decade by decade. When Bix Cameron and the kid, the boy, got iced, the mob still owned at least a piece of most of the major casinos. Those are all legit now, or mostly all. The kinds of things orga-nized crime is into here nowadays are a different sort of animal—drugs, prostitution, that stuff. Your trafficking crimes. Gaming Commission keeps them away from the big money. It's nothing that a high-class woman like Daria Cameron or her mom would have any connection to."

"Okay, but—"

"I'm just saying. She's been missing for, what,

seventy-eight hours now. She has plenty of credit cards, but none of them has been used. Her phone is off, maybe the battery's been pulled, and she hasn't made a call on it or made any calls that we know about on any other phone. She hasn't accessed her e-mail account. Way I hear it, she's a nut about staying in touch. Not so much on the phone, but she's one of those people who check their e-mail ten times a day. And she always calls her mother every day if she's not staying at the house. Since she hasn't done either of those things, I have to think the worst."

"I'm getting that impression myself. Where was she last seen?"

"The estate. She was visiting her mom. Then she left, said good-bye, said she was headed back to her condo. It's in one of those luxury high-rises overlooking the Strip. But she never got there. Staff never saw her come in, she didn't show up on security video. It should be, what, a twenty-minute drive? Maybe up to forty with Strip traffic, if she didn't take the back roads. Which she would have done, since she's a native and knows her way around. Still, say between twenty and forty, tops. But it's been seventy-eight hours." Spitzer glanced at his watch. "And change. Fifteen, sixteen minutes and counting. She's just gone. Poof. Vanished. Like I said, aliens. She's on a flying saucer headed for the Crab Nebula."

"And there haven't been any ransom demands?"

"No communication with the family at all, from her or anyone making any claims about her. They haven't publicized her disappearance, so as not to bring out the wackos. But if it was a garden-variety kidnap for profit, we'd have heard something by now."

"Have you located her vehicle?"

"We're still looking for it."

"You think I can get a copy of the crime-scene report on her condo?" Catherine asked.

Detective Spitzer rubbed the end of his nose. Catherine had never known the cop well, but she had heard stories about him and met him several times on different cases. He had been a hotshot, right out of the police academy, had gone into uniform determined to make a difference. He'd been so gung-ho that it had caused him problems, reprimands for getting in over his head, trying to make busts he wasn't good enough for yet. His approach had soured a few high-profile investigations, ended up getting cases kicked out of court because he had violated procedure or failed to amass the proper evidence.

But that early ambition had been tempered with time and experience. He had become an exemplary street cop and had finally made detective. His career had seemed to be climbing a steadily upward path. Then, in the space of less than a year, his partner had been busted for graft—he'd been taking payoffs, in cash and favors, from a prostitution ring to look the other way when its girls operated—and Spitzer's wife of three years had left him for another man . . . a criminal defense attorney with a big house, a handful of fancy cars, and a seemingly unlimited financial future.

Joe Spitzer had taken the double whammy hard. He crashed and burned, coming to work drunk and getting into fights with fellow officers and suspects alike. He was on the verge of losing his job and his pension when he pulled himself together. He'd been on an even keel since, but his early enthusiasm had never returned. These days, he seemed mostly to be piling up the years to retirement, doing the least he could do without earning a reprimand or another black mark in his jacket.

The way he had investigated the Daria Cameron case did nothing to alter Catherine's opinion of him. He was a smart cop, but he had turned lazy. If he had been one of her CSIs, she would have found a way to get rid of him. Lazy and law enforcement didn't go together. Every profession had its good members and bad, she knew, but when the job was on the cops, she wanted everyone to be at the top of their game.

"There isn't one," he told her. "Condo's not considered a crime scene. She never got there, right? If we find her car, that'll most probably be a crime scene. But the condo? It's clean."

"I see. Does Daria have a boyfriend?"

"She's single and unattached, according to the family. Last guy resembling any kind of steady boyfriend was more than a year ago. She was never big on dating anyway. Way they talk about her, she sounds like kind of a nun. Half a nun, anyhow."

"Does she work?"

"Not that she needs to, with that family money. She did have a job at an art gallery, but she quit when she got sick. Hasn't been in touch with anybody there since she left."

"So she never saw anybody except family?"

"That's about the size of it. The staff at her building, I guess. She had a couple of close friends, other women around her age and social station, but none of them has heard from her, either. They all describe her pretty much the same way. She's serious. She doesn't go out much. She reads a lot. She's very close to her mother. That's the picture I got. Half a nun."

"There are a lot of blank spaces in that picture."

The detective shrugged. "What can I tell you? I'm trying to fill those in. I'm one guy, and I have a caseload like you wouldn't believe."

"Oh, I'd believe it," Catherine said. She was no stranger to the Las Vegas Police Department's ways. But a heavy caseload didn't excuse laziness. "You can trust me on that."

Seventy-eight hours gone by. For evidentiary purposes, Daria Cameron's condo was already a bust. It hadn't been secured, which meant that anyone could have come and gone over the past several days. Anything inside it that might have told Catherine where Daria had gone could already have been compromised, altered, or taken away.

Still, Catherine wanted to see the place. She stopped at the front desk in a marble-floored lobby that soared at least three stories high. The desk was surrounded by a profusion of potted plants, and a young woman with the vitality of a personal trainer at a fitness center greeted her with a smile. She wore a navy-blue polo shirt tucked into snug red shorts, white sneakers, and her brown hair pulled back into a neat ponytail. Her teeth were so white Catherine regretted leaving her sunglasses in the Yukon.

Catherine showed her badge and introduced herself. "I need to get into Daria Cameron's unit," she said. "I'm investigating her disappearance."

The young woman made a face as if she had just bit into something spoiled. "Oh, that's sucky," she said. "But . . . I can't let you into her place. That's totally against the rules."

"I'm sure the rules can be bent for law enforcement."

"Do you have a . . . whaddyacallit?"

"A warrant?"

"Yeah, that!"

"I don't have a warrant," Catherine said. "I just want to take a look around, see if I can find anything that might help us find her."

"Yeah, I get that, only I like my job, you know? Anybody found out I let you in, I'd be back at the mall selling smoothies. And I hated that."

"Is there someone else I can talk to?" Catherine asked. *Seventy-eight hours so far—by the time I turn this ditz around, it'll be a hundred and eight.* "A manager? Building security, maybe?"

"Oh, yeah, totally. Hang tight." The young woman swiveled in her chair, snatched up a telephone, and touched a couple of buttons. In a moment, she explained to somebody that there was a cop outside with no whaddyacallit who wanted to go upstairs to look for somebody who was missing.

A minute later, a well-groomed, crisply efficient woman in a tailored suit emerged from a door at the back of the lobby. In the cool stillness, her heels clicked loudly against the marble. "Yes?" she asked. Her hair was dark and as crisp as the rest of her. She snapped a business card into Catherine's palm. "I'm the chief security officer on duty."

Once again, Catherine explained her mission. "Of course," the woman said. "Come with me."

An elevator door slid open as they approached it. The woman boarded, and Catherine followed her. The woman didn't push any of the floor buttons, but the one for seventeen illuminated on its own. The perky thing at the desk was controlling it, Catherine figured. She had been in other buildings with similar systems, but that didn't mean they weren't always a surprise when she saw one in action.

On the seventeenth floor, the woman led her out into a carpeted, softly lit hallway that had the hush of a cathedral. Downstairs, Ms. Perky had at least given the place a feeling of life, but this corridor felt almost funereal by contrast. "Cheery," Catherine said, unable to help herself.

"Our residents appreciate an oasis of quiet amid the noise and tumult of Las Vegas," the woman replied.

"Tumult," Catherine echoed. "Good word for it."

The woman used a key card to open the door of Daria Cameron's unit. "Here it is," she said. She started to go inside, but Catherine rattled her crime-scene kit. "This could take a while," she said.

"How long?"

"Anywhere between an hour and a day," Catherine said. "It all depends on what I find."

The woman didn't hide her sigh. "I suppose you can be trusted."

"I like to think so."

"Please lock the knob when you leave. Stop by

the office and tell me you're done, and I'll come back up and lock the deadbolt."

"That'll be fine," Catherine said. She entered, closing the door gently behind her, and then took the condo's measure.

It was an expensive unit, and Daria hadn't spared any expense furnishing it. Her tastes were eclectic, mildly funky but in a way that would have won the favor of professional designers. A wooden dining table and chairs were Louis XVI. They stood on what looked like an antique Persian rug, mostly the color of red wine but with blues and yellows and whites and other colors melded into a lovely whole. A couple of large modern art pieces in minimalist frames hung on the wall over a Danish teak sideboard. She made it all work by accessorizing. Colors of dishware on the sideboard picked up accents from the rug, the paintings, and a centerpiece on the table. Above it all hung a contemporary crystal chandelier, with some of the same colors in it.

The other rooms were much the same—although the particular styles were different, they were furnished with a broad range of approaches, all brought together through the use of repeated colors and, in some cases, patterns. In a store, Catherine would never have thought to try mixing and matching to such an extent, but Daria, or her decorator, had pulled it off.

The condo's real appeal, and the reason for the huge price tag that went with it, was the view. Floor-to-ceiling windows in the living room and large ones in the bedroom looked out across the

Strip and toward the mountains beyond the valley floor. For the first time in Catherine's memory, one couldn't look at Las Vegas Boulevard for long without seeing abandoned construction cranes, parked outside half-finished buildings on which work had been halted without any indication of when it would start again. She could see them in both directions, projects begun when credit was flowing, killed when credit dried up.

The place had heavy draperies and shutters that rolled out of the wall at the touch of a button, because conceivably a resident might want the place dark enough to sleep in at night. When the lights of the Strip were blazing, the view from these windows would be dramatic but almost daytime-bright.

Catherine spent a few minutes browsing the bookshelves in Daria's home office. People could, and did, buy books by the yard specifically to fill library shelves, but Catherine believed you could tell a lot about a person who chose books one at a time and read them. From the contents of these shelves, Daria Cameron appeared to be that sort of person. The books were arranged by subject and included a variety of philosophy, science, history, biography, and a great deal of psychology. Fiction was in short supply, as were the sort of big expensive art books displayed mostly to impress visitors.

All in all, Catherine had the impression of someone who bought things one by one, whether books or art or furnishings, because they appealed to her and then figured out how to fit them into the whole. Daria came across as a woman of taste and discretion, not a spoiled rich kid but a woman with some intellectual heft. Catherine hoped she'd have a chance to meet Daria at some point, and not just as one more corpse on Doc Robbins's slab.

More to the point, perhaps, she saw no sign of a struggle, no indication that the condo was any kind of crime scene. From the looks of things, the building management and surveillance video had been right—Daria had never made it home from the estate the night she vanished.

Notwithstanding its uselessness in a court of law, there might still be something in the place that would point to where Daria had gone. If she was in hiding for some reason yet to be determined, chances are she would have made her arrangements there rather than at her mother's house. And if she had been taken by someone else, that person or persons might have come to the condo, either before or after her abduction.

So Catherine went to work, processing the unit as if it was a crime scene, collecting hairs, fibers, and prints, searching through wastebaskets for discarded notes. Daria owned a laptop computer, sitting on her desk, but when Catherine checked it, she found that it was password-protected. Archie Johnson would have to examine it. If Daria owned a planner, it was with her. There was a calendar in her office with a few notations, appointments, and so on, but nothing that seemed out of the ordinary and nothing that gave any indication of where she might have gone. The sun rose into the sky as Catherine finished up the open living and dining area; the office, which was an interior room, windowless; and the meticulous, modern kitchen.

Her only real surprise came in the bedroom. The sheets on Daria's antique four-poster bed were mussed, and there was a pale stain on the bottom one. Catherine played a hunch, based on the tangled condition of the bedding. It was, of course, possible that Daria was a restless sleeper. But to Catherine, it looked more like the sort of disarray that it took more than sleep to accomplish.

She ran a moist swab across the stain, then dripped a combination of Brentamine Fast Blue and alpha-naphthyl phosphate on the swab. Within twenty seconds, it turned bright purple, an almost certain indication that there was semen on the sheet. Just in case, she swabbed a second time and tested this one with a periodic acid-Schiff reagent. The magenta color confirmed the presence of vaginal fluids as well.

So Daria is a woman with no boyfriend, but she's having unprotected sex with someone in her bed? It seemed unlikely to be stranger sex, if what Catherine had already surmised and been told about the woman was true. *Half a nun doesn't fool around with strangers.*

It didn't necessarily factor into her disappearance, of course. But it seemed to indicate that Daria's life wasn't as cut and dried as Detective Spitzer thought. There were complications the detective hadn't found out about.

And where complications came in, trouble could follow.

The Cameron family was looking more and more complicated all the time.

8

SAM VEGA ACCOMPANIED GREG to the nameless tent city.

The place sprawled for what seemed like miles. Greg was amazed and not a little appalled. "I had no idea it had grown so much," he said as they approached it.

"The city's grown, too," Sam pointed out. "More people, more poverty. This place has been around for more than a decade, but it's never been this full before. There are shelters in the city, but they've had funding issues, and most of them are at capacity. The economy has really done a number on Vegas. We were one of the fastest-growing cities in the country, and as long as we were booming, the construction jobs, tourist-trade jobs, even high-tech were booming, too. But when things skidded to a stop nationally, they slowed here, big-time—worse than in most places—and tipped a lot of people over the edge. More houses in foreclosure, more personal

bankruptcies, more jobs lost, more families living in
tents here."

They're not just tents, Greg realized. People there
lived in tents, in parked cars, in shacks thrown together from cardboard, sheets of galvanized aluminum, carpet scraps, and whatever else they had
been able to get their hands on. Some lived in cars
or vans, sometimes with a piece of tarp propped up
on posts or rods as a sunscreen. The homes—they
were homes, Greg knew, however raw, however
mean; they were occupied by human beings, and he
didn't want to lose sight of that—were packed close
together on a vast plain of bare dirt, arranged along
pathways big enough for a small truck to travel.
Some of the places had trash piled up around them;
others were neat, as tidy as their residents could
keep a thrown-together hovel in a field of dirt.

He couldn't see any source of running water.
Someone, probably Las Vegas city officials, had put
up some portable outhouses, but Greg guessed that
anyone who wanted a shower had to find one at a
shelter, a truck stop, or some similar public place.

In the space of a few hours, Greg had gone from
a luxurious estate in one of the city's most expensive neighborhoods to a swath of ground where
probably several hundred people lived. Some of
the homes appeared to be occupied by individuals and others by families. Here and there, he could
see signs of children: a doll in the dirt, a plastic
play structure with one of those two-foot slides
for toddlers, probably sturdier in a high wind than
the blue tarpaulin lean-to it stood in front of. The
combined wealth of all of the residents there prob-

ably wouldn't buy the land on which the Cameron house stood. *From the city's richest to the poorest,* Greg thought, *in a matter of a few miles. Practically neighbors.* With a pang of self-criticism, he realized he had felt more at ease at the Cameron estate than he did at the tent city, even though someone at the estate had just shot a man. As far as he knew, violence in the tent city was nonexistent.

He and Sam didn't have a specific destination in mind, and they couldn't see anything like a central meeting place, a town hall, or any real community organization. It appeared that if someone wanted to move in, all he did was pull up a square of dirt and erect shelter of some sort. There had been that agreement, the rules Greg had found, which were mostly commonsense behavioral issues for people living close together: no loud music after nine p.m., no fighting, no drug dealing, prostitution, or other illegal activity. But that had been from years ago, and for all he knew, whoever had instituted those rules and tried to enforce them had long since found a job and moved away from there.

So they walked from Sam's car up what appeared to be the main road in and out, dirt hard-packed by constant travel. People were out of their homes, sitting in small clutches talking, a couple openly drinking, some just walking without apparent purpose or destination. They spotted Sam and Greg, though, and most of them stared with suspicious frowns or downright hostile gazes.

"Didn't take long for us to be made," Sam said.

"I guess we don't exactly blend in." Even as he said it, though, Greg saw what looked like a middle-class white family, sitting on folding lawn chairs around a Jeep, drinking lemonade. Those people didn't seem to fit, either, but the more closely he observed the residents, the more he saw others who didn't seem as down-and-out as he would have expected. "Looks as if some of the locals don't like the police very much."

"Cops represent the system," Sam said. "Anyone living here, the system has failed."

"I guess that's true."

Sam and Greg approached one resident near the front entrance—*entrance* being a vague term in a place with no fences around it and little in the way of organizational structure but defined in this case by an open space around the dirt path. The man gave them a frank but not unfriendly gaze. He was an African-American guy, wearing clothes that had seen better days but were at least neat and mended. He had long hair, which years of exposure to the elements had turned mostly gray, and he was sitting in a faded and worn outdoor chaise longue in front of a tent that appeared to be well cared for, reading a book.

"What's shakin', Officers?" he asked as they neared him. He put the book down gently on the chair and stood up. "Welcome to our home."

"Thanks," Greg said.

"I'd like to ask you a favor, sir," Sam said. He pulled a photograph of the dead man from the Cameron estate out of his pocket and showed it to the guy. "Do you know this man?" he asked.

The man shook his head. "Just 'cause a dude looks homeless don't mean he lives here."

"It's not that," Greg put in. "He had this, like a rental agreement from here. Who would have had him sign it? Is there some sort of hierarchy here? A controlling authority of some kind?"

The man showed a big smile. "You mean, do we got a government? I remember that agreement you're talking about. I signed it, too. That was with the mayor."

"The mayor of Las Vegas?"

"The mayor of the Happy Hunting Ground. That's what he called this place, anyway, but the name never stuck. And he's the one called himself mayor. Nobody else objected, though, so pretty soon everybody called him mayor." He nodded toward one of the tents with a trash pile behind it, flies buzzing around. "'Course, not everybody abided by the rules on that piece of paper, then or now."

"Can we see the mayor?" Sam asked. "Maybe he remembers this man."

"Wish you could," the guy said. "But he died, what, three years ago now. Hit by a city bus, you believe that? He had lived here almost nine years by then. Lived on in the hospital for three days after he was hit, and some folks said it was the cleanest they had ever seen him."

"This city, I believe anything," Sam said. "I'm sorry to hear it, though."

"And there's no new mayor?" Greg asked.

"Plenty of people wish they were the mayor. Some folks like to make others run through hoops, right? Walk some kind of line. But there's nobody like the mayor anymore. Everybody loved him, most folks wanted to make him happy, so they went along with things like that agreement and his rules."

"So if someone wanted to move in here now . . ."

"They'd find a space and fill it. There are social workers coming around all the time. They try to keep track of who's here, keep some sort of inventory, I guess you'd say. But lately, even they're coming around less. Some of them got fired, I guess, and the ones left got too many cases to follow up on."

"There's a lot of that going around," Sam said.

"Are there any of those social workers here today?" Greg asked. "Someone we might be able to ask about this man? It's important."

"I haven't seen any. Could be some around later, or not. Can't really tell, one day to the next."

"Do you have any other suggestions for us?"

The guy smiled again, shrugging at the same time. "Keep asking around, I guess. Watch out for knives while you do. Some here don't much like the law, but most of us are respectful, decent folks."

"We'll keep that in mind," Sam said. "Thanks for your help."

"Hope you find your man," the guy said.

"Yeah, we're like the Mounties," Greg told him. "We won't give up until we do."

Most of the residents they met were less helpful than the first. Some gave them the cold shoulder, ignoring them altogether. Others simply scowled or spat curses at them. A few turned away at their approach, ducking inside a tent, shack, or van with sheepish expressions, as if embarrassed to find themselves reduced to such a lowly standard of living. Greg suspected he would feel the same way, even if, as was no doubt true in many of these cases, it was entirely bad luck that had landed him there and no personal failing on his part. He supposed if it came to that, he would rather live there than on the street, and he would eventually get past the humiliation he felt. But it would take time to reach that point, and it wouldn't be easy. There was, he reasoned, no shame in making do in whatever way one had to. That didn't mean, however, that he wouldn't feel shame anyway.

Some people were willing to be engaged, though, and they were finally directed to a woman called Crazy Marge. "Crazy Marge, she knows, like, everybody," a kid told them. He was probably ten or eleven, slightly built, with sandy blond hair and a coating of grime over almost every inch of him. He should have been in school, but Greg wasn't about to start in on that when the boy was being helpful. "Talk to her."

The kid pointed out Crazy Marge's home, an almost palatial fifth-wheel pop-top tent trailer with guy lines extending from its corners and bits of colored fabric tied to the lines, creating the effect of pennants. A soft breeze blew through the tent city, making the pennants flutter cheerfully. For someone living in meager circumstances, she made the most of things.

Sam announced them as they neared the trailer. "Hello? Excuse me . . . ? Marge?" he said. "We're with the Las Vegas Police Department. Nobody's in trouble, we're just trying to identify someone and were told you might know him."

"I don't know nobody," a woman said from in-side. "Not till you call me by my right name."

"Your right . . ." Sam trailed off.

"Sorry," Greg took up. "He meant to say 'Crazy Marge.'"

She threw back the trailer door and stepped out-side. "That's better," she said. "Now, who you tryin' to find?"

Greg was glad they weren't trying to identify Crazy Marge, because he could hardly get a sense of her. Her race was indeterminate, her skin dusky and leathery, but whether that was from sun expo-sure or racial identity was anybody's guess. Her hair was dyed a vivid pink and cropped short, blunt at the edges, and uneven around the sides. She might well have done it herself with scissors. Maybe with-out the benefit of a mirror, Greg thought. Her smile was huge, her mouth glinting with gold. She was pear-shaped, narrow above the waist and wide below, and she wore tight-fitting pants, yellow with a bright floral pattern, that accentuated her figure. She also wore jewelry, lots and lots of it, bracelet upon bracelet, necklace overlying necklace, pins and brooches all over her red smock top, what looked like dozens of earrings clipped to or stuck through her ears. None of it looked expensive, but taken all together, it certainly made a statement.

Sam started to show her the photo, but she didn't even look at it. "Someone probably told you old Crazy Marge knows everybody. They all say that. 'Cause it's true." She laughed, throwing her head back, and Greg spotted more gold. *If she sold all the gold in her mouth, she could probably afford to buy a house.*

"Thing is, I'm one of the originals. Only but a few people been living here longer than me, and most of them's passed on. You stay someplace long enough, and you look like I do—" She shot a hip at them and lowered her eyelashes, looking sideways in what Greg supposed was meant to be a coquettish pose. "People get to know you."

"I'll bet they do," Sam said. There was no malice in his tone; clearly, he was enjoying Crazy Marge's performance just as much as she was.

"Ain't nobody like Crazy Marge, that's what they all say. So of course they wants to be my friend. And some of them menfolks . . . they wants to be more than just a friend, if you know what I mean." She gave an exaggerated wink.

"Who could blame them?" Sam asked, playing along.

Crazy Marge *tch*ed at him. "Well, you ain't gettin' any, so don't get you no ideas!"

Sam made a disappointed face and laughed along with her. Greg was beginning to feel like a fifth wheel himself.

"Now, who is this person you're lookin' to find?" she asked. Her face had gone suddenly serious. Greg didn't think there was anything crazy about her, except maybe for the persona she adopted. But it worked for her, as she said—people remembered her, and she had made herself a kind of celebrity among her peers.

Sam showed her the picture, and this time she perused it intently. "He's met with an accident," Sam said. "We're trying to find out who he is, so we can let his family know, if he has any."

"He's dead." Crazy Marge said it flatly, as if it was an acknowledged fact.

"That's right," Sam said. "He is. Does he look at all familiar to you?"

"I know him."

"Who is he?" Greg asked.

She tapped the picture with a long nail. Fake, Greg was sure, with a glittering rhinestone stuck on near the tip. "That's Crackers," she said.

"Crackers?"

She lowered her voice almost to a whisper, dropping the stage act for the moment. "My real name is Lurlene," she said. "But if you asked anybody around here about Lurlene, they wouldn't know who you meant. Most of us old-timers, nobody here knows us by our given names. I'm called Crazy Marge because . . . well, you figure it out. He went by Crackers because that's what he was always eating, always had a box of crackers, or else he was scrounging money to get crackers. Sometimes I didn't know how he survived on nothing but crackers, but maybe when I wasn't looking, he ate a salad or two."

"So he's Crackers."

"That's right," she said, slipping right back into character. "Always had him a cracker in his hand and one in his mouth. Surprised there ain't no cracker crumbs in his beard in that picture."

"When was the last time you saw Crackers?" Greg asked.

She tapped her chin with that same studded fingernail. "Maybe four, five days ago. He kinda kept to hisself. Some people said Crackers really was crazy, but you know, I don't judge people that way. Crazy is as crazy does, right?"

"Did he have any close friends here?" Sam asked.

"Like I said, kept to hisself. Some folks, you can't relate to 'em the way you do to others. He's like that. That's why people thought he was crazy, you know? You couldn't really reach him. He was always in his own head. And I tell you what, there was some scary shit in that head. For a while, my place was close to his, and I heard some screams, when he was sleepin'? Like to curdle my blood. Made me worry about him, wonder what he had been through. Or was goin' through in his own mind."

"Well, can you show us where he lived most recently?" Sam asked her. "Maybe one of his more immediate neighbors can help us."

"You can try," she said. "They all just know him as Crackers, I'm pretty sure, but you give it a shot." She beckoned them to follow. "Come on, you. I gots stuff to do, don't have all day to be directin' y'all around."

Greg felt like part of a floor show as he and Sam followed Crazy Marge, who sashayed through the tent city, waving to some, winking to others, offering a word or two to just about everybody they passed, and usually getting a friendly greeting in return. In her company, he and Sam were more readily accepted by those they encountered.

After about ten minutes, she stopped outside a ragged olive-drab pup tent. It looked like military surplus, maybe from the First World War. There were tears in it, some stitched up, some covered in duct tape, a few just open and catching the breeze. "This is it," she said. "This is Crackers's house."

"You said he's an old-timer," Sam said.

"That's right, like me. Maybe not quite as long. Six, seven years, though, easy. Could be more, I guess. It ain't like I marked it down on a calendar. You know how it is. Some people move in, others move out. Sometimes you don't really notice who's come and gone until it's been a while."

Greg squatted down and pulled aside the tent flap.

Crackers was not one of the tent city's better housekeepers, which did not come as a shock considering how he had looked when he died.

The other thing that didn't come as a shock was that the tent was littered with paper scraps, most apparently written on again and again and again. The ones in his pockets had been just the tip of the proverbial iceberg.

"I'm going to have to get my kit," Greg said. "And process this place. It looks like I'll be at it awhile."

"I'll have a uniform come over and keep an eye on things," Sam said. "I was hoping this would be easier."

You and me both, Greg thought. He didn't bother saying it. Some things were just understood.

Anyway, he would need to save his breath for the task ahead—from the whiff he'd gotten when he stuck his head through the flap, he was sure he would be holding his breath a lot while he worked this scene. The reek clinging to the John Doe's body had nothing over the smell he'd left behind in his tent. Processing the tent would require him to breathe that air for a long time, a task he looked forward to without enthusiasm.

And once Greg got all of those paper scraps collected, the people in the QD lab would have enough work to keep them busy for *years*.

9

"Nɪᴄᴋ?"

Mandy stood in the doorway to the office Nick shared with Greg, her head cocked to one side, dark hair hanging across one eye. She had a clipboard in one hand. Nick had been writing down some aspects of his report on Domingo's house and vehicle while they were fresh in his mind, but he put down the pen. "What's up, Mandy?"

"I got a hit," she said, shaking back the stray hairs. "On those impressions you collected from Robert Domingo's Escalade."

"Good," Nick said, glad something was coming easily for a change. His shift had long since ended, but there he was. Mandy, too. Time could mean everything when it came to catching a murderer, and he knew Catherine and Greg were on a case that involved a missing woman. Both were high-priority and meant that shift times were a flexible concept. "Who do they belong to?"

Mandy consulted her clipboard. "A woman named Karina Ochoa. She's nineteen."

"A young woman was in the nightclub with Domingo, according to Brass. She left with him. If it's the same woman, then she had a fake ID."

"She wouldn't be the first. But I don't know anything about that. I do know she's Grey Rock Paiute, and I have an address here, along with her driver's license photo."

"Let's see."

She brought the clipboard to the desk and handed it over. Nick studied the picture closely. He had seen the video Brass brought back from Fracas, but the quality wasn't great, and the woman had long, straight black hair partially obscuring her face. On the video, she could have been almost anybody. The young woman in the photo Mandy showed him might have been the same one. But this was a driver's license picture, straight on, her hair off her face, with an impatient half smile. He couldn't be sure.

"This is great, Mandy. Thanks."

"I live to serve."

"Yeah, right. Could you do me a favor? Get this and the video Brass got at Fracas compared with facial-recognition software, see if we can confirm that they're the same person."

"Sure. I don't think anybody's busy today. That's a joke."

"I got it."

"I figured. Seriously, I'll take care of it."

"You rock."

"I do, don't I?" Mandy laughed and walked away, leaving the driver's license enlargement with

Nick. He called Brass and described what he had. "If FR gives us anything more concrete, I'll let you know."

"Sounds good," Brass said. "I think we should head up there."

"The reservation?"

"I'll call someone on the tribal police, have him meet us. We don't have jurisdiction there."

"That's right, sovereign nation."

"Exactly," Brass said. "So, you ready for some international travel?"

"You know me, I'm ready for anything."

"Then let's pay Miss Ochoa a little visit."

The Grey Rock Paiute tribal police headquarters was in a steel building, painted white, with the tribe's official logo—a sharply peaked grey mountain jutting up through fluffy white clouds against a bright blue sky, all of it contained within a triangle shape—on the wall facing the gravel parking lot. By the time they had parked Brass's Dodge sedan, a uniformed tribal cop was shuffling across the hot gravel toward them. He was wide, his bulk accentuated by his duty belt with its holster and pouches, and his gut overhung the buckle a little. But he looked sturdy, maybe mid-forties, and he was beaming a smile at them all the way over.

"I was hoping it'd be you," Brass said. "Rico, meet Nick Stokes, with the crime lab. Nicky, Rico Aguirre and I worked a case together a few years ago. How've you been? Looks like your wife's keeping you well fed."

"Can't complain," Officer Aguirre said. He eyed

Nick from underneath a sweat-ringed straw cowboy hat and offered his hand. "Well, at least not where she can hear me." He laughed, then added, "No, really, I'm good, Jim. A little crazed today, because of what happened to Chairman Domingo, of course, but that's what the job's about, right? Pleased to meet you, Nick."

Nick shook his hand, the skin callused and hard. "You, too, Rico."

"You can call me Richie," Aguirre said with a grin. His eyes were hooded, not much more than slits, his nose broad and prominent. Deep-cut lines on his face looked like those of someone who laughed a lot. "Most white people do."

The police headquarters was a few miles beyond the reservation's boundary with Las Vegas. The morning sun shone down on rolling hills in shades of tan and brown, some of them dotted with cacti and other succulents, a few of the valleys carpeted in spring wildflowers. In other places, the land was almost as barren as a moonscape. In the distance, beyond the rectangle of headquarters, a purple mountain with a three-pointed peak shouldered up into an azure sky, almost a match for the logo painted on the building. There was beauty all around, but it was the kind of beauty one had to look for, the subtle beauty of a desert springtime.

Aguirre noted Nick's gaze. "What do you think of our land? Did the Great White Father rip us off?"

"I don't know," Nick said. "It's pretty empty, but that's not a bad thing. Maybe you guys got the better end of the deal by not getting the Strip."

Aguirre laughed again. "See, you're only here a

few minutes, and you're already thinking like an Indian." He turned to Brass, suddenly all business. "So you want to talk to Karina Ochoa?"

"Do you know her?"

"Jim, I'm Rico Aguirre. I know everybody."

"Is that a fact?"

"No, but I thought maybe you'd buy it anyway. I do know Karina, though."

"That's good, because I tried to get a map to her place online, and it seems the mapping services don't do too well on the reservation."

"'Cause we put a magical protective shield over it."

"Right," Brass said, sounding less than convinced.

"Man, you just can't be fooled." Aguirre addressed Nick. "Most people believe we're all mystical and spiritual and stuff. If I told them I solved a case through diligent police work, they'd think I was full of it, but if I told them I magically made the guilty party appear in a dream, they'd be all over it."

"We're a little more reality-based at the crime lab," Nick said.

"Not that I *can't* do magic, mind you . . ."

"Can you keep the day from being hot?" Brass asked. "Because it's starting to feel like it might be a scorcher, and that kind of magic I could go for."

"Sorry, Jim. I can only do so much."

"Okay, then, why don't you start by taking us out to Ochoa's place? If we need you to extract a confession from her magically, we'll let you know."

"That I can manage." Aguirre led them to a white Jeep with tribal police markings, parked in the shade of a spreading mesquite tree. His duty belt creaked as he walked, spinning his key ring on his finger. "Our chariot awaits."

When they were settled inside, he started the Jeep and drove out of the parking lot, turning right on the road Brass and Nick had taken to get there. "What do you want to talk to Karina about? She a witness to something?"

"She might have killed Robert Domingo," Nick said.

Aguirre let the Jeep slip off the side of the road, then corrected his course. "No. You've got the wrong person, then."

"How do you know?"

"I just know Karina. She wouldn't do anything like that."

"People can surprise you, Richie," Brass said.

"That's true. And I don't know her all that well. But from what I do know . . . it just doesn't sound like her. She's kind of a political type, hangs around with some people who like to make a fuss. But she's liberal, a peacenik type, not someone I can see getting involved in murder. I don't believe she would ever get violent."

"We know she was at a club with Domingo last night," Nick explained. "We know she left with him and went for a ride in his Escalade. Someone smashed in one of the windows with a brick. We think that was her, too, but we're still waiting for DNA results on the epithelials. A little while later, someone smashed his skull with a heavy cigarette lighter."

Aguirre was nodding along as Nick spoke. He had pulled off the main road and was driving up a steep hill, taking tight switchbacks with comfortable familiarity. The road was jarring, every bump feeling as if it was compacting Nick's spine a little more. "I'm sure you guys have your reasons for being here. I just have to believe there's a disconnect somewhere along the way. I read the report on Chairman Domingo, and that was some brutal stuff. Maybe she broke that car window, but I don't see her bludgeoning anybody to death." He pulled into a packed-dirt driveway that led around a smaller hill, and parked in front of a tiny pink-stucco house. "You'll find out for yourselves in a minute. This is her place."

The yard was nonexistent, just raw desert right up to the front door. A couple of window air-conditioner units poked out, dripping into the dirt and breaking the smooth planes of the walls, but otherwise, the house was a flat-roofed box. White lace curtains in the windows added a homey touch. "She live here alone?" Nick asked as they got out of the Jeep.

Aguirre scanned the desert beyond the house, alert for anything. Nick wasn't sure what he was watching for, but the murder of their chairman must have had everybody on edge. The tribal cop had seemed loose, casual, but Nick had noticed that his gaze caught every motion on the way over, every roadrunner or snake in the road, every hawk wheeling overhead. "No, her mom and a couple cousins live with her."

"Crowded."

"That's what poverty's like," Aguirre said simply. He strode to the front door and knocked twice.

"Karina Ochoa!" he called. "Get your clothes on, it's the law!"

Guess they have different legal standards here, Nick thought. *If I announced myself that way, I'd be written up for harassment.*

A slim young woman opened the door, laughing. "You crack me up, Richie," she said. She saw Brass and Nick looking at her, and her smile faded. "Who are they?"

Brass showed his badge and walked toward the door. "Miss Ochoa, I'm Jim Brass with the Las Vegas Police Department, and this is Nick Stokes with our crime lab. May we come in?"

She glanced at Aguirre, who nodded. She looked like the woman in the driver's license photo and could easily have been the one in the video as well. Her hair was long and straight, as black as spilled ink. Her eyes were dark brown, and there was a light, metallic eye shadow above them, a heavy black line around them. Her plump lips had dark lipstick on them. She wasn't dressed as she had been at the club but simply, in a blue tank top and black shorts. Metallic green polish, like a beetle's back, decorated her toenails. Nick couldn't help noticing her slender legs, accentuated by a silver chain around her right ankle, but he was professional enough to put them out of his mind and focus on her as a human being—and a potential suspect. "Sure, I guess," she said.

Inside, she sat them down on a faded sofa in a living room covered in toys and children's books. At the back of the room was a small kitchen with a table and six chairs. Two doors led out; one was closed tight, the other slightly ajar. Brass took a photo from his jacket pocket, a still from the surveillance video at Fracas, and put it down on the table in front of her, on top of a pile of Dr. Seuss. "That's you, isn't it?"

She barely glanced at it. Her mood had changed from jovial to sullen. Aguirre leaned against a wall, arms crossed over his deep chest, watching quietly. "Looks like it."

"And that's Robert Domingo with you."

"If you say so."

"And this was taken last night, at a place called Fracas."

She tilted her chin up, as if warding off any inference that the nightclub was an improper place for a girl her age. Oddly, the gesture reminded Nick of how young she was, underage for the club, a child trying to pass as a grown-up. "So?"

"So you may or may not have heard, but Robert Domingo was murdered last night."

"I heard." Her voice betrayed no emotion, and her expression didn't budge. Nick noted a thin blue vein in her neck pulsing, and he wondered how much effort it was taking for her to remain so outwardly calm. A lot, he guessed.

Brass sighed. "Okay, I guess I have to come right out and ask. Did you kill Chairman Domingo?"

Finally, emotion flashed across her face, her brow furrowing, her mouth dropping open in a scowl. "Hell no!" she said. "Of course not!"

"But you were with him at the club and then later in his vehicle."

"Yeah, I was with him."

"Were you and Domingo close?"

"No."

"Then why—"

"Just tell them, Karina," Aguirre suggested. "Tell them about your buddies."

"Okay, whatever. You see the way we live, right? My mom is keeping my little cousins in her room because you cops are here, but normally, this house is crazy with noise and activity. Domingo, though, he had, like, two houses at least, one here on the rez and that big one in town. I have these friends, that's what Rico's talking about. I guess you'd call them activists or whatever. Always making signs, trying to hold protests, whatever."

"Protesting against Domingo's chairmanship?"

She kneaded her hands together. "Against anything related to him. His lifestyle, his policies, everything. I mean, a few people on the rez have plenty of money, but most of us don't. He always seemed to represent the ones who do, and he ignored the rest of us."

"Okay," Brass said. "I guess that makes him a politician. Par for the course. That still doesn't explain—"

"I'm getting to that! I wanted to see if the things they said about him were true, about his houses and his spending and all that. So I watched him for a while. When I heard he was going to Fracas, I dressed up and went there, arranged to meet him."

"A little face time with a constituent. What happened then?"

"And I guess it was all true. He dropped, like, a grand or something, buying drinks for people.

Champagne and whatnot. I played nice, you know, stroking his thigh and purring like some damn cat, and he thought he was going to score with me. He sent the others away and paid attention to me for a while, you know, telling me how pretty I am and all. He thought he was pretty smooth. I left with him, got into his Caddy, and then while he was driving, I just laid into him. I went off about his spending our money, Grey Rock money, on women and strangers and whatever, about his car and his houses and how he was always ignoring the little people. You should have seen how fast his attitude changed. All of a sudden, he knew he wasn't getting any, and he got pissed off. I was a spy, he said. Wanted to know who I was working for. I told him no one, everyone, the whole tribe. He was stealing our money, and he needed to stop it."

"I don't imagine he liked that," Brass said.

Her brown skin had flushed as she relived her anger. She let out a deep breath, trying to cool down a bit. "Not at all. He stopped the car and told me to get out. We had only gone a few blocks. This was close to the Strip, you know, over near where Fracas is on Sahara. There was this construction site where he put me out, so before he drove away, I grabbed a brick off the ground and threw it at the car. It went right through the side window."

"So we've seen," Brass admitted.

"He yelled something at me and drove away. That was the last I seen him. He was alive then."

"So you never saw his house. The one in town."

"Hell no," she declared. "I walked back to the club, got in my junker, and drove home. Breaking his window was good enough for me. I didn't even expect to do that, but I didn't like the way he was talking to me."

"Did you call anybody on your way home, Karina?" Aguirre asked. "Is anyone able to back up your story?"

"I didn't call anyone," she replied. "I just came home. My mom can tell you what time I got in. She knew I was pissed, too, but I didn't tell her about Domingo." She glanced at the closed interior door, which Nick could tell wasn't much thicker than a sheet of paper. "I guess she knows now."

"Okay, Karina," Brass said. "Tell you what, we'll keep looking into this. You stay close to home in case we need to talk again, all right?"

"Yeah," she said. She looked relieved somehow, as if she had been wanting to tell her story to somebody but didn't know who. "Yeah, I'll be right here."

"One more thing, Miss Ochoa," Nick said. "I need to collect the clothes you wore last night."

"To the club?"

"That's right."

"They're in my room, in the hamper."

"Can you get them, please?"

Aguirre nodded again, and she left the room. The three police officers waited silently until she came back carrying a bundle of black clothing. Nick unfolded a big paper bag and put the bundle in. "Thank you," he said.

Whoever had killed Domingo should have been covered in blood. Nick hadn't smelled any when she handed him the clothes, just perfume and sweat.

"Thanks, Miss Ochoa," Brass said, standing up. "Either we or Officer Aguirre here will be in touch soon."

"See how I can barely contain my excitement?" she said. She shot Aguirre a look as if she considered him a traitor, and the three cops went out the front door.

"See what I mean?" Aguirre asked when he was back behind the wheel. Nick was in the back again, with Karina's clothing on the empty seat beside him.

"What? I saw an angry young woman who didn't think twice before throwing a brick through a man's car window," Brass said.

"But she's no murderer," Aguirre countered. "She destroyed property, and even that's rare for her. She had to be pushed hard to get to that point. Karina's not a firebrand, not any kind of real troublemaker. She's had a few run-ins with us, but always minor beefs, trespassing because she's carrying a picket sign on private property, that kind of thing. Maybe a couple of drunk-and-disorderlies, at parties and the like."

"Well, Nick here will check out her clothes, and if we find any traces of her presence in the house, then we'll have to have another conversation."

"Understood."

"In the meantime," Brass said, "is there anyplace to grab a late breakfast around here? I'm starving."

10

THE WESTERN LAS VEGAS University campus still felt like home. Ray knew every walkway, every window, every landscaped planter, all of it as familiar as if he had never left. Even the call of a mockingbird that roosted in a tree in one of the landscaped areas sounded like a hail from an old friend. Sunshine filtered through the trees and cast mottled shadows on concrete walkways.

Only a few students were around this early, most of them wearing jeans, backpacks slung over one shoulder. They hurried to classes or lounged on wooden benches. Couples held hands and leaned their heads together. A few people clutched paper to-go coffee cups as if they held the elixir of life itself.

Ray guessed that whenever he got around to retiring, the campus might, in his memory, be his favorite workplace. The crime lab was endlessly fascinating, with new challenges every day and interesting people to work with. At the hospital, he had felt fulfilled by the prospect of saving lives and helping the sick and distraught at every patient he lost. But as a university professor, he had the satisfaction of helping to mold young minds, to instill in people an early love of learning that they would carry with them the rest of their lives. Students loved to challenge their professors, to test their intellectual wings, to throw off the tethers of old ideas, so he was constantly being confronted, and the intellectual stimulation that provided kept him forever engaged and excited. In the campus environment, he could count on each day bringing at least one student who was convinced that Ray knew nothing of the world, and that kind of adventure was worth its weight in dead bodies and ninhydrin.

But his new life, his new career, came with a certain amount of adventure of its own. On campus, he didn't usually have guns pointed at him or have the opportunity to put murderers in prison. The guns he could do without, but the knowledge that every shift he worked left the world a little safer was hard to beat.

Still, walking across campus sent a blade of nostalgia right through his heart, and it brought with it an undeniable longing for times gone by. He couldn't split himself in three, though: one to work at the hospital, one to teach, and one to perform crime-scene investigation. Failing that, he had to take one job at a time, and for now, he was a CSI.

Ray went into the history department's building, stepping into the cool hush of an air-conditioned hallway, and headed toward an office he had visited many times. He was looking for Keith Hyatt, who taught American history with an emphasis on the Western United States and Native American issues, and whose wife Ysabel was Grey Rock Paiute. Not only did he hope for some explanation of what "Quantum" might mean in relation to the late Chairman Domingo, but he also hoped that Keith could offer some insight into any other tribal issues that might have led to murder. Domingo's slaying wasn't necessarily connected to his role as chairman—it might have been a simple break-in gone bad—but the possibility couldn't be discounted.

Ray couldn't remember Keith's office hours, but the door was open, so he tapped twice and went in. Keith's side of the office was as neat as ever. Keith, he had often thought, was not really cut out to be a university professor, because Ray had never seen another one who kept his office so tidy, every book in its place in the bookcase, student papers in crisp manila folders, pens and pencils contained in a made-in-China "Indian" vase a student had given him once as a gag. He had never looked inside Keith's filing cabinet, but he suspected it would be every bit as orderly.

That side of the office was as shipshape as always, but Keith himself wasn't there. On the office's sloppy side—Keith and his office mate, Brandon Romero, were sometimes called the Odd Couple of WLVU—Brandon sat, engrossed in a paper, red pencil in his right hand. From the amount of red Ray could see, the paper's author would not be getting a very good grade. "If you're looking for Keith, he's not here," Brandon said without looking up.

"Well, I was, in fact," Ray said. "But how are you, Brandon?"

At that, Brandon lowered the paper and raised his head. "Ray! It's good to see you."

"You, too. Everything going okay?"

"For me, yeah. I mean, you know, students being what they are and everything." He rattled the paper in his hand. There was a pile of similar papers on his desk, along with several books, other sheets of paper, pens and pencils, a computer, a paintbrush, a rubber monkey's head in a net bag, what appeared to be six marbles, and a telephone only partially visible beneath it all. "What do you do when someone tries to argue that rural electrification was a cause of the Civil War?"

"Send them back to high school?" Ray offered. "Or junior high?"

"Would if I could."

"On the other hand, sometimes students with outlandish ideas also come up with some of the best insights."

Ray was thinking specifically of a student's essay Keith had told them both about, which had prompted a lively lunch-hour debate about whether or not the surrender of Geronimo to the United States Army had been a net positive or negative for native peoples. The student had argued that if he had remained free, Geronimo might have been able to lead a revolution that could have resulted in a separate native homeland within what was now the U.S.-Mexico border region. The three professors had discounted that idea but taken different sides on the overall question. Ray had believed that since the white population wasn't going anywhere and the reservation system was already established, achieving a lasting peace was a necessary step toward some workable reconciliation. Keith had argued that Geronimo was most valuable as a symbol of freedom and that he should have tried to remain free no matter what. Brandon's theory had been closest to that of the student: that Geronimo should have kept up his raiding, trying to achieve concessions that would have bettered the lives of the reservation Indians as long as he could. They had achieved no certain outcome, but the conversation had been loud and lively.

"That's true," Brandon said. "And it's always fun to be surprised." He put the paper down on the stack of similar ones. "Like I said, Keith's not here. You know about Ysabel, right?"

"Is there something new?"

Brandon turned the red pencil in his hands. "She's taken a turn for the worse. Keith's at home with her. He's still hoping she'll pull out, but . . ." He shrugged.

"I'm sorry to hear that." Ysabel Hyatt had been fighting lung cancer, and the last Ray heard, she had been doing well. He felt sorry for Keith and Ysabel, and the knowledge that his new responsibilities at the crime lab had kept him out of the loop where old friends were concerned gave him a searing ache high up in his chest.

"Is there anything I can help you with, Ray?"

Ray considered the question, but the things he needed enlightenment on were really in Keith's area of expertise, not Brandon's. "No, that's all right."

"I'm sure Keith and Ysabel would love to see you. They're up and about. I've already talked to Keith twice today."

"Maybe I'll drop by," Ray said.

"You should. It'd do her a world of good."

"Thanks, Brandon. I hope you don't have to flunk too many students today."

Brandon picked up the paper again, his gaze already landing where he had left off. "Someone's got to. Someone should have done it a long time ago."

Keith and Ysabel Hyatt lived in a comfortable house in a long-established neighborhood, with tall palms offering some shade against the desert sun, actual grass lawns around some of the houses—although the city was working to phase those out—and neighbors who knew one another. The house had two stories, real wood siding painted a soothing periwinkle, a pitched slate roof, and contrasting dark red shutters. It reminded Ray of an East Coast beach house. He had always liked coming there, and the Hyatts had loved entertaining, holding regular barbecues, faculty mixers, and dinner parties featuring fascinating conversation and great food.

Ray parked on the brick-paved driveway, and by the time he reached the door, Keith was there opening it for him. He greeted Ray with a broad smile and a firm hug. "Come on in, man," Keith said when he finally released Ray. "Ysabel will be so happy to see you."

"How is she, Keith?"

"She's good." Keith glanced away, and Ray thought he saw moisture glint in his old friend's eyes. "You know, not *good*. But considering. She's in fine spirits."

"She's a strong lady," Ray said. "Always has been."

"Stronger than me, that's for sure." Keith dabbed at his eyes. "I would have given up years ago."

"I don't know about that."

Keith opened the front door and led Ray inside. "Ysabel, we've got company!" he called. Ray understood that he was giving his wife fair warning. The life of a cancer patient was not easy, and if Brandon Romero's report had been correct, she might need a couple of minutes to steel herself for guests.

"We turned the den into a bedroom for her," Keith said. He was a silver-haired man, lean and professorial. Even here in his own home, he was wearing a blue Oxford shirt and a vest, a natty navy blue with gold and red alternating pinstripes, over khaki pants. On his feet were deck shoes, worn without socks, giving extra credence to the idea that he'd have been happier on the coast at Nantucket or Martha's Vineyard. "Easier than having to climb the stairs. Not that she can't—still does, probably a couple times a day. I guess I'm just overprotective."

"There's nothing wrong with that, my friend. She's worth protecting."

Keith took him through the dining room, where Ray had met more interesting people than he could count. A door led from there into a short hallway, then to the kitchen and then the den. As they neared it, Ray caught what he thought of as hospital smells, disinfectant and medicine. He tried to brace himself. It had been months since he had seen Ysabel.

She was sitting up in bed, weaving one of the traditional baskets for which she had become locally famous. Spread out on the bed was her traditional toolkit, with a couple of cactus-spine awls that were rolled up into a yucca carrier and tied with cord. For years, she had exhibited at Indian fairs and pow-wows across the West, and now her baskets were in museums in Santa Fe, Phoenix, Denver, and Las Vegas. Her once thick, lustrous hair was short and thinned out, and her complexion was sallow, but she looked delighted to see Ray. The troubling thing was that her smile did not bring to her eyes the crystal brightness it once had, and that lack shot a bolt of ineffable sadness through Ray's heart. "Come here and give me a kiss, stranger!" she demanded. "I'd hug you, but I got this basket all over my lap."

"Not a problem," he said. He went to her bedside, clasped her offered hand, and kissed her cheek. Her skin had always been the softest of anyone he had ever known, and that remained true. She wore a cotton nightgown containing all the colors of a desert sunset. "I'm sorry it's been so long, Ysabel."

"You've been busy fighting crime," Keith said. "We try to keep up with the news."

"How is that going?" Ysabel asked. Her voice rose at the end of the question, more than most peoples' would; it always made her sound as if she was singing.

"It's good," Ray admitted. "It's hard work, but I feel it's worthwhile."

"I'm sure it is," she said. "You're making the world a better place. Of course, you always did that."

Not as much as you, Ray thought. Her presence in the world was like a beacon of life, a message of joy. People who bought her baskets without meeting her acquired things of beauty, but those who had the chance to get to know her acquired a knowledge that true goodness really existed. Or so he had always believed.

"I would think your years dealing with college students would be good preparation for handling hardened criminals," Keith put in, smiling as he said it.

"Generally, the people I deal with are already deceased," Ray replied. "But I remember a few students that might have been true of as well, at least judging by their participation in the class."

He chatted with them both for a few minutes, until Keith suggested that Ysabel was getting tired. She denied it, but Ray allowed Keith to lead him out of her room and back through the entryway to the couple's living room. The furniture there was worn and comfortable, arranged for easy conversation. A bookcase held well-thumbed volumes, and posters advertising powwows and old rock concerts decorated the walls. They weren't prints, Ray knew, but originals. He had always been especially impressed by a Mouse and Kelly poster featuring a blue and red Day-Glo Native American holding a pipe, its colors almost as crisp and vibrant as the day it was printed. The Hyatts had hung it in a position of honor above the fireplace. The concert was an appearance by the Youngbloods, the Sparrows, and the Sons of Champlin at San Francisco's Avalon Ballroom in 1966.

"She's a great lady, Keith," Ray said, admiring the poster.

"She sure is. She has the energy of a racehorse. Honestly, I'm sure she would have wanted to visit with you for hours, but it would wear me out."

"You've been under a lot of stress, Keith."

"And not sleeping as well as I should, I'm afraid."

"That's hardly surprising."

"Tell her. She thinks I should be taking all this in stride. It's just another part of life, she says." Keith sat down in the chair that had been his as long as Ray could remember, dark brown leather, worn on the arms. Ray took a seat on a sofa opposite him.

"She's right, in a way. Not that it's easy, or should be. But it's as natural a part of life as anything else."

"So they tell me." Keith studied Ray for a long moment. "You didn't just come here to visit."

Ray met his gaze with a sheepish grin. "You're right. I do have an ulterior motive."

"What is it? Anything you need, man . . ."

"It's actually work-related, Keith. I don't know if you've heard yet, but the chairman of the Grey Rock Paiute tribe, Robert Domingo, was—"

"Yes," Keith interrupted. "I heard. It's a terrible thing. Are you working on that case? What can I do?"

"We've kept it out of the news so far, but there was a word painted on the wall near his body," Ray said. "Painted in blood, actually. 'Quantum.' Does that mean anything to you, in this context?"

Keith didn't even have to think about it. "Blood

quantum? That's the formula that tribes use to determine their membership rolls."

Ray wished he had known that from the beginning. "Fascinating. Can you tell me how that works?"

"Well, every tribe can set its own standard. For the Grey Rock Paiutes, as of last fall, anyway, it's been fairly restrictive. Someone has to be able to show that they're at least half Grey Rock to be officially enrolled."

"That seems fair."

"It's a very controversial subject," Keith said. "Say someone marries outside the tribe, like Ysabel did, but for purposes of this discussion, let's say she married an Apache or a Cherokee and has kids. If Ysabel was three-quarters Grey Rock, then her kids are already out of the tribe. They might live on the reservation their whole lives, they're still native, but they're not half Grey Rock. Depending on what the other tribe's blood quantum is, they might not be Mescalero or Chiricahua or whatever, either. Then what are they? We're talking about peoples' identities, determined by the decision of a tribal membership board that might have financial motivations behind its standard."

"Financial motivations?"

Keith had clearly given the topic some thought. "Some of the poorest communities in the country are Indian reservations, Ray. But there are a few that are doing well—better than well, even. A successful casino or some energy leases can put a lot of money into a tribe's pockets. Some tribes are happy to share the wealth, but others get greedy, start cutting people out of the tribe so that the wealth doesn't have to be spread around so much."

"Is that what Grey Rock did?"

"The membership committee doesn't have to give a reason for its determination, but when they changed the standard last year, a lot of people thought that was why. The casino and spa have been making good money. With the recession, though, tourism is down, so the money they're used to pocketing has dropped some. People think they changed the blood-quantum standard as a response to the recession, so that those who make the most out of the tribal businesses can continue their standard of living, at the expense of those who are cut out."

"I can see why people would be upset about that."

"Also, some of the profits have been plowed back into the business. There's a new, higher-end casino hotel opening soon, and that's expected to be very profitable once the economy starts to come back. Most casino expansions in the city are on hold, but the tribe is cash-rich, and the project is self-financing. Whenever people start coming back to Vegas to gamble—which everybody in the city believes will happen—the Grey Rock rez will have the newest place in town. And with hotel rooms at cut rates, compared with the privately held places in the city. Which will mean yet more money divided up into fewer pieces. I don't even know that it's the money as much as the personal identity, though," Keith continued. "How finely do you want to chop yourself? Are you five-eighths Indian? Thirteen-sixteenths? Where does it end? As generations go by and there's more and more intermarrying, fewer and fewer people are left who can meet the most exacting standards. When the Grey Rock decision was made, a lot of people were ticked off. Some of them made a lot of noise, but the committee's decision is final."

"Was Domingo on the committee?"

"The way I hear it, Domingo owned the committee."

"So painting that word on the wall, in blood . . . the implication is that the murder was about the blood-quantum controversy. Maybe one of those angry people decided to strike back."

"That's quite possible, Ray. When you tell someone who always thought he belonged to a particular tribe that he doesn't, that tears right to the heart. Honestly, I'm a little surprised there wasn't some violence earlier on."

"You said there were complaints. Is there anyone in particular who you think might be especially angry over this? Anyone mad enough to kill?"

Keith gave a wry chuckle. "That's above my pay grade, man. I know there are some activist types who held some demonstrations, put up posters. Firebrands, you know, the kind who run every social movement. The main one, I guess, kind of a ringleader, is a filmmaker named Meoqui Torres. He's called for Chairman Domingo's resignation, demanded the blood-quantum requirements be restored to what they were before. He rubs some people the wrong way, but he has his followers, too."

"Do you think he's capable of murder?"

"I couldn't tell you that. Honestly, I barely know

the guy, Ray. I'm just saying he has the loudest voice out there."

"Okay. Thanks, Keith, I appreciate it." Ray rose, extending a hand to his old friend. "If I can do anything for you—or for Ysabel—you'll let me know, right?"

Keith took Ray's hand and drew him into another hug, more awkward this time because of the living-room furniture around them. "Definitely," he said. "Listen, that reservation, with the blood-quantum debate going on and everything? It's a powder keg. Something like Domingo's murder could be the match. If you have to go out there, you watch your back, okay? Just be careful."

"I will," Ray promised.

"Good. And drop by again soon. Ysabel loves having visitors, and I know you made her day."

On his way back to the lab, Ray called Nick Stokes, who was already on the Grey Rock reservation, and told him what Keith had said. "A powder keg?" Nick asked. "Only powder I've seen is the powdered sugar on the fry bread. But I got mine with beans and salsa, so I'm cool."

"His concern sounded genuine, Nick."

"Okay, Ray. Thanks for the heads-up. Brass and I are here with the tribal police, and everything's copacetic so far. All we've learned is that Karina Ochoa definitely broke Domingo's window but probably not his head."

"Ask your tribal police escort for the two-dollar lesson on blood quantum, Nick. And maybe check on this Torres fellow. Meoqui Torres—I don't have a spelling on that first name."

"I'll check on it as soon as possible. Thanks again, Ray. I'll talk to you soon."

"Don't mention it," Ray said. But as he ended the call, he hoped Nick was taking him seriously.

Because when Keith Hyatt had talked about it, he had sounded as serious as the grave.

11

CATHERINE WAS ON THE phone when Wendy Simms tapped on her office door. Catherine now spent her life on the phone, it seemed, or dealing with paperwork or attending meetings. That she still had time actually to go out into the field seemed to be the result of a flaw in the time-space continuum—surely there weren't really that many hours in any given day.

But the phone call was about her water bill, a matter she would have handled at home if she had expected to make it back there today, so she cut it short. The DNA tech had a sheet of paper in her hands and an expectant look on her face, and her slender body bobbed from side to side impatiently, making her ponytail wag. "Sorry, Wendy," Catherine said as she lowered the phone. "What's up?"

"Good news, I think," Wendy said. "Well, news anyway."

"What is it?"

"Those sheets you brought in? I've got a preliminary result."

"Let's have it," Catherine said. She was thrilled to have something back so soon. She didn't know if Daria Cameron's disappearance was at all connected to the man killed on her mother's estate, but she didn't like coincidences. If a link between the two events existed, she intended to find it.

"I've only tested the seminal fluid so far," Wendy said. "Assuming—and before you say anything about assuming, I know, it's just a prioritizing tool— that the vaginal fluid belonged to Daria Cameron and she wasn't letting someone else use her place as a . . . play pad."

"That's probably a safe assumption. Temporary assumption," Catherine added. "Which will be checked out shortly."

"Absolutely. Anyway, the other fluid came from one Dustin Gottlieb."

"The Camerons' estate manager?"

"I guess so, if he lives on the estate. He has the same address as Helena Cameron, anyway."

Catherine raked her memory, turning up what she had heard about Gottlieb at the scene. "He was fired recently, a couple of months ago. I'm not sure on what grounds. Then a few weeks ago, he was re-hired, put back in his old position. Apparently, some of the other people on the staff were unhappy about that. As, presumably, would be whoever had the job in his absence."

Wendy nodded along. "And screwing the boss's daughter . . ."

"He wouldn't be the first guy to advance his career that way."

"Probably not the first guy to end his that way, either," Wendy pointed out.

"True. Whatever happened, there seems to have been a reconciliation between him and Helena Cameron. When I was there, he seemed genuinely concerned for her well-being."

"Wouldn't you be, if she was your meal ticket?"

"Well, of course. But it can go beyond that, too. Maybe he really does care for Daria and her mother."

"In different ways, let's hope."

"Oh," Catherine said, making an involuntary grimace. "Yes, let's hope that. Very strongly."

Greg was on his way to his office when he saw Wendy coming out of Catherine's with a sheet of paper in her hands. "Wendy," he said. "Just who I was looking for."

"You were? I can usually be found in the DNA lab. Which is, you know, next to your office."

Greg tugged his collar away from his neck. He felt as if he needed a shower after spending time in that filthy tent. More than a shower, a whole series of them, increasingly hotter and more sterile, until his entire outer layer of skin was burned off. "Okay, I just got back. But I was going to go looking for you in a minute."

She walked with him toward the DNA lab and his shared office. "What for?"

"I have something that needs analysis, stat."

"Is it evidence?"

"I think so."

"Log it in with the evidence clerk, and he'll bring it to me."

Greg stopped in his tracks, stared at her, then realized she was joking. The evidence clerk was in his office so seldom that Greg had a hard time remembering what he looked like. Maybe they didn't have one at all. Maybe he'd been fired as a cost-cutting measure. *That's an excellent idea*, Greg thought. *That one's going in the suggestion box. Even if it's already happened.* "That's very funny," he said. "Do you want it now, or should I bring it to the lab?"

"What is it?"

"Fingernails."

"Without fingers attached?"

"Just the nails."

"Eew. Bring them to the lab."

"They're strange."

"Besides being disembodied, how strange can fingernails be?"

"These are strange," Greg said again. The paper scraps in the tent belonging to the man called Crackers had been almost geologically layered, like the Grand Canyon. But he had found the fingernails and some long, fine, straight hairs right on top, along with shorter brown hairs that he thought belonged to Crackers himself. He didn't know if they meant anything other than that someone had visited Crackers sometime in the relatively recent past. But at this point, he would take any clue he could find that might point to someone who could identify the dead man. "They're actually pieces of nails.

They're very brittle. And they have these weird yellowish-white longitudinal lines running through them."

"Yellowish-white lines?" Catherine asked from behind them.

Greg's heart jumped into his throat, pounding feverishly. "Yes! I didn't know you were there."

"Sorry, Greg," Catherine said, "I didn't mean to startle you. Wendy, you were going to give me the data on Gottlieb." She gestured toward the paper Wendy still clutched. "But then you left with it."

"Oh, right." Wendy handed it over. "Sorry."

"No problem," Catherine said. "Lines in the nails. I have a feeling your nail donor isn't well."

"That would be my guess," Greg said. "I was going to do some research, see if I could find something that would cause that."

"You do that. I'm going to do some checking of my own. I have a little bit of a hunch . . ."

"What is it?"

"You'll know when it's more than a hunch," she said, walking away.

They both watched her go, then Wendy turned back to Greg. "Okay, you're bringing me diseased nails. I can't wait. Anything else?"

"Some long red hairs. Also very brittle."

Wendy eyed him for a moment, letting her gaze drift to his feet and back up to his head again. "What?" he asked.

"You have a certain . . . aroma about you today. Or should I say reek? You bring a girl diseased nails and brittle hair. And you're still single? Imagine that."

* * *

David Hodges watched Wendy and Greg out of the corner of his eye. It didn't look as if Greg was really getting anywhere with her, and it wasn't as if Hodges would have been jealous if he had.

Well, maybe a little. He and Wendy had so much in common. They were both smart—okay, brilliant, at least in his case. They both loved the old sci-fi TV series *Astro Quest*. He was sure she thought he was cute, and he agreed with that assessment.

But he had blown his one real chance with her, and he wasn't likely to get another one. Not really his fault, of course, that was just the way things shook out sometimes.

Still, he couldn't help watching her and wondering what they might have been like as a couple. Perhaps in some alternative dimension, an alternative Hodges was raising adorable little geniuses.

But this dimension's Hodges had more immediate concerns. He had to analyze the trace evidence from Robert Domingo's murder scene. Ray Langston hadn't been able to bring him much, but Hodges didn't know if that was because there wasn't much to be found or because he possibly had left some behind.

He had some hairs, which weren't whole enough still to have their follicles attached. The follicle cells were the parts of hairs that stored nuclear DNA and would have been most helpful to discover. A couple of the hairs had gone to Wendy just the same, because mitochondrial DNA could sometimes be extracted from hair shafts. Mitochondrial DNA was passed by maternal lineage, and it mutated very slowly, so it could identify not only a person's mother but also grandmother, great-grandmother, and so on, going back potentially for generations. It wasn't as commonly used in criminal cases as nuclear DNA, but that didn't mean it should be ignored. Finding it would be Wendy's problem.

The rest of the hairs were his problem. He would have to study the color and width, the distribution pattern of the pigment. He would run them through an infrared microspectrometer to determine if the color was real or fake. Through neutron activation analysis, he could determine the chemical content. There was plenty to be learned from hairs, even without DNA, it just took some doing. He might be able to determine the gender, race, and even age of the person the hair had belonged to, maybe even a place of origin if there was something unique in the chemical composition that pointed to a specific place. If it was dyed, he might be able to pinpoint when that had happened and what substance had been used.

And then there were the plant fiber samples. He would have to finish analyzing them to determine what type of plant they had come from and maybe to find the plant DNA that could differentiate the original plant from every other example of its type. If it was a local plant, he might be able to isolate where in the city it was found.

His shift had ended. He could go home, and no one could say a word about it. Day shift had come on, and everybody had to share space. Hodges hated sharing space with the day shift. They crowded him.

But Greg was still there, and Wendy and Mandy. And Catherine. Nick and Captain Brass were out in the field, as was Ray Langston.

No, he was trapped, like a rat in a faulty maze.

He was there for the duration, like it or not.

12

"THERE ARE A FEW huge nations," Aguirre was saying, "like the Navajo and the Cherokee, for example, where it's not that hard to find fullbloods anymore. Smaller tribes like ours, though, we're full of what they call thinbloods. Intertribal marriage was commonplace even back before the Europeans came here, so it's not like it's a new thing."

They were back in his official Jeep, cutting across the reservation, Aguirre driving fast over roads in serious disrepair. Every now and then, they passed a house or a trailer, some with wash hanging out on lines, kids in the yard, maybe a couple of goats or some chickens in a pen. Nick had filled in Aguirre and Brass on what Ray had told him about blood quantum, and Aguirre took over from there.

"Story is, blood quantum was invented by the white government as a way to winnow down tribal membership. Drive us into extinction bureaucratically, since they couldn't do it with bullets. I don't know if I believe that, but a lot of people do."

"That sounds a little far-fetched," Brass observed. "I thought the conspiracy theory was more modern than that."

"You want to talk far-fetched, how about those treaties you guys had us agree to?" Aguirre countered. "Look, I'm not some radical, I just try to understand the different points of view. I have to, to keep tabs on what's going on around here. People who grew up poor on the rez want some mechanism to keep newcomers from claiming tribal identity—pushing them to the back of the line when it comes to health insurance, housing, other tribal benefits. But if circumstances you couldn't control, you know, who your grandmother married, mean you suddenly don't belong to the people you thought you did, that's no good, either."

"It's a complicated thing, all right," Nick said. "Seems going by parentage would be easier. If your dad or your mom, depending on if the tribe is matrilineal or patrilineal, was a member, then you are."

Aguirre turned around in his seat and glanced at Nick. "Then what happens if my tribe goes by the mother, but your father's goes by him? Do you belong to both? Or what if you're in a patrilineal tribe, but your mother married into it, moved to the reservation years before you were born, and you've never lived anywhere else or considered yourself a part of any other tribe? It's not so bad if the rules are consistent for generations, because then at least people know what to expect. But when a tribal commission can change them in midstream, then people get messed up."

A snake slithered across the road, pink as a heavy-duty garden hose. Aguirre was watching the road again, which Nick appreciated, considering the sheer number of rabbits, ground squirrels, birds, and other creatures that kept darting into the road. "Some think the line should be cultural, not connected to bloodlines at all. What matters most is how well someone has assimilated the values of the people, not how much of any type of blood they have. Do they speak the language? Do they participate in traditional tribal activities? That's hard to measure, too, but it hurts to see someone raised as white, identified as white, who can claim membership with a piece of paper, when you're fully native but you're knocked out by some intertribal marriage way in the past."

"So . . . this guy you're taking us to see," Brass said, bringing them back around to the subject of Robert Domingo's murder. "What's his story?"

"Calvin Tom," Aguirre said. "He's exactly the kind of case I'm talking about."

"How so?" Nick asked.

"Calvin is part Grey Rock Paiute and part Navajo. That's not an uncommon mix around here. He was raised on the rez and always considered himself Grey Rock. His mom was almost full Grey Rock and had divorced his dad when he was very young. So all the family he knew was here. He never even met his daddy's people. As a young man, he moved away for a few years, worked in Los Angeles for a time, then I think Seattle. Recently, he came back here, to the place he had always thought of as home. When he got here, the whole membership thing was going on. He applied for membership, but he was turned down."

"I bet he wasn't happy about that," Nick said.

"Not a bit. He bitched and moaned, you know. He complained to Domingo, then threatened him."

"Anybody take his threats seriously?" Brass asked.

"They didn't sound serious, according to witnesses. I mean, he was pissed off, no question. But it was all that 'I'm gonna freakin' kill you, Domingo!' stuff. Every cop hears that crap. I'm sure you hear it every day. If we tried to intercede every time someone said he was going to kill somebody else, that's all we'd do."

"Except in this case, somebody did," Brass said.

Aguirre cranked the wheel hard to the right, and the Jeep shot around a corner, fishtailing a little. *If he always drives like this,* Nick thought, *it's a wonder there are enough people left on the reservation to make the membership rolls a problem.*

"Somebody did," Aguirre echoed. "And that is why we're going to visit Calvin Tom."

Tom's place was up a little hill, set well back from the road. A couple of scrawny dogs sprawled in the shade of a broken-down, rust-scaled pickup truck outside. The home itself was a double-wide trailer, blue with brown trim, listing to the left where some of the cinder blocks propping it up had started to crumble under its weight. The whole property looked as if a stiff wind could blow it into the next state. "I'm not saying it's a bad place to grow up. I love it here, wouldn't trade it for anything. But like I said," Aguirre reminded them quietly as he parked, "there's a lot of poverty on the rez. You okay with that?"

"I wish it was different," Nick said. "But we're here to investigate a murder. It doesn't matter to me if the people we're talking to are rich as kings or poor as dirt."

Aguirre chuckled. "I'll try to line up a few of those rich suspects," he said, stepping out into the sun and blinking. "Till then, we're gonna have to go with poor."

Nick and Brass followed the tribal cop to the door. One of the dogs perked up and followed their progress with ears raised, while the other just snoozed. Aguirre banged loudly enough to wake someone three houses over. "Calvin doesn't hear so good. Screwed up his ears working construction."

Heavy footsteps sounded behind the door, the floor groaned, and Nick was afraid for an instant that the whole structure would tip over. Then the door swung open. "Yeah?"

"Hey, Calvin," Aguirre said, at a level just this side of a shout. "You doing okay?"

"Fine," Calvin said. He was a big guy, six-five or six-six, almost as broad as the whole doorway. Compared with him, even Richie Aguirre looked petite. He eyed the Las Vegas police through eyes narrowed with naked suspicion. "What do you want?"

"These guys are cops from the city," Aguirre replied. "They have some questions for you."

"I'm Captain Jim Brass, LVPD," Brass said. "Did you kill Robert Domingo?"

"Huh?" Calvin asked.

Brass repeated the question, louder. Calvin Tom cocked his big head toward Brass, then answered him with a sorrowful expression. "I wish I did."

"That right?"

"Yeah. I hate that bastard."

"But you didn't kill him?"

"I just said no, didn't I?"

"That's right, you did. You ever been to his house in the city?"

"I didn't know he had one."

"Where were you last night? Say, from midnight to two a.m.?"

"I was drunk," Tom said. He hadn't had to ponder the question for long.

"Drunk?"

Calvin Tom tugged at the hairs of his left eyebrow, already so thin it almost appeared plucked. His cheeks and chin were so smooth that Nick wondered if he had to shave more than twice a week. "I got some drinks at a bar in the city. On the way home, I got sleepy, so I pulled over by the road. That's why my truck isn't here."

"I'm not following. Why isn't your truck here?" Brass asked.

"A cop brought me home."

Brass met Aguirre's gaze. "Okay, Mr. Tom. Thanks for your time." He turned away from the door and started back toward the Jeep.

"Thanks, Calvin," Aguirre said. "You stay out of trouble now."

"Okay." Calvin Tom slammed his door hard enough to rock the trailer.

"That's it?" Nick asked angrily as they climbed back into the Jeep. " 'You didn't do it, did you?' That's how a captain does things?"

"Did you get a load of his feet, Nicky?" Brass asked.

Nick was almost embarrassed to answer. "I, uh, I was still kind of stunned by the rest of him."

"I'm talking Shaquille O'Neal feet. You could raft across Lake Mead in one of his shoes. The footprints you found at the house were, what, eight and a half?"

"Yeah," Nick said. "But that doesn't mean—"

"Sometimes you gotta go with your gut," Brass said. "Mine tells me that if that guy wanted to kill Domingo, he would have squeezed him between his paws until he popped. He wouldn't hit him with something like a cigarette lighter."

"You're probably right about that," Aguirre said. He started the engine and backed away, watching for the dogs the whole time so he didn't run into them. "I remember this one football game when we were in high school. Calvin accidentally made an interception. Nobody passed to him, because he just wasn't that good, but he happened to be standing between the other quarterback and his receiver, and he was like this wall. The ball just fell against him, and he got his hands on it. He started for the end zone, and by the time he got there, I think there were six or seven guys hanging off him. They looked like Christmas ornaments on a tree."

"Still . . ." Nick said. "Can you check on his story? About a cop bringing him home?"

"Sure," Aguirre said. "Nothing to it. I figured maybe

that's what happened when we got there and I didn't see his truck."

"That happens a lot around here?"

"Yeah, once in a while. We don't mind giving people a ride if it's not too busy. Calvin's a big man, but when it comes to drinking, he's a lightweight."

"Tell you what, Nick," Brass said. "If we turn up some physical evidence connecting Calvin to the scene, we can come back here and pick him up. It's not like the guy can hide, right? I think you can see him from space."

13

Because the paper scraps found in the John Doe's pockets and tent were so numerous, Catherine had called in forensic document examiner Professor Rambar to assist Ronnie Litra, the lab's night-shift Questioned Documents tech, along with the day-shift tech, to try to find out if anything in all of those pieces of paper pointed to the dead man's identity.

The review hadn't been completed yet—Catherine thought it could take days, if not weeks—but progress had been made, and now Rambar had come to Catherine's office to summarize their findings so far. Rambar was a distinguished-looking gentleman, with thinning gray hair, a goatee, and thin glasses. He sat with his spine erect, right leg crossing the left at the knee, his fingers interlaced on his lap. Greg was there as well, leaning against a filing cabinet, listening intently.

"I appreciate you coming in on such short notice," Catherine began.

"I'm just happy that I was available," Rambar said. "I wouldn't have wanted to miss this for anything."

"That good?"

"That . . . let's just say interesting. It's not every day one comes across such a trove of documents. All in all, these appear to illuminate what seems to be a very disturbed man."

"Disturbed how?" Catherine asked.

"That's a question for a psycholinguistics expert, which I can't profess to be," Rambar replied. "You could feed these documents—or a transcription of them, anyway, since it would never be able to read them as they are—into a computer and no doubt learn much more about the man who wrote them. I'm afraid I can't tell you a whole lot about him; I can only address the documents themselves."

Greg knew that in the trade, a note jotted on a crushed toilet-paper tube was still considered a document, but even so, it sounded odd to his ears to hear those bits of random paper described that way. They looked more like trash than documents—the word seemed to give them more importance than they deserved. But then again, maybe not—maybe somewhere in them was the clue that would crack the case. He'd had to find them, photograph them, and bag them in huge plastic trash bags, and he was glad that interpreting them was someone else's responsibility.

"I understand," Catherine said. "What can you tell us about them?"

"First, and perhaps most significant, virtually all of them were written by the same person. Over a period of years but definitely the same hand. I checked overall form, line features, format, to the extent that I could, and the consistency is undeniable. There are changes, of course—most handwriting changes a little, month to month and year to year. But there are also enough markers that don't change that we can tell when the same author writes two separate notes even a decade apart.

"It was harder to get a sense of content, because the sentences themselves are often disjointed, or portions are missing, torn off, or what have you. Plus, as you know, much of it was obliterated by overwriting, even charring in many cases. Still, I can tell you that the author is a male, most likely older than twenty and younger than forty. As I said, the notes themselves were written over time, so I can't narrow down the age range much more than that."

"How can you read the writing that's covered by other writing or burned?" Greg had seen it done, but he still marveled at the fact that seemingly impossible-to-read text could be deciphered.

"We can't always," Rambar admitted. "Sometimes the best we can do is to establish that something has been altered or removed. Erasure through scraping or actually eliminating layers of paper will leave rough patches, and if someone tries writing over those patches with ink, the ink will usually spread more than it would have on the original paper. Chemical erasures leave stains that can be detected through infrared luminescence, oblique lighting, and so on.

"The difficulty here," he went on, warming to his material, "was that we had overwriting—probably not deliberately obscuring the original text but simply the result of a man of limited means, making notes to himself on paper he had already used, perhaps years before, to make other notes to himself. The result is notes that might have meant something to him but only to him—to us, they simply look like confused scribbling. Again, oblique lighting, alternative light sources such as infrared or ultraviolet, and the use of filters helps, especially in those cases where the color of the layers of writing varies. If he wrote in blue ink over gray pencil, then viewing through a blue filter subtracts the blue, making the gray reasonably legible. Or as legible as this man's handwriting ever is.

"In the reverse case, pencil over ink, the pencil can be erased to reveal the ink below. That destroys the document's usefulness in court, although in this case, if the deceased wrote all of the documents himself and they're not all likely to become part of a court case—or any, since he's already dead—we can certainly do that in order to see what the underwriting says. Of course, your staff and I have made every attempt to preserve the integrity of the original documents. We've been busy photocopying those that are legible on their face and preserving the others in transparent plastic so that we're handling them no more than absolutely necessary."

"Of course," Catherine said. "The most important thing is to find any clues to his identity that they might contain, but we don't want the documents to be destroyed during analysis, if possible."

"Especially given what I had to live through to collect them," Greg added. He still felt as if he could smell the tent's interior, as if subatomic particles of it had become lodged in his nasal membranes. Which, no doubt, they had. More precisely, the chemicals causing the smell would have floated into his nose, binding with the cilia lining his nasal cavity, which would cause a nerve impulse to send the information through the olfactory cell, up the olfactory nerve fiber into the olfactory bulb, and from there to his brain. It would take a while before that all cycled out, but he didn't like thinking about tiny bits of the dead man's belongings living inside his head for any length of time. He turned his attention back to what the professor was saying.

"Yes, well, we try to be careful," Rambar said. "Then, of course, we move on to the more sophisticated techniques. Hyperspectral imaging can create true three-D images of the individual lines, allowing us to differentiate even same-colored inks or the identical ink written at different times. To examine charred documents, we stabilize them first with polyvinyl acetate, to make sure they don't flake apart in our hands—or forceps, more accurately— float them on a solution of glycerin, chloral hydrate, and alcohol, and photograph them. You'd be surprised at how much can show up if you just know the right way to look."

"I'm sure," Greg said.

"At any rate, it turns out that most of the notes are attempts to jog the writer's memory about various things or else written so that he won't forget something. Directions to a shelter or a church serving Thanksgiving meals. The day of the week he had a shower at the Y. 'Rainy today.' That sort of thing. Most of it trivial and not pointing in any obvious manner to the identity of the person who wrote them. You couldn't even go back and trace who got a free Thanksgiving dinner on such and such a date, because even on the rare occasions when he did note a specific date, he didn't write the year."

"So you're telling me that it's all useless to us?" Catherine asked.

"Nothing of the sort," Rambar said. "We've only really just started, as I said. We have a long way to go, but I wanted to tell you where we are so far, since I know there's a certain urgency. And there are a few things that are more intriguing than others, things that show up again and again."

"Such as?" Greg asked.

"Well, one of the things that struck me is a particular set of directions. Judging by the landmarks noted, they seem to lead from open desert into the city, at least to the city's edge. It's very detailed, although not necessarily the sort of thing one could follow now. 'Left at the gas station,' that sort of thing. What if there are two gas stations close to each other? It doesn't tell you which one. What if it's no longer a gas station? Without a date, you couldn't even go back and determine that there was a gas station in this location at this time."

"Then why do you bring it up?" Catherine asked.

"Because of what we've been able to examine so far, it's the one thing that has been repeated most often. And verbatim, or very nearly so. He wrote it down many, many times, on different pieces of paper, as if to keep it fresh in his mind. The phrasing changes only slightly, and the details are always the same."

"Maybe he was afraid he would lose, or had lost, the other papers," Greg suggested. "And wanted to make sure he had it in enough places that he couldn't lose them all."

"Certainly possible. The main thing is that these directions, for whatever reason, were vitally important to him. To lose them would have been tragic, in some way that I can't yet determine."

"We have to keep in mind, this guy had a bullet in his brain all this time," Catherine said. "That's bound to affect someone's habits and perceptions."

"True," Greg said.

Professor Rambar uncrossed his legs and put his hands on his knees. "I should get back to it," he said. "I'll let you know if we find anything else interesting."

"Thanks, Professor." Catherine watched him stand up and leave her office, then turned to Greg. "What do you make of it?"

"I don't know," Greg said. "I guess if we can determine where in the city those directions lead to, I could try to backtrack it. Find out what it was in the desert that was so important that he needed to keep the directions no matter what."

"It's already been a long shift, Greg. And Professor Rambar said they would be impossible to follow."

"Tell me about it. But he's a documents guy, not a CSI. He doesn't know how often we have to do the impossible. Anyway, we have to figure out who this guy is. And like you said, what if there's some connection between him and the disappearance of Jennifer Cameron? I'd be glad to take a crack at it, if it's okay with you."

Catherine smiled the way people did when addressing tiny children or the hopelessly confused. Or hopelessly confused small children. "You be my guest, Greg," she said. "Knock yourself out."

14

Rico Aguirre was driving Nick and Brass back to tribal police headquarters and checking out Calvin Tom's story on his handheld radio at the same time, when the voice from the other end said, "Hold on a minute, Richie."

"Okay," Aguirre said. Static took over the airwaves. Aguirre kept driving one-handed, holding the radio in his right hand. Nick liked the man, but if he never had to get into a vehicle with him at the wheel again, that would be just fine.

A moment later, the voice came back over the radio. "Richie, there's been a shooting reported. Multiple shots fired, multiple victims. Can you head over to Meoqui Torres's house?"

"Yeah, I'm not too far from there. I got these LVPD guys in the car with me—"

"Ray mentioned that name," Nick whispered to Brass. "I think we should check this out."

"We'll tag along," Brass said.

"Other units are responding, too," the radio voice said. "You won't be alone for long."

"Okay, I'm on it," Aguirre said. He handed Brass the radio. He usually wore it on his belt, but Nick supposed that, for all his terrifying driving habits, he didn't intend to try to put it back there while he was behind the wheel. Probably, he usually just dropped it onto the passenger seat. Aguirre hit the lights and siren and started driving even faster. Desert whipped past the windows, and although the wheels gripped the road, when he took corners at speed, he slid over the shoulder and spat gravel and dust into the air.

"What's the scoop on this Torres?" Brass asked. "Our colleague Ray Langston mentioned him."

"Meoqui is one of the most obnoxious guys in the whole tribe," Aguirre said. "Real political, always bitching about something or other."

"Like the blood-quantum standards?" Nick asked.

"Sure, that. Or whatever. When the new casino hotel renovation was announced, he was the guy complaining about environmental issues, demanding an impact report. When we were negotiating with an energy company about putting in a coal plant, he was the one who ended up getting it killed. Plus, he makes movies about it all, so just in case you didn't get tired of listening to him the first time around, you can watch him on DVD. Don't get me wrong, it's not that I don't like the guy. And he's smart as hell. It's just . . . you know, sometimes even someone who means well can get tiresome. You just don't want to hear about what's bad about everything all the time."

"I know what you mean," Brass said. "Some people just aren't happy unless they're throwing dirt on someone's campfire."

"Sometimes you've gotta have those people," Nick put in. "They can be annoying, but they can keep everybody else honest."

"We're a better tribe with him in it than we would be without," Aguirre agreed. "He's kind of holier-than-thou—like he always knows what's best, and everybody else should just listen to him. And like I said, he just gets old. But I don't wish him any harm."

The Jeep whipped through open desert and past more homes of various sizes but mostly small. Almost all of the people watching them race by had dark hair and dark skin, Nick noted—not surprising on the reservation, but every now and then, he was surprised to see a blond or a redhead with pale skin outside one of the houses, and the contrast always reminded him of how overwhelmingly homogeneous the population there was.

A few minutes later, Aguirre made a screeching left turn onto a smaller paved road. The tires spat gravel for a quarter-mile, and then they reached a yellow ranch house with an open porch across the front. The windows behind it were shattered, and bullet holes pocked the walls. A young Native American man holding a rag over a bleeding wound on his left biceps released his arm when he saw the Jeep and waved the bloodstained rag over his head. He was tall, his head shaved and polished, and in spite of the warmth of the day, he had on a plaid flannel shirt, open to reveal the chest and abs of a guy who took his weight lifting seriously. The sleeve of his shirt was dark with blood.

"This is the place," Aguirre said.

"So it seems," Brass said.

As they ground to a stop in the front yard, Nick saw more people, mostly men but one woman, sitting in chairs or sprawled out on the balcony floor. Blood pooled on the floorboards like spilled paint.

Nick, Brass, and Aguirre were all out of the Jeep before the roostertail of dust they'd kicked up had settled, rushing across the dirt yard toward the porch.

"The shooters still around?" Aguirre asked urgently. He went into the back of the Jeep and brought out a battered first-aid kit.

"Gone," the guy with the rag said. "Bastards didn't stay long."

"There's an ambulance coming," Aguirre told him.

"It better hurry."

This was the worst-case scenario for a crime-scene investigator, Nick knew. People had been shot. They were bleeding, possibly dying. Finding out who had shot them might depend on keeping the crime scene clear and uncompromised. But saving lives definitely depended on getting to them as quickly as possible, offering first aid, and making sure the wounded were transported to someplace they could get real medical care. Preserving the scene had to give way to the other priorities, Nick understood, even when it made the CSI in him cringe.

"START triage!" Brass called.

"Right," Nick said. He was already sprinting toward the porch. He had a crime-scene kit with him, but he wished he had brought the first-aid kit from his vehicle as well. He beat Brass to the porch by a couple of steps. Aguirre, slowed by having to go for his first-aid kit, brought up the rear.

START meant Simple Triage And Rapid Treatment and had been developed for just this sort of event, when people without a lot of emergency medical training arrived at a disaster before those who did have the training and proper equipment. Nick ignored the guy who had waved them in, since he was upright and, although wounded, not critically so, and went to the closest one on his left, who was down on the ground. Brass went right.

The man Nick reached first was lying facedown, blood spreading from beneath him. Nick put a hand on his back, to let him know he was there and comfort him but also to find out if he was breathing. "You okay, buddy?"

But he didn't feel any motion beneath his hand. He moved it up to the guy's neck, feeling for a pulse. Nothing. He turned back to Aguirre, kneeling beside another victim. "You got any tape, Richie? To mark these guys?"

Aguirre fished around inside the first-aid kit and found four rolls of tape: red, black, yellow, and green. He tossed them to Nick, who tore off a long strip of black and adhered it to the dead man. Black didn't necessarily mean the person was dead, but he wasn't expected to live long enough to reach medical care, so he should be skipped over until the more urgent cases were dealt with. The highest-priority victims would be tagged with red, then yellow, and finally, those whose needs were least urgent got green.

In this way, Nick worked from victim to victim, while Brass and Aguirre did the same. Most of those he came across were alive, with wounds of varying degrees of seriousness. One had been hit in the scalp, the bullet digging a furrow just beneath the skin from forehead to crown. Another had taken two rounds to the abdomen and was bleeding like mad. He was told to put pressure on the wound and got a red tag. Another had a through-and-through that had been hit in his popliteal artery. He got a wide-cuffed tourniquet and a yellow tag.

The eleven victims were all Native Americans, most in their twenties or early thirties, Nick judged, although a couple were significantly older. They wore jeans, T-shirts, and sneakers or cowboy boots. For the most part, they wore their hair long and loose. From the glimpses Nick had of the house's interior, it was a combination home and studio— he saw a lot of lighting equipment, a good-quality video camera on a tripod, and gear boxes in what would ordinarily be a living room with bare floors and plain white walls.

"What happened here?" Brass asked as he wrapped his own belt around a man's leg as a tourniquet.

The guy with the bloody rag was the most coherent one. He dropped down into a wicker chair, its cushion already sopping with blood, not that he seemed to care at that point. "We were just sitting out here, you know, slinging the shit. These dudes pull up in a truck, slow down, and then all of a sudden they got guns out and they're blasting away at us. Couple of us were strapped, we shot back, and they rolled out."

"Can you identify them?" Brass asked.

"Never saw them before."

"What about anybody else?" Brass asked loudly. Nick recognized the commanding tone Brass could take when he wanted cooperation, and in a hurry. "Anyone able to ID the shooters?"

No one answered in the affirmative. Nick didn't believe that no one had recognized the shooters, but, as in the city, there were occasions where no one wanted to identify their assailants, preferring to mete out their own brand of justice.

"Hey," Aguirre said, "where's Meoqui?"

"Over there," someone replied, pointing to an unconscious man, crumpled on the floor, whom Nick had bandaged as best he could and tagged with red. He had been hit in the left thigh by a large-caliber round that had exploded a big chunk of his upper leg. Apparently spinning around from that wound, he took a second shot through the right trapezius, back to front, and then fell and hit the back of his head on the windowsill. He'd been bleeding badly when Nick found him. There was still hair and tissue on the corner of the sill, which Nick had observed with professional detachment. That was the sort of thing he would ordinarily be looking for, except in this case, he was more concerned with patching and tagging. *This isn't your turf,* he kept reminding himself. *Even if you could work the scene, you don't have the authority.*

Aguirre went down on one knee at the activist's side. "Meoqui, you okay?" he asked. The concern in his voice sounded authentic. Nick supposed the cop had been telling the truth. He ran short of patience with Torres but liked him in spite of that.

Torres didn't answer. Nick didn't expect him to. Best case, Torres had a concussion. Nick hoped the young man hadn't suffered any permanent brain damage, but that crack in the head was a bad one. And he'd lost plenty of blood from those bullet wounds, as well as from the scalp laceration.

His gaze ran down Torres's body. The man was short and lean, with long legs and a swimmer's build, powerful shoulders and arms revealed by his red muscle shirt. His Nikes were on the small side. Nick would have to measure to be sure, but he believed they were eight-and-a-halfs. The marks behind Domingo's house hadn't been clear enough to lift treads from, but those shoes could have made them.

Sirens wailed down the street, vehicles skidded in the dirt, and suddenly, the little yard and porch were overrun with cops. Nick, Brass, and Aguirre gave up what they were doing and huddled in the yard. "No EMS yet?" Brass asked.

"The closest real hospital is in the city," Aguirre said. "We've got some medical clinics and a couple of traditional healers. Nothing like a trauma center, though. Best thing for these guys will be to get them into town, but somehow the ambulances never seem to hurry real fast to get here."

"That's just wrong," Nick said.

"You don't have to tell me."

"Who was the target here?" Brass asked. "Torres?"

"Maybe," Aguirre replied. "Like I told you, he pisses a lot of people off. He makes these movies, documentaries. Last one was kind of a hit on the film-festival circuit, I guess. Even played on cable TV. It was about one of our tribal elders, a man who's had a lot of success steering reservation kids away from joining gangs by getting them interested in traditional Indian skills and practices. He teaches them the old ceremonies, you know, some of the old ways, and then they don't want to take drugs and get into trouble, because they have a connection to the land and their ancestors."

"Sounds like a great guy," Nick said.

"Yeah, he is. A real treasure. Meoqui got a lot of attention and some money because of the movie's success, and I think maybe it went to his head. The film he's working on now is about institutionalized poverty on Indian reservations. He's been traveling around, shooting on different reservations, but also shooting a lot of it here. From the stories I've heard, it's very critical of some of Chairman Domingo's policies and decisions. In return, Domingo threatened to revoke Meoqui's permission to film on the rez."

"Which could be motive for murder," Brass said. "If the revocation is still a threat and hasn't taken effect yet—"

"I don't think Meoqui's a killer."

"You didn't think Calvin Tom was, either. I don't know if you have a lot of killers on this reservation, but you've got at least one whose handiwork I can see from here."

"True. Anyway, yeah, you're right. I'm sure Meo-qui was pretty upset with Chairman Domingo."

"And if other people know how angry he was, they might reach the same conclusion you did, Jim," Nick said. "Somebody thinks Torres killed Domingo, so they came here and shot up Torres in revenge."

"That's what I was getting at," Aguirre said. "That's what this feels like to me. A gang-style drive-by but not a random one. These guys meant to take Meoqui out."

"While I was at Domingo's house last night, these two guys came by in a dark pickup truck," Nick said. "Black, navy blue. I reported the tag, or as much of it as I was able to catch."

"We got the report," Aguirre confirmed. "We weren't able to get anything nailed down, though."

"They could have been gang types." Nick described the two young men, the smaller one with long hair and his big tattooed friend who would have stood out in any crowd.

Aguirre squinted into the sky. "The smaller one could be a guy named Ruben Solis. He's kind of a punk. One of Chairman Domingo's thugs, really, the kind of guy who'll do whatever he's told without thinking too hard about the morality of it. He hangs with a big guy named Shep Moran, who's done hard time over in Jean. Shep's got tats all up his arms, across his neck and chest. And Ruben drives a dark truck."

"Would they do something like this?"

"I hate to think anybody would," Aguirre answered. "But I wouldn't put it past them. Solis especially. Shep's the one who's done prison time, but Solis is a mean one, with a nasty temper. Definitely the ringleader of that pair. Thing is, if word gets out that he shot Meoqui—or even a rumor that he might have—then they're in trouble, too. Meoqui has a lot of friends on the rez, and some of them are just as ruthless as Solis is."

"So, what, you think we're going to see a domino effect of revenge shootings?" Brass asked. "Sure glad I came out here today. I could be home sleeping or pulling weeds."

"Hey!" Aguirre called abruptly. Nick followed his gaze. Three of the less badly wounded men were carrying Meoqui Torres to a bright red pickup truck. "Where are you taking him?"

"Tired of waiting for the ambulance," one guy said. "We're going to get him to a clinic."

Aguirre beckoned one of the tribal police officers over, a young guy who was standing around watching other people work but not doing anything particularly useful. "Follow them over there, Wilbur," he said. "Park outside the clinic, make sure there's no trouble."

"Will do," Wilbur said. He hurried to his car, an old Ford station wagon with a faded tribal police logo on the door, and got in. When the pickup truck pulled away with Torres and one other man in the back, Wilbur followed right on their tail.

Aguirre called another cop, a woman with a broad, flat face and a solid build. "Canvass the neighbors, Juanita," he said. "See if anybody saw anything." Nick couldn't see any neighbors from there, but the street curved around some low hills, and there might have been houses out of sight but within earshot. "And don't let 'em tell you they didn't hear it. This many rounds, anybody within a mile or two would have heard."

When she was walking to her vehicle, Brass approached Aguirre. "I think you and I should go find Ruben Solis and Shep Moran before someone else does."

"Probably not a bad idea. What about Stokes?"

"I'll stay here, if it's okay," Nick said. "We stomped all over this crime scene, but it should still be processed. I can work it and hand over whatever I find to you for your investigation. You'll know where to find me if you need me."

"Till the Fourth of July, from the looks of it," Brass said with a grin.

Nick held out his car keys to Aguirre. "Richie, can you have someone bring over my Yukon? I have a kit with me, but there's more equipment in the back I could use."

Aguirre took the keys and whistled for one of the other uniformed officers. "I'll take care of it," he said.

Brass put a hand on Nick's shoulder and gave him a stern look. "Keep your guard up, Nick. I got a feeling this is a long way from over."

15

After Keith Hyatt told Ray that Meoqui Torres was a filmmaker, Ray called Archie Johnson and asked him to track down some of Torres's work. Now that he had made it back, Archie summoned Ray into the A/V lab and showed him what he had turned up on the Internet.

"He's been posting clips online," Archie said, smoothing his crop of thick black hair. "I've pulled together a few for you. These are from a work in progress, he says. The working title is *Epic Failure.*"

"A nice optimistic note."

"From what I've seen so far, optimism isn't his strong suit."

Archie clicked a couple of keys, and a computer screen filled with a blurred image that quickly focused in on the exterior of a shack on a windswept desert plain. There was one plant in the shot, something that might have been classified as a tree but was stunted and bent and provided little, if any, shade for the building. If the place had ever been painted, wind and blowing sand had scoured it down to a raw gray-brown color. The camera zoomed in on a window and then through it on a man sitting inside on a folding metal chair.

Then the shot cut to an interior, lit by the natural light flooding in the window. The man was middle-aged, Native American, with short hair going gray, a shirt open to the waist showing a lean, wrinkled torso, and a cigarette burning in one hand. Smoke wafted up into his face, forcing him to squint. A title at the bottom of the frame identified him as Herbert Acosta, Grey Rock Paiute.

". . . thing is, it was the white people, the ones in the nineteenth and early twentieth century who were making policy at the Bureau of Indian Affairs—Bureau of Extinction Affairs, I call it—who were determined to hold us down. They couldn't destroy us militarily, but they could make us wish they had."

"Do you really think that, Herbert?" an off-screen voice asked.

"That's Torres," Archie whispered. "He's on the screen later."

"Hell yes!" Acosta jabbed at the camera with the lit cigarette. "Just look at the evidence, little cousin. It's everywhere. See, fetal alcohol syndrome? The health-care system they devised encourages that. It's easier to keep a population compliant if the individuals in it are damaged from birth. And even those who weren't damaged are then so occupied with taking care of the little ones that they're easy to push around, too." He stopped long enough to take a drag and blow out a plume of smoke, then the shot switched to a close-up of his hand, burning cigarette between his fingers. Age spots marked the back of his hand, and the webbing between the second and third knuckles was yellowed by nicotine.

"It's all about finding legal ways to keep us poor, keep us dependent, keep us like children they can manipulate. Fetal alcohol is one. Controlling our jobs is another, keeping them limited and low-paying. And casinos, don't get me started on them. They're a great way to legally steal money from the poor."

"But some of the profits go back to the tribe, right?" Torres asked

Another cut, back to the original framing. Acosta sucked on the cigarette, the tip glowing so brightly it seemed it would burn a hole through the screen. "Key word is 'some,' brother. As little as they can manage. And I'm not just talking about the Great White Father now, I'm talking about Indians, too. People like Chairman Domingo, who cut and cut the tribal rolls so they can concentrate the wealth in the hands of the few. At the expense of the many, of course. Instead of rolling the profits into services that would benefit the people who need it most, they try to make themselves and their friends—the people who are already the richest—even more wealthy. Throwing their own brothers and sisters under the bus to line their fat wallets. You ask me, Domingo and his kind are no better than the whites who stuck us on these reservations in the first place. Keeping us there, keeping us down. Squashing us like bugs if we try to stand up. One of these days, he'll get his."

"I think I've seen enough for now," Ray said. Archie stopped the video. "Send the rest to my computer, and I'll look at it when I can. I have to make a phone call." He started out the door but stopped and swung around. "And thanks, Archie. That's good stuff."

Ray called Nick as he headed for his "office," a cramped space in the morgue that Doc Robbins had made generously available to him. It was small, but it suited him, and it was better than hauling all his gear around all day long.

"Stokes," Nick answered.

"How's it going out there, Nick?"

"Could be better. It's a bloodbath here, Ray. A bunch of people were shot, and I'm afraid that more might be on the way."

"Oh, no. Any fatalities?" Ray asked.

"Yes, some. Not everybody. That guy Meoqui Torres you mentioned is among the wounded. Shooting was a drive-by at his place."

"I'm sorry to hear that. Speaking of Torres, I just watched a clip from his new movie. It's pretty incendiary."

"That's kind of his reputation."

"If you can, check into a man named Herbert Acosta. He's Grey Rock, and I think he lives on the reservation. He made an implicit threat against Robert Domingo, on tape."

"Herbert Acosta, huh? I'll let Brass know. I'm working the shooting scene while he and our tribal police escort are running around."

"He got the easy part, huh? Okay, I'll finish up

what I'm doing here, and then I'll head out your way to see if I can help. Watch your back, Nick."

"Always, Ray," Nick said. "Thanks."

Nick called Brass and told him what Ray had said about Herbert Acosta. He heard Brass relay the information to Aguirre, heard Aguirre chuckle without humor.

"Acosta?" the tribal cop said. "Tell him he's too late."

"What do you mean?"

"You see that older guy at Meoqui's? Skinny guy, gray hair?"

"The dead one."

"Yeah, the dead one. That was Herbert Acosta."

"You catch that, Nick?" Brass asked into the phone.

"Yeah, I got it. Paramedics just rolled up. I'll try to process Acosta before he's taken away, see if I can connect him to Domingo's house."

"You do that," Brass said. "I'll talk to you later."

16

"I'M CERTAIN, DETECTIVE WILLOWS—"

"I'm not a detective, Doctor Boullet. I'm a criminalist. You can call me Supervisor Willows, or you can call me Catherine."

"Very well, Supervisor Willows," the doctor amended. Somewhat pointedly, Catherine thought. Hutch Boullet had a pinched face, with a pursed mouth, small eyes, and a high forehead. He looked as if he spent more time playing tennis than examining patients, but the dramatic view of the city's skyline from the window of his spacious office suggested that he had a profitable practice. Of course, with the Cameron family as patients, he might not need any others. "At any rate, you're a law-enforcement officer, so I'm sure you understand that I cannot release any information about my patients without their express consent. You're familiar with doctor-patient confidentiality, of course."

"I am, Doctor," Catherine assured him. She had

come there on a hunch, and he had not been happy to carve out some time from his day to see her. She could have called first, but for all she knew, that might have sent him scurrying to the nearest tennis court. At least this way, she had caught him in the office. "And I wouldn't ask if it wasn't vitally important."

"I don't care if the fate of the free world depends on it. I can't do it."

"Here's the thing," she said. She had to get through to this guy somehow, but so far, he had proven difficult to crack. "My DNA tech has made a positive match between some hairs and fluids found in Daria Cameron's condo and some other hairs and pieces of fingernail found inside a tent at a homeless encampment."

Boullet looked uncomfortable about the direction of the conversation. He was sitting behind his expensive wooden desk, his lips pursed, his gaze locked on the desktop as if afraid to look away. There was more color in his cheeks than there had been a moment ago. "That seems most unlikely. Are you sure there isn't some mistake at your lab? I understand there have been some issues of contamination—"

"Not in a very long while, Doctor. I can assure you, our lab is very clean. And while some forensic science is considered to be questionable, DNA isn't. It's as definitive as fingerprints."

"Very well," the doctor said. "Go on."

"The hairs and fingernails that were found are very brittle, and there are whitish striations in the nails. You'd know better than I what that means. The point is, Daria is missing. And we know from the household staff that she's not well. But if she's critically ill in some way, then that changes the whole dynamic. It increases the urgency of finding her, wouldn't you say?"

"Certainly, people are looking for her anyway," the doctor said. "I'm not sure what—"

"Of course they are," Catherine interrupted. "But there's looking and there's *looking*. She's young, she's not currently employed, there haven't been any signs of abduction or foul play. And she's well off, and this is Las Vegas. For all we know, she's missing because she took a penthouse suite at the Romanov, or she went to Europe for the month. But if she's in need of constant medical attention or if being away from treatment might result in her death, then it's a different story. Not only does it give us new places to search—hospitals, pharmacies, doctor's offices, and the like—but it changes the importance of finding her quickly. That information might free up more resources for the search."

"I see." The doctor sat there, steepling his fingers. Catherine let the silence build. Keeping the pressure on him. If he truly had his patient's best interests at heart, he would have to make the right decision. "All right. I don't like to do this, because it's a violation of the first rule of patients' rights. And I'll trust you to keep this information as closely held as possible—it would be very bad if it became public. But if it's a matter of her life and death, I suppose I really have no choice."

Jackpot, Catherine thought. Not wanting to spook him into changing his mind, she didn't allow her triumph to show on her face. "That's right."

"Daria is quite seriously ill. I'm afraid I still haven't been able to diagnose her condition adequately; it has only presented itself recently. She has what appears to be congestion in her heart and a bit of an orange-brown discoloration of her skin, which is getting progressively more pronounced. For her heart, I've prescribed digitalis and aspirin for the time being, and I intended to schedule her for a battery of diagnostic tests, but there were . . . obstacles, and then she stopped returning our calls. On one of my visits to the estate, I checked with her mother, who told me she had gone missing."

"Can you tell me what those obstacles were?"

"Scheduling conflicts, I was led to believe."

"You don't sound convinced."

"Let's just say that if it were me, I would put the rest of my life on hold until I found out. But there seem to be other factors at work here, other people making decisions for her. Beyond that, I'd rather not go into detail."

Catherine let it go. "So she'll need access to a pharmacy to keep getting the digitalis," she said. "And the skin condition will be something our officers can watch for. That's a big help."

"The family has an adequate supply of medication, at least for the time being. But at some point, yes, she'll need to get more. And I hope this helps her, honestly." He was staring at his desk again, looking stricken. "I take my responsibilities seriously, Supervisor Willows. You presented a quandary, with two competing and mutually exclusive priorities. I hope I chose correctly."

"I'm sure you did, Doctor Boullet," Catherine said. "Thank you for your help."

She was standing up when something he had said struck her. He said he talked to Helena Cameron on one of his visits to the house and that the family had plenty of medicine. Did that mean Helena was suffering from the same thing? She hadn't seen the woman when she had gone to the house—she wasn't well, either, and she had gone to bed, tranquilized, the estate manager had said.

Dustin Gottlieb, in fact, the same estate manager who had sex with Daria before her disappearance.

He would need talking to again.

She started to ask the doctor about Helena, then stopped herself. He had told her everything he was going to and wouldn't talk about Helena, she was sure, without her permission, since she wasn't missing. He had noticed her hesitation, though. "Yes?" he asked. "Will there be something else, Supervisor Willows?"

"No, Doctor. That's quite enough. Thank you again."

She called Wendy from the car. "Thanks for that quick work on the Daria Cameron DNA," she said. "It was exactly what I needed to pry some information out of her doctor."

Wendy didn't ask what information, and Catherine appreciated that. "Glad it was helpful," she said. "I was just about to call you again."

"You've got something else for me? You're on a tear today."

"I just want to get everything wrapped up so I can go home."

"Well, you've been a big help today. We all would like to call it quits, but—"

Wendy cut her off. "I know, Catherine. I wasn't really complaining. Much. Anyway, here's the scoop . . ."

Catherine knew she was risking Undersheriff Ecklie's wrath by returning to the scene of the crime— the Cameron estate, in this case. She was doubling her jeopardy by demanding to talk to Helena Cameron herself. But after she made her case to Bradley Gottlieb (all the while promising herself she would have a few words with him before she left the premises), he parked her in a sitting room and went to fetch Mrs. Cameron, Drake McCann, and Craig Stilton.

During the few minutes she was waiting there alone, Catherine took in the artwork on the walls— an original Thomas Moran Yellowstone landscape, which was almost as big as one of Catherine's entire walls, a pastoral piece by John Singer Sargent, and more. Many paintings appeared to be at least a hundred years old, most depicting somewhat romanticized landscapes. All were hung in frames that appeared just as old as the paintings themselves.

"I love the out-of-doors," Helena Cameron said in a voice quavering with age and ill health. Catherine was staring at the Yellowstone painting, depicting a brilliant sunset over the mountains, and hadn't heard her come in. "Sadly, I hardly get to see it in person anymore. Bix and I used to travel the

West in a style that might surprise you, to look at me now, Mrs. Willows. We drove around in a station wagon with wooden panels on the sides, slept in tents, cooked our meals on campfires. Even after the money was coming in and the children were born, we loved to be outside, in nature. Now I can only experience what little nature there is here on the estate or enjoy it through lovely paintings and photographs."

"I sympathize, Mrs. Cameron," Catherine said. "I've always been more of an indoor girl myself, but I do appreciate natural beauty when I get the chance to see it."

"To what do we owe this visit, Supervisor Willows?" Stilton asked, remembering the right title for her. He and McCann flanked the lady of the house, as if ready to catch her if she fell. Helena Cameron was barely five feet tall and girlishly petite, with white hair cropped boyishly short and skin that looked a few shades past tan. "Is there some development in the case?"

"There are two cases ongoing," Catherine said. "The man who was shot on the property last night and Daria's disappearance. I'm becoming more and more convinced that there's a connection between the two."

"Oh, I don't see how there could be," Helena scoffed. "I'm told the man was a filthy bum, perhaps some sort of degenerate—"

"Careful how you talk about him, Mrs. Cameron," Catherine said, interrupting as gently as she could. She didn't want to let Helena become too riled up, since she was clearly not well. But she was here, and the poor woman had to know the truth. Next of kin notification could be the hardest job any police officer had to do. Sometimes, though, valuable information could be learned through the process, which was one of the reasons detectives preferred to do it themselves instead of delegating it. "In fact, it might be best if you sat down."

"Anything you have to say, Mrs. Willows, I can hear standing up."

"Very well," Catherine said. She noted that Craig Stilton took Helena's elbow, offering support. Catherine took a deep breath. Conrad Ecklie would be pissed, but that was a risk she would have to run. "The man Mr. McCann here shot last night? He was Troy Cameron, your son. I'm very sorry for your loss."

Helena wobbled, and McCann caught her other arm. Her face went white, or as white as someone whose skin was taking on a distinct terra-cotta cast could go, and her dainty, fragile left hand curled before her lips. "That's not possible."

"This is outrageous," Stilton fumed. "How can you come in here and say something like that? What proof do you have?"

"I have enough common DNA markers to be sure, at odds of about eight trillion to one," Catherine said.

Helena's legs threatened to give out. Stilton and McCann got her onto a couch that didn't look as if it would have been comfortable when some French craftsman had made it in the 1700s, much less today. "He . . . I haven't seen Troy since he was seventeen," she said in a faltering voice. "I can't believe he's been . . . *alive* all this time, and . . . and now that I find him, he's . . . he's . . ."

Her head drifted backward. Stilton got a hand behind it just before it hit the wooden rail at the back of the couch. "We need to get her to bed," he said. "She can't take this. I can't believe you came in here and told her that."

"She has a right to know," Catherine said. "We always tell the next of kin." She knew that Ecklie would hear about it, and she would hear about it from him. But what she had said was true. Helena Cameron had to be told. Better in person than through an intermediary. And Catherine had needed to see her reaction, if at all possible.

One thing was certain now: Helena had not known her son was still alive.

And another thing: whatever illness Daria Cameron suffered from, Helena had it, too. Her flesh was definitely on the orange side, and when she had put her hand to her mouth, Catherine had seen yellowish-white streaks on her nails.

"I'm afraid you'll have to leave, Supervisor Willows," Gottlieb said as he marched into the sitting room. "I understand you've upset Mrs. Cameron terribly."

"That was not my intention," Catherine said. "But I'm sure you'll agree that a mother has a right to know her only son has been found."

"There was surely a better way to tell her."

"Perhaps. I believe in the direct, honest approach myself. Unlike some people."

Gottlieb crossed his arms over his chest, perhaps

unintentionally swelling his biceps. "What does that mean?"

"It means," Catherine said, "that you didn't tell investigating officers about your relationship with Daria Cameron. She's missing, and her family is concerned. Don't you think your relationship is something the police might want to know about? Or were you afraid that it would make you a suspect?" She knew she was pushing it, maybe going a little over the top. But her certainty that this guy would complain to Ecklie, combined with his lame attempt to intimidate her by showing off his muscles, had ticked her off.

To her utter surprise, Gottlieb backed down, deflating in an almost physical way. "Okay," he said. "You're right. Daria and I were seeing each other. But you have to understand that we agreed to keep it a secret because she was afraid it might disturb her mother, and I was worried that it might affect my relationships with the other people here at work. There was nothing more sinister about it than that. I didn't say anything to the police because I didn't think it mattered. I knew that nothing I had done had anything to do with Daria's disappearance, so if they spent time investigating me, it would just distract them from what was really important."

"You should have let the detectives make that call."

"I know. I understand that now, really. At the time, I was just thinking of the promise I made to Daria."

"Would her mother honestly have been upset? I thought maybe she knew, and that's why she—"

"That's why she took me back? No way. She wasn't like that. She might even have canned me if she'd found out about me and Daria. But see, I just knew that's what people would believe. Helena took me back because she tried two other people in my job, and neither of them was any good at it. We fought sometimes, because I'm a person who says what he thinks and doesn't stop to think about how someone else might take it. Which is why she fired me the first time, because I said some things about other people around her that she didn't like. But when she found out no one could run the estate the way she likes it, she personally called me and asked me to come back."

"How long has the affair with Daria been going on?" Catherine asked.

"Six months, give or take. We've been friends for ages, and it just kind of moved to a new level one day. Believe me, if there was anything I could have told the police that would help find her, I would have. I've been worried sick about her."

"Okay," Catherine said. She had plenty of experience reading people, living ones as well as dead, and he came across as someone who was telling the truth. "I won't say a word, unless I have reason to believe it would affect the investigation in some way."

"Thank you!" he said. He was so effusive she was afraid he would try to hug her. "You're an absolute lifesaver! I do love my job here, and I wouldn't do anything to jeopardize it."

"I'll do what I can," Catherine promised him again. "But if you think of anything—anything—

that might help us find Daria, it's absolutely crucial that you let us know." She handed him her business card, even though she had given him one the night before.

He slipped the card into his pocket without looking at it. "I will," he said. "I would have already, except that—"

"I know. You made a promise. Promises are fine, but when lives are on the line, sometimes they have to be broken."

17

RAY DIDN'T LIKE THE idea of Nick processing such a complicated scene on his own, out there on the Grey Rock reservation. Not that CSIs didn't have to work alone sometimes, but a multiple-shooting scene was always a big job. And if there was the possibility that the shooters might come back, then a difficult job became a nightmare.

He wanted to get out there, to lend a hand if he could. He wrapped up what needed to be done in his office and started to head out, then remembered he wanted to check on progress in the trace lab before he went to the reservation. One never knew when the most seemingly insignificant fact would turn out to be the key to the whole case.

Then again, insignificant facts were often, in fact, insignificant.

Hodges was in the lab, peering into a comparison microscope, when Ray entered. "Excuse me, David?"

With a dramatic flourish and a rustle of fabric,

Hodges whipped his right hand into the air, holding up his index finger. Ray got the message—*one second.*

As the seconds trailed on and Hodges kept staring into the binocular lens unit, Ray thought maybe he had meant one minute. He hoped it wasn't one hour. He had no intention of staying that long. But it didn't look as if Hodges had any intention of addressing him until he was good and ready. He just kept that finger in the air, as if he was testing the wind.

Finally, Hodges raised his head from the scope and turned to face Ray. He still didn't speak, simply fixed what Ray supposed was meant to be an expectant look on his face and waited.

"Hello, David," Ray said, determined to be polite. "I was wondering if you've made any headway on the materials from the Domingo scene."

"Actually, I have," Hodges replied. "I'm not through all of it yet, but I have some results for you."

"Excellent," Ray said. Hodges stood there for a moment, his expression unchanged. "May I know what they are?"

"Oh," Hodges said, blinking as if his mind had been somewhere else entirely and he had just remembered whom he was talking to. "Sure." He flipped open a folder and glanced at some papers inside. "There was some plant matter found on the body. I've determined that it's from a soaptree yucca plant. Possibly more than one plant. I haven't gone so far as to have Wendy run a DNA comparison on the individual fragments, but I can if you need me to."

"That shouldn't be necessary. Soaptree yucca—that's a pretty common plant in Nevada."

"As common as slot machines."

"Right," Ray said. "Anything else?"

"You brought in some hairs that were found on or near the body."

"Short orange ones, yes."

"Cat."

"Excuse me?"

"Those hairs were from a cat, not a human. An orange cat. I did you the favor of making a couple of phone calls. Robert Domingo's next-door neighbors have an orange cat. The cat is outside at night, and it loves to visit Domingo's place. They're pretty sure he feeds it sometimes, although they've tried to discourage that. They said it came home with something brown and sticky on one of its paws this morning, and they washed it off. I told them it was probably blood."

"So chances are, the cat went inside because the door was open, wandered around, rubbed against Domingo, shed some hairs, and left."

"Unless you're planning to revise your theory about the murder weapon and suggest that maybe the victim was bludgeoned with a cat."

"I don't think so. Thanks for making those phone calls."

"Don't mention it. Seriously. It was a whim—I don't want everybody thinking I'll go that far for them."

"My lips are sealed, David. Is that it?"

"It just so happens that I was talking to Mandy about the cat thing, and she told me she hadn't been able to raise any finger impressions off the lighter. She got a partial palm print, but that's all. She can't match it to anybody yet, but if you come up with a suspect, there's a chance that it can be confirmatory."

"Best we can hope for, I suppose. Thanks, David. I'm on my way to the Grey Rock reservation to join Nick."

"Okay," Hodges said. "One thing, though. When you get back? Don't look for me. If there's any mercy in the world, I'll be home in bed."

"Catherine asked me to give you a call, Greg," Wendy said.

"That was good of her," Greg answered. "It's a little lonely out here."

"I think she had something more specific in mind than just checking in. Where are you?"

"Hang on," Greg said, scanning out the Yukon's windshield. At the next corner was a sign he could barely make out from here. "West Warm Springs."

"Where is that?"

"It's off South Rainbow."

"You mean five ninety-five?"

"The guy who wrote these directions knew it as Rainbow. At least, that's what I'm counting on. I spent about twenty minutes looking for something that could be described as a rainbow before I realized that, for a change, he had used an actual street name. I'm really only guessing about Warm Springs. On the directions, he wrote that there were bulldozers and noise. I'm guessing he meant construction, and there are a bunch of relatively new houses down here. New since he wrote this, anyway. But I could be wrong. There's so much here that's just wide open to interpretation. Whoever this guy was, he was kind of . . . kind of crazy."

"That's actually why Catherine asked me to call you," Wendy said.

"To tell me he's crazy?"

"No, to tell you who he is."

"We know?"

"We do now. Isn't DNA a wonderful tool?"

"So who is he?"

"He's Troy Cameron. The one and only son of Bix and Helena Cameron."

Greg had been ready to hear almost anything, since he really had no idea who the John Doe was. But that . . . that took him off guard. "He *is*?"

"He definitely is. Not only that, but those hairs and fingernail pieces you found in his tent? They belong to his sister, Daria."

"The one who's missing?"

"The very same."

"Wow. Small world, I guess."

"I guess so."

"Listen, Wendy," Greg said. "I have to cover a few more blocks here, then I'll have to get out and hike, so I should go."

"Hike? Like, in the desert?"

"Looks that way."

"Carry water," she said. "Plenty of it. And Greg?"

"Yes?"

"Are you talking while you're driving?"

"I pulled over when the phone rang," he said. "But I need to drive now."

"That's good. Don't be a dope, okay?"

"Always an admirable goal," Greg said, but she had already hung up.

He had, over the course of the past few hours, often had to park and walk around, searching for anything that looked like it might have ten years ago and could potentially correspond to the notes Troy Cameron had scribbled down over and over again.

Some of it was virtually impossible. At one point, he had written, "Left at laundrymat." There was no Laundromat anywhere in the vicinity. Greg had gone into some of the shops that were there, in a strip mall that had probably not existed a decade ago, and asked if anyone remembered a Laundromat in the area. An elderly woman working in a card shop said that she did and spent fifteen minutes telling Greg about the surly man who ran the place and about the mouse she saw run underneath the dryers once. He was sure she would have told him precisely how many items she had washed there if he gave her enough time, but he had finally managed to extricate himself and continued on his way.

Some of Troy's landmark descriptions had been surprisingly astute, in their own strange way. Greg had spent several minutes at one point looking for a half-moon, wondering if the guy had first written out these directions at night and how that would affect the attempt to follow them, before noticing an old iron manhole cover in the middle of the street with a smiling crescent moon on it—a little less than half a moon, to be precise, but close enough. At another point, Troy had written, "Left by woof woof woof." Greg wondered how in the world he was supposed to turn at a decade-old sound, but after a few minutes, he spotted an old chain-link dog run behind a ramshackle house, with the remains of a couple of wooden doghouses inside it. The fence drooped now, and the house was vacant, its windows boarded over. It didn't appear that any dogs had used it in ages, but they certainly had at some point. He made the left and found the next landmark shortly thereafter.

He had never expected, when he first became a CSI, that he would spend a day doing something like this. Especially a day after he had already pulled a night shift. Walking around the city following old handwritten directions wasn't something they taught in school. But you did what the job demanded. The task of the moment set the agenda. If you tried to tailor the job to your preferences, you burned out fast.

He parked the Yukon and got out, carrying the directions in one hand and a backpack, which contained water and survival gear, in the other. He had known there would be some desert travel and prepared for it, wearing hiking boots, a T-shirt with a long-sleeved cotton shirt over it, and a ball cap. He didn't look much like a CSI, but at least he wouldn't perish in the wilderness. And his cap had the word "Forensics" printed across the front, so he had that going for him.

Warm Springs Road ended at Fort Apache. He doubted the road had extended that far back in Troy Cameron's time—at least, when he had described this route. Most of the houses Greg had passed had been newer than ten years old—the bulldozer stuff Cameron had mentioned. But Cameron did say that he walked for a long way in a straight line, away from the afternoon sun. That meant he was walking toward the east, and Greg, backtracking his way, had been driving into the west.

From this point on, all of the descriptions were of desert scenery. Fortunately, Cameron hadn't used a lot of plants as landmarks, instead picking rocks that reminded him of animals or places, the shapes of individual hills, and in one case a cloud formation. Greg figured that one wouldn't be too helpful.

He moved slowly into the wilderness, looking for a rock like a sheep's back, which was how Troy had described it. He guessed that would mean it had a woolly texture to it, maybe lots of lumps that would look like tight curls. It was, according to Cameron, on the side of a steep hill, and it was where he had turned toward the road.

Greg scanned the hills rising before him. They were dotted with desert scrub: low yellow-blossomed rabbitbrush, spindly ocotillo, bright green creosote, mesquite bushes with thorns like stilettos. One slope was particularly steep, although farther from the road than Greg expected, and high up on it was something that might have been a sheep rock. He made his way to it, tramping across soft dirt and then hard, bare rock. On the way up the slope, he leaned forward, into the hillside, for balance. A walking stick might have been a good idea—the last thing he wanted to do around here was grab the local plants for support, since most of them had barbs or thorns, daggers waiting to impale the unwary palm. He also kept an eye out for rattlesnakes. It was a little early in the year for them, but he didn't want to happen across one that didn't own a calendar.

When he got to the rock he had his eye on, not only was the upper surface oddly bumpy, but there was a broad main section and then a slightly offset smaller section on a top corner that, if he squinted a little, looked like a sheep's head.

Almost every time he began to despair, to think that whatever Cameron had observed ten years ago no longer existed, he came upon something that did. Cameron might have suffered brain damage if that bullet in the head predated the directions he wrote out, or he might have been a little off all along. But he had a good eye for permanence— for all of the landmarks that were long gone, such as the "laundrymat," there were others, such as the sheep rock and the half-moon, that were still around and not that hard to find.

After the sheep rock, he was looking for "the white cliffs of Dover." Las Vegas was a long way from the real Dover, a city facing onto the English Channel. Ferries and hovercraft from the European continent docked there, making Dover England's busiest passenger port, and Greg knew that even people who had never been there were familiar with its white cliffs.

The folded hills grew progressively steeper and rockier, beyond the sheep-shaped rock, so Greg assumed he was looking for a sheer cliff face, pale in color. He turned the indicated way—really, the opposite of the indicated way, since he was still working in reverse—and started off, eyeing the hillsides.

Tiny flies buzzed around his head—Grissom could probably have identified them from the sound alone, but as far as Greg was concerned, they were just airborne nuisances, nothing more—and he had to perfect a double-handed swat to keep them from just circling his head, avoiding first one hand and then the other.

He hiked for fifteen minutes before he rounded a bend and saw it—a high cliff, almost directly perpendicular to the desert floor, with a light yellowish cast to the exposed surface. Greg probably would have made the Dover connection even if he hadn't been looking for it.

He was walking toward the cliff, less than thirty yards away from it, when he saw the footprints.

The prints had been made by hiking boots, small but new, the tread still so sharp it cut deep, clear grooves in the dirt. And they were headed straight toward the white cliffs of Dover.

This was wide-open land, and there could have been a perfectly innocent explanation for them. Some nature lover out for a stroll on a spring afternoon. In another month or so, the weather would make it more difficult to do so, but desert rats loved these conditions, warm and bright.

Still, the direction they were headed made Greg wary. He kept hiking in toward the cliffs, but he made sure to watch ahead and to check his back trail, as well as looking at his directions and searching for the next landmark.

Believing in perfectly innocent explanations rather than expecting the worst was a good way to find himself faceup on Doc Robbins's slab.

18

NICK HAD BEEN RELUCTANT to let someone else drive the department's vehicle. But he had been even more reluctant to leave the crime scene, and Brass hadn't objected to the idea. The cop who took the keys returned in twenty-five minutes with the Yukon, bearing no obvious new dents or scrapes, so Nick was glad Aguirre had been willing to send him. Those twenty-five minutes could have been crucial at the scene.

Nick was under no illusions that the work he did there would ever wind up in a courtroom. The scene was way too compromised for that. And he was far out of his jurisdiction.

But crime-scene investigation had different purposes at different times. For the most part, it was meant to seal a conviction, to help a prosecuting attorney present an ironclad case to a jury. But it could also help point the finger at the right suspect in the first place. That was what Nick was trying to do now—to see if he could figure out who had shot up Meoqui Torres's house. As a corollary to that, because he believed the two cases were somehow connected, he wanted to learn if that information pointed back at whoever had killed Roland Domingo. If one led to the other, it would more than justify the time and effort he spent there.

The police who had arrived just before Brass and Aguirre left—and the EMS team that followed almost twenty minutes later—destroyed most of what little was left of the crime scene. The cops swarmed the porch, went into the house, stood around outside talking and smoking, trying to re-create the incident. They helped the remaining wounded, stabilizing them until the paramedics showed up, which Nick was glad of. But in their haste, they trampled what should have been evidence. The paramedics were worse; at least the cops recognized that they should have been more careful. And Nick didn't blame them for being anxious about the victims. He saw tears in the eyes of some as they tended to people who might have been brothers, cousins, or close friends.

By the time the paramedics came, Nick had retreated to the street. It was paved in front of Torres's house, and someone had scraped his tires against the curb and left rubber in the street as he peeled out. After setting rulers next to the tread marks for scale, Nick photographed them. He had shot some pictures of the porch, too, but mostly just so he would remember the layout. The photos would have no standing in court at all, after everybody had moved around so much. Then he flaked some rubber bits off the curb into a plastic evidence bag, in case he had occasion later to match it to actual tires.

In his experience, most people underestimated how truly unique a tire mark was. They thought if someone took an impression of their tires from a crime scene, all a suspect would have to do was point out how many similar tires were purchased in any given year. But Nick could point to all of the different variables in a tire track, the grooves and ribs, the sipes and lugs and slots, and show how an individual tire print was almost as good as a fingerprint at singling out a specific vehicle. He actually enjoyed being in court on those occasions, watching the faces of suspects when their certainty of exoneration turned into terror of certain conviction.

As long as he was out in the road, he also took pictures of brass shell casings, ejected from the automatic weapons as they were fired out the window. One of the shooters had used 9 mm ammo, standard fare for urban thugs, but the other had been firing .50-caliber cartridges. That made Nick nervous, because that shooter was armed for war. He collected the casings, bagging each one individually and labeling each bag, just as he would if the evidence was intended for his own crime lab. The shell casings would have rifling marks that could be compared with any weapons recovered later, and they might carry fingerprints.

When he had gathered all of the evidence he could get in the street, he turned his attention back to the porch. The paramedics had taken away all of the gunshot victims, and there were only a couple of tribal cops left behind. They paid little attention to Nick, interacting with him only occasionally and for the most part letting him do his work.

Something about the shooting of Meoqui Torres bothered him, but he couldn't put his finger on what it was. When he had arrived with Brass and Aguirre, Torres had been lying on the floorboards, and it had seemed cut and dried. But he had learned not to disregard his instincts in cases like this. He stood on the porch again, eyeing the scene, re-creating in his mind what he believed had happened.

Torres had been leaning against the wall, shooting the breeze with his buddies, talking about Domingo's death, most likely, and how it would affect the tribe. Maybe Torres had even been sitting on the porch—not in one of the chairs but on the floor, back against the wall or cross-legged—and he stood up when that pickup truck came to a stop at the curb. Perhaps he recognized the truck, knew that the men in it weren't friendly. Either way, when the shooting started, that's where he was, standing there just beside the window. One of the first rounds struck him in the thigh. That had been one of those big .50-caliber rounds. Reeling from that shot, Torres had turned away from the street, and the next bullet, one of the nine-mils, caught him in the shoulder. He had fallen then, hitting his head against the corner of the windowsill.

Nick realized what wasn't sitting right with him.

He had found Torres on the ground a foot or so from that window. The wall behind the porch was pockmarked with bullet holes, but he couldn't see any that corresponded directly to Torres's shoulder wound. The window was open, and more rounds had gone inside, but Torres had been too close to the wall and too far from the window for the shot that hit his shoulder to have flown through that.

So where had it gone? The shot was definitely a through-and-through, leaving a good-sized exit wound on its way out.

Besides, if Torres had spun around so that he faced the house, he should have struck the windowsill with the front of his head, not the back. He might have continued spinning, the trapezius shot even increasing his momentum. But Nick was beginning to think it hadn't gone down that way after all.

He went back to the Yukon and took out a dummy and some trajectory rods with built-in laser pointers. These would help him better visualize Torres's position and locate the bullet.

Getting the dummy placed where he believed Torres had been standing at first, he inserted one of the rods into Torres's thigh. He wished he'd been able to get pictures of Torres's wounds before those guys had spirited him away, but he thought he remembered the positions well enough at least to get close to the mark.

With the dummy and rod in place, he checked the laser beam. It shone straight into the street. Just to make sure, Nick walked over there, waving his hand in front of the beam to check its location. When he reached the street, he looked at where the beam landed in comparison with where the tire marks he'd found against the curb were. Based on that, he adjusted the dummy slightly and repeated the process. The laser ran straight through where the pickup's passenger window would likely have been. No one had mentioned the truck being jacked up, so Nick had to operate on the belief that it was a standard truck.

That part done, he tried to reenact Torres's motions using his own body, then to duplicate what he came up with using the dummy. He imagined the brute force of that big slug's impact, the heat of entry, the shock that Torres must have felt as his thigh muscles were torn away. He would have fallen backward, spinning around—

"Hey, you okay?" One of the tribal cops stood in the yard, a young woman with her hair in a long ponytail, watching him. Nick must have looked as if he was having some kind of seizure.

"Yeah, I'm fine. Just trying to re-create one of the shootings."

"Is that what the lasers are for? That's pretty cool."

"That's right," Nick said. "They're for determining trajectory, showing where someone shot from."

"That's awesome." She turned away, as if she was afraid that she had intruded on some personal moment, and walked back to where a clutch of other cops stood together at the edge of the yard.

Nick went back to what he was doing, trying to work out how Torres had spun. But no. That's where the theory fell apart. Now that he acted it out and tried to make the dummy go through the motions, he knew that Torres would not have spun away from the first shot. His damaged leg wouldn't have supported that sort of movement. He would have fallen back, past the window, bounced off the wall, and dropped to the floor.

No matter how Nick tried to make it happen, that second shot, through the trapezius, had not come from the truck. It couldn't have.

Which left only one option: the window.

The people on the porch and inside the house had returned fire, they said. Nick had seen plenty of spent rounds out in the street and beyond to back up that story. He didn't think it would be possible to isolate which one had hit Torres, at least not without a lot of lab time testing each one for his DNA. But when he put the dummy through the paces he had laid out for it, the trajectory rods confirmed his theory. The shoulder shot had to have been fired from inside, behind Torres, and at pretty close range. Torres started to fall forward, hit the porch's front rail, and bounced off that. His legs gave way, and he fell back, striking his head on the windowsill and then slumping to the floor.

Which meant the second shot was an accident, someone pulling the trigger as Torres fell into his line of fire . . .

Or else someone had intentionally shot the activist from inside the house. Someone he had probably trusted.

Torres had been taken to a clinic by some of his friends. One or more of those "friends" might not be so friendly after all.

Nick tossed the dummy and the rods into the back of the vehicle and approached the young female officer who had spoken to him. "Hey," he said, "can you tell me how to get to that clinic they took Torres to? I've got a few more questions for him."

Being deceitful with fellow cops tied his stomach

up in knots. But he was on shaky ground—literally inside a sovereign nation, where he had no authority. He didn't know anyone but Aguirre and didn't know who could be trusted and who couldn't. Domingo had been the chairman, in charge of tribal government, including the police. If they were loyal to him and they thought Torres had something to do with his murder, what might they do to get back at him? Even the cop Aguirre had sent to watch over Torres might be in on the plot.

Torres had trusted whoever shot him in the back. Nick wouldn't make that same mistake. Once the cop had jotted down directions for him, he jumped into the Yukon and tore off down the road, dialing Brass as he went.

Whenever Catherine was called into Conrad Ecklie's office, she knew she was in for bad news. But when Ecklie came to hers—especially when his narrow face had that lovely eggplant coloring to it that it did now—she knew the news would be even worse.

"Have a seat, Conrad," she offered.

"I'll stand. I won't be staying long."

"Suit yourself."

"You went to see Helena Cameron."

She had already guessed that's what this visit was about, had known this chat was coming. She felt the way her daughter, Lindsey, probably felt when Catherine went into her room or took her aside for one of those critical mother-daughter "chats" about hanging out with the wrong people, using a fake ID to get into a club, doing poorly on a test, or committing some other infraction that seemed minor to a teenager but major to that teenager's mother. "I did."

"You told her that her son is dead. To be more precise, you told her that her head of security killed her son on her property last night."

"I did tell her that," Catherine said. "Because it's true."

"The way I hear it, you could have been a little more diplomatic about it."

"And just how did you happen to hear it at all, Conrad?"

"I heard about it from the mayor. As in the mayor of Las Vegas. He heard about it from Marvin Coatsworth, Mrs. Cameron's attorney. Do you have any idea how many times the mayor has called me directly over the course of my career?"

"I don't have a clue."

He held out his right hand, fingers splayed. "Not very many times, Cath. Not many times at all. I can count them on this hand, probably. And when he does call me, I don't like it. At all. It's never a good thing."

"I'm sorry you got that call. But I had to see her, and I had to give her that information."

"You didn't have to inform her yourself!" Ecklie argued. His facial color was fading, back to its typical hue, but Catherine could still see a vein in his neck twitching spasmodically. "Need I remind you, you are a CSI, not the lead detective on this case. From now on, if you want to communicate with Mrs. Cameron, you'll do it through Sam Vega, who will talk to Coatsworth. You know how to reach Sam, right?"

"Yes, I do. But Conrad, you've done this job. You know that sometimes you have to see someone in person, to observe a reaction or to check for some physical attribute. No, I'm not a detective, but in this case, seeing her in person was crucial."

"I know that's often the case. It isn't here, not anymore. You've seen her. You know what she looks like. That's all you get." He stared at her for a moment, as if daring her to disagree, to protest. It reminded her of something else Gil had told her about Ecklie once. "Some people avoid conflict, or shy away from a fight," he had said. "But not Conrad. Sometimes I think he seeks them out or intentionally incites them. It might even be good for his mental health—at least he isn't internalizing his anger. But it can be hard on everyone else around him."

"Are you hearing me?" Ecklie asked when Catherine didn't respond.

"Yeah, I hear you," Catherine said, deciding that she wouldn't avoid the conflict, either. She thought Gil might have been proud of her next statement. "Now you hear me. I'm sorry the mayor called you. I will make every effort not to contact Helena Cameron directly again. But by seeing her once, I obtained information valuable to the case."

"The case is open and shut, Catherine. We know who the victim was, and we know who shot him and why. McCann won't be charged. What else matters?"

"It's not that simple, I'm afraid. What was Troy Cameron doing at the estate? Where has he been for the last ten years? And more important, where is Daria Cameron now, and does her disappearance have anything to do with her brother's reappearance? That's the case, and there's nothing simple about it."

Ecklie paused, then let out a long sigh. "All right, you made your point. I'm not going to second-guess you, and I'll back you up as far as I can. You know that. But do us all a favor, and go through Vega and Coatsworth, from now on, okay?"

"Okay, Conrad. I'll go through them if I can. And I won't disturb Mrs. Cameron if I don't absolutely have to. Good enough?"

He nodded wearily, letting his shoulders droop and rubbing his temples with his fingertips, as if trying to ease a sudden headache. He hated backing down, but Catherine had made it clear that she wasn't going to. More important, she was in the right. *Gil definitely would have loved this.* "I guess it'll have to be."

"Looks like it," she said. "Now, if you don't mind, I still have a lot of work to do."

"Sure, get to it," he said. Halfway through the doorway, he stopped. "Just wrap it up tight, okay?" he tossed back over his shoulder.

"No problem," Catherine said. "You can take that to the bank."

Doc Robbins was still in the morgue, which both astonished and pleased Catherine. He was a family man, and she knew he liked to get home after his shift to be with them. And although he never let on that it bothered him, he was a double amputee, and pulling a double shift had to involve a fair amount of pain on his part. He looked weary, and his shoulders were slightly hunched. He was probably putting more weight on his forearm crutches than he usually did.

But it pleased her because he knew more about medicine than most MDs she had known, having been one himself before switching to a career as a medical examiner. She knew he kept up on the latest medical developments, too, even when they didn't appear to affect his work directly. She needed a doctor now, and she didn't think Hutch Boullet would be interested in talking with her any further.

"Long day, Catherine," he said. Coming from him, it didn't sound like a complaint, simply an observation. He said it with a grin on his face, and he was one of the few men she knew whose eyes actually did twinkle when he smiled. She liked him a great deal, even though, for all the twinkling and smiling and genial conversation, there was something about him that he kept hidden, not just from her but from everyone.

Everyone at the lab, at least. And she was positive that there were things about his working life that he kept from his family. He seemed intent on separating the two facets of his life, as if to guarantee that they did not start to impinge on each other, to flow together like two rivers joining. She couldn't blame him for that; she liked to keep Lindsey and her work, which so often involved violence and death, as far apart as she could. Nobody wanted to go home and tell the kids about the victim found facedown in a house with claw marks from a hammer on her head and insects infesting her body. You shared the good stories, the ones with happy endings, and the others you talked about only at work—or, for some people, on a therapist's couch.

But she often wondered about the parts of Doc Robbins she didn't know, would likely never know. He was a sweet man, a kind man, and she would have liked a glimpse at the private man away from his morgue.

"Ain't it the truth?" she said, aware that she had been silent for too long, and he was looking at her in puzzlement.

"I won't waste your time, then. You wouldn't be here if there wasn't something I could do for you."

"Albert Robbins, talking to you is *never* a waste of time."

He performed a shallow bow. "Compliment accepted. I sense a 'but' lurking behind it somewhere, though."

"But . . . there is something you can do for me."

"Name it."

She described Helena Cameron's skin color and what she had heard about Daria's, what Dr. Boullet had told her of Daria's condition, the congestion of her heart, the lines on the Cameron women's fingernails, and the brittleness of Daria's hair and nails. Robbins listened quietly, nodding along from time to time, one finger to his lips. "I don't know if it's some kind of a genetic condition or what," said Catherine. "Something passed from mother to daughter?"

"I do have an idea, but let me confirm something," he said. He went into his office and returned with a heavy volume.

"Do you want a hand with that?" Catherine asked. "Looks like it weighs a ton."

"The publishers of medical reference books rarely make a priority of concision," Doc Robbins said. "If one word is good, ten are better. But I've got it, thanks." He opened the book on one of the stainless steel counters and started flipping pages. Catherine watched his back, appreciating his efforts. He must have had better things to do. Like getting out of there and going home.

"Here we go."

"You found something?"

"I thought it was this but wanted to make sure. There's nothing worse than a doctor who doesn't double-check a diagnosis. Well, maybe there is, but not many things. Anyway, what you're describing sounds very much like selenium poisoning."

"Poisoning," Catherine echoed.

"That's correct, yes."

"Not a virus or anything like that. They're not actually ill."

"Not precisely, no. The only diagnosis I can think of that fits the symptoms you've described is selenium poisoning. Keep in mind that I haven't examined the patient myself, so it's obviously only a preliminary diagnosis. But I have some confidence that an exam would bear it out."

"Would their family doctor reach this same conclusion?"

"Not necessarily, at least not at first. A general practitioner would be most concerned about the heart and might, for a while, see the skin discoloration as jaundice, until the orange color became more pronounced. But it would take a while for anyone without forensic training to get to selenium poisoning."

"I thought maybe that was it," Catherine said. "But it's been years since we've encountered it, and I figure medical diagnoses are best left to the pros. Is selenium poisoning always fatal?"

"Usually, if it's not caught in time. Its effects can be reversed, as long as the patient isn't too far gone."

"Okay," she said. "Thanks, Doc. I have to go." Her shoes clicked across the morgue's tile floor as she hurried toward the exit.

She called Sam Vega on her way to her car. He answered on the second ring. "You're still working, too?" she asked.

"I am."

"Good. Meet me at the Cameron estate."

"When?"

"Now. Or sooner."

"Sounds important. I'm on my way."

"It is," Catherine said. "I'll see you there."

She got into the car and jammed her key into the ignition. As she turned it, the engine roared to life.

She wondered if Ecklie's head would make that same noise when he heard about this.

At least she would have Vega along with her. He could report that she'd only had Helena Cameron's best interests in mind.

She even thought about calling Ecklie, briefly. But he would tell her not to go, and then they would waste time arguing.

Time that Helena Cameron might not be able to spare.

19

Keith Hyatt led Ray once again to the comfortable living room where Ray had spent so many hours in the company of friends. Out of habit, Ray took his usual position, at the right end of a couch that was broken in just right, with all the wrinkles and soft spots of an old friend. Ray's elbow slotted into the armrest as if it had been custom-made, instead of just worn down in that precise place. Keith occupied the leather chair he always used.

"We so seldom see you twice in one day anymore," Keith said. "I guess you're not here again by happy accident."

"I'm afraid not."

"Is it about Robert Domingo?"

"It is," Ray said, dropping his chin slightly. He had talked to Nick again on his way there, but Nick had been racing someplace, unable to spend much time elaborating on the situation.

Keith straightened in his chair. He took naturally to the role of professor, as he always had, and Ray felt a little like a student dropping by the teacher's house after hours for advice. He had been on both sides of that situation, many times. "What do you need, Ray?"

"Context," Ray said. "You told me about the blood-quantum issues, and I believe you were right, that plays a part in this somehow. But there's more going on than just that. One of our guys is on the Grey Rock reservation now, and he says it's like a war zone. There was a shooting today, multiple victims, including Meoqui Torres."

"Oh, no," Keith said. His face blanched, and he gripped the arms of his chair so tightly that his knuckles went white. "I hadn't heard about that."

"Two guys in a pickup truck pulled up outside his house and opened fire. Nobody expects that to be the last of it."

"No, I wouldn't, either," Keith said. "I suppose I'll have to tell Ysabel, although it will upset her terribly. Is Meoqui . . . ?"

"He's wounded, but he's alive," Ray told him.

"That's something, at least. I assume he's getting medical attention?"

"He was taken to a clinic."

"Good, good. So what can I do to help?"

"Here's what I need. Alive or dead, Domingo's got his people, right? Torres must have his supporters as well. Where are the lines drawn?"

"In what way?"

"Who would be on whose side? Would the police support Domingo's side, for instance?"

"Oh, yes, for the most part. I mean, cops are working-class people, right? But there's that eternal conflict, because the whole point of police is obedience to authority, right? Maintaining the status quo. For working-class folks, and often union members, they tend to be on the conservative side. I'm not, um, not trying to be offensive—I keep forgetting you're a cop now."

"I'm a scientist," Ray said. "I just work for the same side as the cops. But don't worry, I get your meaning, and I'm not offended."

"Anyway, Chairman Domingo made sure the tribal police were in his pocket. He couldn't pay them a lot of money, but they made a decent living, especially by the prevalent standards on the rez. When he could, he got them new equipment. He made sure the blood-quantum rules were a bit more relaxed when it came to them and for anyone else he wanted to curry favor with. It's astonishing how flexible supposedly inviolable standards can be under the right circumstances. And in the event of any disagreements or controversies surrounding tribal law enforcement, he tried to side with the police. There'll be individual cops with different loyalties and, of course, some who are genuinely fair-minded and impartial. But as a group? Yes, they would be with him. Or with whoever his designated successor is, if he has one."

"That's something else I wanted to ask about," Ray said. "If you know of any obvious successors."

Keith considered for a moment, head back on the chair, eyes toward the vaulted, beamed ceiling. "No one in particular," he said. "I would look at the people running the enrollment eligibility office, because they're obviously people he put a lot of trust in. That's one of the most powerful offices in the tribe. And look at whoever he's put in charge of the new casino and spa, because the people who'll be handling the big money would be high up on his list. I mean, if you're looking for who would benefit financially from his death."

"That's part of it," Ray said. "Although, honestly, that's more a job for the detectives. For my part, I just want to understand what I'm getting into."

"You're going out there? To the rez?"

"I have to. My colleague Nick is out there on his own, and I think it's too dangerous for that."

"From the sound of things, you could well be right."

"What else do I need to know, Keith? What's going to happen next?"

"Money and power have flowed through Domingo's hands for a long time. He really cemented his hold on that office through the judicious application of those two forces. Now that he's gone, there's going to be a power struggle. I don't mean armed combat, although I certainly wouldn't rule that out. There's a lot at stake. It will be heated, if mostly political. Nobody will completely trust anyone. But for the most part, the sides will still be about where they are now. The power players are the ones who were close to Domingo, and they'll remain, by and large, in those same roles. The activists, the people pushing for social change, the ones you would equate to labor leaders, perhaps, will still be on Torres's side."

"Okay, that's pretty much what I suspected, but I needed to have it confirmed. Thanks, Keith."

"One more thing?"

"Yes?"

"Since Domingo died, he won't be around to represent himself anymore. That means a lot of people will be saying they know what he would have wanted, whether they really do or not. And if Meoqui dies, he'll be a martyr to the opposition. Martyrs and dead men talking through the living are dangerous to be around."

"Point taken," Ray said.

"Since you're here, can you come in and say hello to Ysabel? If that's all you needed? She knows you're here, and she'd be crushed if you didn't drop in."

"I'd be glad to. I really need to get up to the reservation, but I wouldn't think of not looking in on her."

"Great." Keith pushed out of his chair, straining with the effort, and Ray followed him across the house to Ysabel's room. His wife's illness was weighing heavily on the man, Ray observed. Since his visit to the house earlier that morning, Keith looked as if he had aged five years.

"Twice in one day?" Ysabel said when he walked through the door. "I thought I heard your voice. Is everything okay?"

"I had a few questions for Keith." Ray leaned over and kissed her cheek.

"About that awful business with Robert?"

"Yes, I'm afraid so."

"Are you going to catch whoever did it?"

"We'll catch him, Ysabel. I promise you that."

"Well . . . I'm glad you came back, whatever the excuse. I have something for you."

"For me?"

"Yes!" She reached for something on the bedside table. Ray couldn't see what it was until she brought it around to hand him.

"That's the basket you were working on earlier."

"It is. I was almost finished, but it hadn't told me yet who it was for. Then it spoke up and said it wanted to go home with you."

"I'm honored."

"I'm making them for some of my most special friends to . . . to remember me by. When I'm gone."

"Ysabel," Ray said firmly. "You're not going anywhere."

"Oh, I am, too. Look at me. Don't worry. I'm a little sad about it, because I'll miss all of you. But I'm not scared."

"And anyway," Ray went on, "do you really think anyone who has ever known you could possibly forget you?"

Ysabel laughed and squeezed his hand. Her hand felt as light as a bird's wing. "You're a charmer, aren't you? If I didn't have Keith . . ." She lowered her voice to a stage whisper. "You could be my boyfriend."

"I'd like that," Ray said. He held up the basket she had given him, admiring the workmanship. It was naturally colored, the tan of the main material, which Ray knew was some kind of desert plant, with darker browns and blacks from other local plants, all in a precise pattern of jagged lines and occasional swooping arcs. "It's beautiful. Like its maker."

"Speaking of beauty, Ray . . ."

"Yes?"

"Tonight Keith and I are going on one of those dinner cruises, out on Lake Mead. That's one of my favorite places, and I want to feel all that water under me one more time, and look out at the dry desert hills in the setting sun. Will you come with us, Ray?"

"I would be delighted to."

She clapped her hands together, almost childlike in her glee. "Oh, goody!"

"If I can," Ray added. "I'm working today, and it has already been a very long day. But if I can get there in time, I'll meet you at the dock."

"You'll try?"

"I'll try. I promise."

"That's the best you can do. Thank you, Ray. And thank you for accepting the basket. I hope you like it."

"Better than that," he said. "I absolutely love it."

Aguirre drove Brass to Grey Rock Tobacco, the reservation's original smoke shop. It was off Interstate 15, visible from the freeway, and Brass knew from experience that there had been billboards along the side of the road for ages promoting it. He had never bothered to stop, but he knew the appeal was that, as a sovereign nation, the reservation didn't have to charge the same state excise taxes that off-reservation stores did. As a result, they could undercut the prices people paid in Las Vegas, and they had always done a brisk business.

On the way, Aguirre's police radio crackled with

new information, none of it good. Shots had been fired at a recreation center. Someone at a public swimming pool had been stabbed three times. Two store windows had been shattered by flung bricks. Fights were breaking out across the reservation, it seemed, neighbor against neighbor, brother against brother in some cases. Police and emergency services were being stretched thin.

"Can you afford the time to keep looking with me?" Brass asked.

"I can't afford not to. We need to find a way to bring a peaceful end to all this."

"It's not always this way, is it?"

"What, you think we're living in the Wild West?" Aguirre said with a not-so-nice laugh. " 'Course not. It's all about Domingo. Like him or not, he was a stabilizing influence, because he held the power, and everybody knew it. With him out of the way, people are drawing up new sides or cementing their old ones. Add to that the shooting of Meoqui and his friends, and . . . well, there's a lot of tension around here today. What was it that guy in L.A. said? 'Can't we all just get along?' Something like that."

"Rodney King," Brass said, remembering the African-American motorist pulled over and beaten by white highway patrol officers in Los Angeles. The acquittal of the officers in that case had touched off citywide riots in which fifty-one people died. Brass hoped the current situation didn't get anywhere near that bad. "Guy might have had a point."

"Ruben Solis and Shep Moran hang out here a lot of the time," Aguirre said as they approached the smoke shop. "Domingo always had a soft spot for this place, even after the bigger, more profitable businesses got up and running. He had kind of a clubhouse in back, lots of his guys would come around, smoking and telling lies, you know."

"You think Solis is there now?"

"I don't know," Aguirre replied. "He doesn't have Domingo to follow around anymore, but my guess is that the people who were close to him are going to want to be together today. This is one of the places they might be."

The smoke shop had been built in the early 1960s but remodeled in the late 1970s. It was an adobe structure, a single story on the wings but a big A-shaped peak in the middle that must have soared two stories higher. The A was all windows, offering clear views of the sales area inside, its shelves stacked high with cigarette cartons. The adobe section to the left of the A had four vertical window slits, while the walls of the section to the right were smooth and solid.

Brass and Aguirre got out of the Jeep and walked casually to the front door, just two guys getting out of an official tribal police vehicle and going in for some butts. Inside, pink neon script identified a cigar room off to the left. On the right, the door into the solid section on the other side was unmarked.

When Aguirre pushed the front door open, an electronic tone sounded. A Native American woman tossed them a friendly look from behind the sales counter. She wore a black Western-style shirt with embroidered cigarettes on it, smoke wafting up her shoulders in ornate curlicues. "Hi there, welcome to

Grey Rock Tobacco," she said. "If there's anything I can help you find, just let me know."

Aguirre snatched his straw cowboy hat off and tilted his head toward the unmarked door. "We'll be in there," he said.

The woman's welcoming expression vanished. "I'm sorry, that's—"

Aguirre tapped the badge on his chest and made for the door. As he reached it, a buzzing noise sounded, the young lady at the desk passing them through without further argument. Aguirre yanked the door open, and a cloud of smoke welled out. Brass quickly sucked in a deep breath of clean air and waded into the miasma.

He had entered a stockroom, lined with steel shelving units holding cardboard cartons of tobacco products. Most of them had familiar printed logos, but there were also brand names Brass didn't know and others that weren't identified at all.

In the middle of the room were a table and chairs and beyond them a separate seating area with a plush sofa and a couple more chairs, arranged around a low table. Ashtrays were everywhere, most of them full to overflowing.

Half a dozen Native American men glared at the doorway as the two cops entered. They were older than the men Brass had seen at Torres's house, strands of silver icing their black hair in places, lined faces frowning. Brass noticed a lot of jewelry, most of it silver and turquoise but some also featuring accents of red coral, bone, and other materials.

"This is a private area, Richie," one of them said. Deep furrows ran from the sides of his nose to the corners of his mouth, as if sliced there by a carving knife. "You know that. You have a warrant?"

"We're looking for Ruben Solis and Shep Moran," Aguirre said. "Trying to help them dodge some trouble. Don't need a warrant for that."

The man shrugged. "You see 'em here?"

Aguirre made a show of looking around. "No, I sure don't. So maybe you can tell me where they are."

"I run into 'em, I'll tell them you're looking. Maybe they'll give you a call."

"That would be good," Aguirre said. "There's a lot of bad stuff going down around here, Russell. You know I don't have to tell you."

"I know a great man was killed," Russell said. The other men murmured agreement. Most of them didn't look directly at Brass, but he knew he was being sized up just the same.

"And we're trying to find out who killed him," Aguirre said. "I know you all were close to Robert, and I'm sorry for what happened to him. You can be sure nobody's taking it sitting down." He then said something else that Brass couldn't understand. Brass assumed he was speaking in the Paiute tongue. The men acknowledged his words with glances and gestures, and a couple said something back, something that was equally unintelligible to Brass's ears.

"Look, just track down Ruben and Shep, and tell them to get in touch with me," Aguirre said. "I'm not trying to jam anybody up over this—just trying to keep a lid on things so they don't boil over. Okay?"

"We'll spread the word, Richie."

"That's exactly what I need, thanks."

Aguirre gave Brass a look and a nod, and they retreated from the smoke. On the way out the shop's front door, Brass asked him, "You think they'll really help us find Solis and Moran?"

"Not a chance," Aguirre said. "But I wish I had taps on all their phones, 'cause I bet you one of them is calling those guys right now."

"Warning them?"

Aguirre chuckled dryly. "Yeah. They'll already know we're looking for them, so that's not going to make any difference in the long run. We'll just keep going till we find them, or we don't. I'm hoping we do."

"That makes two of us," Brass said. "And maybe half a reservation who hope we don't. I'd hate to see the odds against us on the screen at a sports book."

"So what's the deal with you guys and tobacco?" Brass asked. "I mean, I know you can sell it at lower prices than off-reservation retailers because of the tax thing. But it seems like there's more to it than that."

"Indians never used tobacco casually," Aguirre told him. "And we were using it long before you Europeans showed up here and started throwing up strip malls everywhere. We used it in ceremonies, for spiritual purposes or political ones, even medicinal. Shamans used to smoke larger amounts of it to get high. One cigarette won't do much, but try a pack or two at a time, and see what happens to you. Of course, it wasn't just about getting wasted; there was a ritual element to it. Tobacco was a part of Indian life. When the Europeans came and created a big new market for it, it became important to us commercially."

"And it looks like it's stayed that way."

"Yeah. There's a downside, though. Some researchers think that early prevalence in Indian society set us up for greater susceptibility than the white population. Lots of Indians smoke, and lots of them are addicted to tobacco. That and alcohol are both big problems in our communities. At least some of it comes from the way we used it in precontact days."

Brass was about to say something else when his phone rang. He flipped it open. "I gotta take this," he said.

"Go ahead," Aguirre said. "That's one thing I'm not addicted to. When I'm not on the job, I like to be miles from the nearest telephone."

"What's up, Nicky?" said Brass.

Nick was driving fast, on unfamiliar roads, not the best conditions for making a phone call. At least he wasn't texting, but that didn't mean some other driver wasn't. "I just got off the phone with Ray."

"And?" Brass asked.

"He's heading out here. But on the way, he stopped to talk to his friend who's married to a Grey Rock woman."

"What did his friend say?"

Nick twisted the wheel right for a sharp turn, then cranked it left as he headed into an S-curve.

"It's not good. He said the tribal police might take sides. I guess Domingo treated them pretty well, made sure they were taken care of. In turn, they watched out for his interests. Now, if the powder keg blows, he thinks most of them will back whoever Domingo's likely successor is, trying to maintain the status quo."

Brass hesitated before answering. Nick could tell from the background noises that he was in a vehicle and probably had Rico Aguirre right beside him. "Okay, thanks. That's something to keep in mind."

"That's what I thought."

"And Nick?"

"Yeah?"

"The fuse has already been lit. And it's burning fast."

20

THE BODY WAS DESICCATED, shrunken, its skin dark, wrinkled, and leathery. Greg's first thought was of beef jerky. Wisps of hair still clung to the head, but the clothing had deteriorated, with only a few scraps of fabric strewn around the makeshift cavern giving testimony to the idea that the mummy had once been clothed at all. Whoever it was must have been there for years.

Greg's trek through the desert had taken a couple of hours, following landmark after landmark. As opposed to the city streets, out here not much had changed—or, to be more precise, the author of the directions, who was presumably Troy Cameron, had noted landscape features that wouldn't change instead of plants that might have grown taller or withered and died in the intervening years.

For the last twenty minutes or so, he had seen a pair of turkey vultures wheeling overhead, then a trio, like ragged black shadows against the bright blue sky. He had been starting to wonder how much longer this would take, worrying that he hadn't brought enough water after all. The number of landmarks listed didn't help him gauge his progress, because some were close together while there were great distances between others, even though each was within line of sight of the one before. He was out in the desert with no company but a line of footprints, the carrion birds, dirt, rocks, and the long-enduring desert plants, the creosote bushes and yuccas and mesquites.

The earth appeared too hard, dry, and unforgiving to be susceptible to the fragile charms of wildflowers. But there they were, broad yellow blooms and brushlike red ones and lavender blossoms growing close to the ground like a lace handkerchief someone had dropped. And this was late in the season; early in March, the desert would have been carpeted in places by flowers coaxed from the rocky soil by winter rains.

Flowers were only one aspect of desert life that seemed to defy scientific reason. Mesquite could push a taproot down a hundred and fifty feet, through hardpan and caliche and maybe even limestone, looking for water, but most of its root structure was within three feet of the surface. They were hardy trees, almost unkillable, and chances were good that some of the ones Greg passed had been there, albeit smaller, in Troy's day. He thought there was a lesson to be learned from them, something about survival and resilience and the willingness to do whatever it took to make it until the next rain, but he was too distracted by his list of landmarks and growing uneasiness about his task to dwell on it.

He had pressed on, heartened by the fact that three of the landmarks near the end of his list were almost right on top of one another. Finally, he spent some time wandering around a broad cliff face, the rocky patina smoothed by wind and weather. Dark, uneven vertical streaks were probably rust stains from the iron in the rock leaching out to the surface. He was certain he was in the right general vicinity but didn't know exactly what he was looking for. He guessed that Troy Cameron had known his own starting point, so he didn't bother writing it down with the precision he had used on the other notations. All he had written was "Bleeding rock," and the cliff face certainly gave that impression.

The other person who had come this way had encountered the same problem, so following those prints (*her* prints, Greg was largely convinced, although it could have been a man with very small feet) was little help. That person had wandered this way and that, looking, no doubt, for the same thing Greg was. Troy hadn't meant the entire cliff, had he? Could Greg have spent hours following a trail that led nowhere at all?

Finally, he had found a rock shelf, sheltered by the cliff face. On the face itself, someone had marked a crude X, as high as a tall man could reach, above the shelf. The mark might have been an ancient pictograph, except that it was alone, and it had been inscribed there with no particular grace or skill. Someone had simply taken a harder rock and scratched it there, marking the cliff like a treasure spot on a pirate map.

The shelf was jammed with rocks, so it looked less like an open space than a jumble of fallen stone. But there were some on the ground in front of the shelf, and they looked to have been placed there recently, as they weren't covered with the film of dirt that coated everything else. Looking more closely, Greg saw that others had been removed and then put back, as if by someone trying to ensure that whatever was behind them stayed hidden. The hole that was left was almost wide enough for him to squeeze through but not quite. Behind it was a dark, open space, but he couldn't tell how big it was or if there was anything in it until he could get at least his shoulders inside.

The other footprints were all around there. Whoever had preceded him into the desert had been the one who had taken the rocks out, then replaced some. Why?

He took a few pictures of the rocks as he had found them, then slipped on three layers of latex gloves—knowing that handling the rocks would tear through at least one or two—and started pulling them away, setting them carefully on the ground behind him. Within a short time, he had cleared enough rocks to give him limited access. He took a flashlight from his backpack. Maybe he should have brought his whole crime-scene kit, but not knowing how far he'd have to walk, he hadn't wanted to risk carrying the extra weight, not to mention the weight of the additional water he would have needed had he done so.

He beamed the light into the opening, turning it this way and that until he saw the dried, shriveled form inside. It didn't look human at first, but then he spotted the hair, and with that as a starting point, he was able to make out the basic shape, the shoulders collapsed and curled slightly in toward the chest, knees drawn up, feet together. It looked more like some dark, carved wood than human flesh.

Greg knew that dry desert air could do that to a person. The aridity sucked the moisture from a body, and the rock wall that had been built in front of this one would have protected it from animals. Every schoolkid knew about the carefully embalmed and wrapped mummies of Egypt, but the fact was that anyplace dry enough or cold enough could mummify corpses, as could immersion in such natural preserving substances as peat bogs.

He took a few additional pictures before dislodging any more rocks and regretted once again the decision not to bring his crime-scene kit. Not that there would be much physical evidence left after ten years, but there might be some. And if there was, he wanted to find it.

Considering who had written the directions and saved them for so long, he had a feeling he was looking at the corpse of long-missing casino mogul Bix Cameron.

Since the space was now wide enough for him to wriggle through without worrying about dislodging any more of the rocks, Greg stuck his head and shoulders in. He expected to encounter the close, dry smell of a desert cave, but there was something else in the air, something unexpected. He took another whiff.

It was sweat. Human sweat, mixed with something else, something with a little of the bite of alcohol, leavened with a floral scent. He smelled himself. Not exactly fragrant but different from the smell in the air inside the cave. The body on the floor hadn't been sweaty for a very long time, nor had it worn any perfume, so the smell didn't come from him.

Greg tried to picture the footprints, to remember, without climbing back out of the tight space, if any of them had led away from there. He couldn't envision any, but they had strayed all over the place, as his own certainly did, since the other person had seemingly had just as much trouble as Greg finding the exact spot he or she was looking for.

Instead of turning around to look, he pushed forward. The floor of the rock shelf was dusty, and there were bug carcasses and bits of rodent feces scattered about—he checked his hands, pleased to see that the gloves were holding so far—but the piled rocks had kept the interior relatively clean. He saw scuff marks in the caked-on dust, though, leading past the mummified body. Aiming the flashlight that way, he saw that the cave curved around, and he couldn't see its endpoint from there.

"Hello!" he called. "Las Vegas Police! Is there somebody in here?"

He might have heard a faint intake of breath, but he couldn't be sure. He continued past the body, careful not to touch it, moving on hands and knees and trying to keep the flashlight pointed ahead at all times.

No way of telling what's around that corner, he thought. The cave might continue on for five feet or a hundred or more. There might be someone waiting to ambush him with a gun. The idea made his heart pound in his throat, but there was no way around it. He had to see what was there. And if the mummy was indeed Bix Cameron, he couldn't risk going for backup and letting someone dispose of or damage the body. The casino magnate had been missing long enough.

"Las Vegas Police Department!" he announced again as he neared the corner. Then he shoved the flashlight around and beamed it into the darkness. No one shot at it, so he risked following it with his head.

No one would be doing any shooting in that cave, not that day.

The cave spur reached back only about seven feet. Lying on her side, against the back wall, was someone Greg recognized from photographs as Daria Cameron.

As Catherine had suggested, there was an orange cast to the young woman's skin. Moving closer, he saw white streaks on her broken fingernails. She wasn't moving, but as Greg crawled nearer still, he saw that her chest rose and fell slightly as she took shallow breaths.

She wore brand-new hiking boots on her small feet, the tread matching the tracks he had seen outside.

"Ms. Cameron," Greg said. He couldn't tell if she heard him or not, but she gave no sign of it. He touched her arm gently. "Ms. Cameron, I'm going to get you some help. I'll be right back, okay?"

She didn't answer. He had not expected her to. If she was conscious at all, it was just barely. He backed out of the space, climbed out the hole through which he'd entered, and tugged his cell phone from his pocket, fully expecting to see the words "No Service" on the display.

Ten years ago, when Bix Cameron had come there—or been brought there, probably along with his son, Troy—there certainly would not have been service there. But in those ten years, Las Vegas had grown fast, and cellular-phone use had risen dramatically. Coverage areas had expanded as well, and he had two bars. That was plenty. He made the call, then went back inside the cave to wait with Daria Cameron.

She had come there to die where her father had, where her brother had been badly wounded and had lost touch with his own identity.

Greg didn't intend to let that happen.

He was still sitting beside her in the dark, speaking in quiet tones, telling her about his life, current events, sports, whatever he could think of, when he heard the *thwap-thwap-thwap* of the Life Flight helicopter's blades, muffled by the stone walls but still distinctly recognizable. He touched Daria Cameron again—she had not budged but was still breathing—and raced out of the cave, waving his arms in the air to bring the chopper down as close as it could come.

21

ROBERT DOMINGO HAD TAKEN a swipe at someone, presumably his assailant, and as a result, there were bits of tissue under his fingernails, more than enough skin cells for Wendy Simms to run DNA tests on.

The usual tests hadn't turned up much useful data. There was no match to anyone in the databases, although that wasn't necessarily telling. There were far more people *not* in the databases than people who were, and although it would have made her life easier if everyone on earth was sampled at birth, she knew that was not only impractical but would have been an enormous violation of personal privacy.

Failing any progress there, she turned instead to one of the not-so-usual tests, a brand-new method of evaluating DNA data that had been developed recently at the University of Arizona. The idea wasn't to match the DNA sample with any specific individual but to see what other information it could tell the careful investigator about its source.

When she had printed the results out and studied them, she grabbed for the phone and called Ray Langston.

"It's Wendy, Ray. I found out something interesting about the Domingo suspect."

"You have an ID for me?" he asked. She could hear the excitement in his voice and hoped what she did have wasn't too much of a letdown.

"Not a suspect . . . but I think I can narrow the field a bit."

"Narrow is good." He managed not to sigh, but just barely. "A name and address would be better, but I'll take narrow."

"It's a male," she said. "Or he's a male, I guess. And he's not Native American."

"He's not?" He sounded as surprised as she had been.

"Nope. He's probably blond, in fact. With blue eyes. You are definitely looking for a Caucasian. If you guys are only considering people from the reservation, I think you're missing the boat."

"I'm trying not to miss the boat," Ray said.

"What?"

"Never mind. Do you have anything else for me?"

"That's it for now, Ray. White male, blond and blue-eyed. It may not be a lot, but I bet it rules out a lot of suspects among the Paiutes."

"That it does, Wendy. Thank you."

Catherine had already turned into the Cameron driveway and was sitting at the front gate waiting for the loud buzz that would admit her, when her phone rang. Did Conrad Ecklie have spies watching her? Maybe he was keeping tabs on her with satellite surveillance.

It was not the undersheriff on the other end of the line, though, but Archie Johnson. "I've been doing some snooping around online," he told her.

"Which is basically your job."

"It's like getting paid to play," he said. He loved technology of every stripe, and if he hadn't been employed by the crime lab, she had no doubt he would have been involved with it in some other way. "But this snooping was mostly into financial data, which is pretty dry stuff, not all that much fun at all. Still, it's intriguing. Do you have any idea how much someone can find out about your personal financial matters if they know how to look?"

"I'd have to have money even to have personal financial matters," Catherine answered. "Instead, I have a teenage daughter."

"Well, let me tell you, Helena Cameron's daughter isn't a teenager anymore. And Helena Cameron is not the wealthiest woman in Las Vegas anymore, either."

"Was she ever?"

"Top ten, anyway, once upon a time."

The gate buzzed and parted in the middle, each side rolling away from the other, and Catherine inched forward until she could safely pass between them. "I'm at the house now, Archie. Talk to me."

"Okay, here's the short version. She *did* have a lot of money, mostly in investments—stocks, real estate, and such. But that's all past tense. Her stocks have been cashed out, buildings sold, casino holdings gone. What she is left with are a few bank and money-market accounts, some small-time stocks and bonds, the stuff that was never worth much to begin with. Everything that was really valuable has been liquidated."

"Over what time period?"

"Mostly the last five to seven years."

"That's interesting."

"I don't know if I've described her situation clearly enough," Archie went on. "She's close to bankruptcy. The estate you just drove onto? It's in foreclosure."

"I'll try to finish up and get out before she's evicted," Catherine said. "Anything else?"

"Just that her daughter's condo is in the same boat. Helena bought it for her, but she's stopped making payments, and Daria hasn't made any. The foreclosure sharks are circling there, too."

"Thanks, Archie. This is fascinating stuff."

"I thought you'd want to know."

"You thought right. Now, go home—you've put in enough hours today."

"I'll go home," Archie said. "As soon as you and everybody else from night shift goes home."

"Then it'll be a while. Tell you what, as long as you're sticking around anyway, do one more thing for me . . ."

Catherine parked in what was fast becoming her usual spot, shaded by mature palms and facing onto the reds, yellows, pinks, and greens of the rose garden. Her hand was on the door handle when her phone rang already. Archie already? Or Ecklie this time, having observed her driving onto the estate and listened in on her phone call?

Neither, as it happened.

It was Greg, but there was a lot of background noise. "We have her, Catherine!" he shouted.

"You have who? Where are you, Greg?"

"I'm in a helicopter," he replied, which explained the roar around him. "With Daria Cameron!"

"You found her!"

"Her and Bix Cameron, too. He's long dead, but she's alive. The chopper's taking us to Desert Palm Hospital. There's a bus bringing Bix to the morgue."

"I guess I'll have a lot to discuss with Helena Cameron and her people. Thanks, Greg, that's great work."

"No problem. I'll talk to you again after we land, when I get a better sense of Daria's prognosis."

He hung up, and Catherine sat in the car for another couple of minutes, gathering her thoughts. This was going to be a very different conversation from the one she had expected to have.

When it was over and Ecklie heard about it, she hoped she'd still have a job.

22

BRASS AND AGUIRRE MADE several more frustrating stops before they could begin to claim any real progress. They talked to some of the senior staff at the old Grey Rock Casino and the project manager at the construction site for the new one, a tall, triangular-shaped structure that mimicked, in steel, concrete, and glass, the real Grey Rock territory. They stopped at Ruben Solis's home and Shep Moran's.

The only thing everybody they talked to had in common, besides their heritage, was the fact that they all claimed to have no idea where Solis and Moran might be.

At the casino, there had been four police vehicles and an ambulance, because a verbal argument had escalated into a physical one, and a guy had been slammed onto a roulette wheel, injuring his back and totaling the wheel.

Finally, they stopped at the home of one of Solis's aunts. She was in her late twenties, not much

older than her nephew. She had long black hair and
dark skin and a tired look on her face. The dusty
front yard was littered with tricycles, a slide, a sand-
box (which seemed more than a little redundant to
Brass, given the home's nonexistent lawn—sand
was in more plentiful supply than almost anything
else), a couple of Razor scooters, and an assortment of balls and other sporting equipment. But the
house was as large and modern as anything in a Las
Vegas suburban development, the only apparent
concession to the bare desert surrounding it a pau-
city of windows, and those few remained blocked by
heavy drapes.

"Nice place," Brass said as they approached from
the road. "Does that mean she's on Domingo's good
list?"

Aguirre eyed Brass without turning his head. "I
hope I haven't given you cause to underestimate us,
Jim. There's a lot of poverty on the rez, but we're
not just that. There are Indians who leave the rez
and stay poor and others who stay here and get
rich. Some have jobs in town, some here at one or
another of the tribal businesses. Some of us have
college degrees, advanced degrees. I'm one of them.
I was recruited by the FBI, but I thought I could do
more good here than in a Bureau office in California
or Rhode Island or someplace."

"My apologies. I didn't mean—"

"It's okay, Jim. I have a problem seeing slights
that don't exist outside my own head. Forget I said
anything."

When Solis's relative came to the door, she had a
toddler clinging to her left leg. "Hello?" she said.

"Hello, ma'am," Aguirre said. "Are you Ruben Solis's aunt?"

The toddler hid behind the woman's leg, peeking out at Brass as if afraid the police captain might like to have him for an afternoon snack. "Yes," she said. "Is there something . . ."

"No, ma'am," Aguirre said. "We're just concerned about him. I don't know if you've heard about all the trouble, the fights and things going on around—"

"Just a little," she said. "I've been pretty busy, but I had the radio on, the rez station, and they said something about that."

"Well, we have reason to believe that someone might try to hurt Ruben," Aguirre told her. "But he's hiding out someplace, and we're having a hard time finding him to warn him."

Brass didn't like it when cops lied to civilians. He had already called Aguirre on it, in private, after Aguirre had used the same story earlier. But the tribal cop said he was just stretching the truth in a good cause. A rubber band could be stretched, Brass thought, but sooner or later, it would snap, and as often as not, it would come back and sting the person doing the stretching. He hoped that wasn't the case here.

The baby started to fuss, and she clucked at it, rocking it back and forth in her arms. "Did you try Shep Moran's mom's place?"

"No, we haven't looked there," Aguirre said. "Does she live on the rez?"

The young woman shook her head. "No, Shep's mom isn't Grey Rock, but his father was. After they broke up, she had a place in the city, but it got fore-closed on. She's moved to Phoenix with her new boyfriend's parents. But the house is sitting empty, and sometimes Shep and Rubin go out there and party."

"We'll try it," Aguirre said. "Thank you for your help. You don't happen to have the address—?"

Brass cut him off. "That's okay, we can find it."

"Thank you," Aguirre said again.

The woman closed the door, aided by the toddler, who pressed his hands against it and shoved, just in case Brass might change his mind and lunge for him.

"She could have given us the address," Aguirre said as they climbed back into his Jeep.

"And while she had it handy, she could have made a quick phone call to let him know we were coming," Brass pointed out. "This way, she still has her hands full with the kids, and she's less likely to dig for the number."

"But how do we—?"

"We know the place belongs to Shep Moran's mother. You get me her name, and I can track that down in ten seconds."

Aguirre shrugged. "Okay," he said. He started the engine and reached for his radio at the same time. "I won't have any authority there."

"We'll be on my turf," Brass said. "So now I'll be the escort, and you can be the guest."

"I can't wait," Aguirre said, thumbing the button for the mic. "That means you buy dinner."

Shep Moran's mother had lived in a neighborhood about twenty minutes from the edge of the reservation. The good-sized single-family homes were built on quarter-acre lots, so there was some space around each one for the now-standard xeriscaped yards. The whole development wasn't more than ten years old, and some of it appeared newer than that. Probably built in phases, Brass guessed, and her place was in one of the later phases. What little vegetation grew there was immature, so the houses were exposed to the full strength of the Nevada sun.

They had stucco walls and tile or shingle roofs, covered entryways, dormer windows. Brass could almost picture the flags snapping in the breeze, the signs offering easy terms and upgrades and low, low interest rates, back when the developer had been trying to entice people to buy these houses. Back when money flowed freely and credit was cheap.

The place was a ghost town.

It wasn't hard to tell which houses were still occupied. They had curtains hanging in the windows, maybe a vehicle in the drive and flowers in the garden.

But even most of those homes had For Sale signs standing out front. Anybody who was stuck in one of these houses wanted to get out, once all the neighbors had been forced from their homes. Brass couldn't blame them. They had moved into a neighborhood, which implied the presence of neighbors, friends for the kids to play with, block parties. Instead, there was the forest of For Sale signs on those posts that looked disturbingly like gallows.

He had been in too many Las Vegas neighborhoods just like this one recently. The recession had hit the city hard, and one of the nation's most

booming markets had gone bust practically over-
night. The foreclosed homes sat there like silent
ghosts, with gaping windows for eyes and Realtors'
lockboxes on doorknobs standing in for a little bling
in the mouth. Yards were no longer tended, and
even in the desert, weeds grew. Broken windows
were fixed with tape or boarded over. When no one
was buying, no real estate agent wanted to invest in
maintaining the houses, and the banks holding the
paper weren't about to put money into upkeep.

Shep Moran's mother's house looked just like the
others. They watched the addresses as they cruised
through the development, and they parked the Jeep
well out of sight of the house. Cutting through back-
yards (and it was worse there, with pools filled with
stagnant, algae-filled water or black mold crusting
their sides, more broken windows, more signs of ne-
glect), they reached a spot from which they could
get a view of her house. It was a pale tan, almost
cream, two-story, with a dark brown shingle roof. It
sat in a cul-de-sac, with houses on each side but behind it a steep hillside choked with boulders almost
the size of the house itself.

Parked out in front were two pickup trucks, one
dark blue, the other white, scaled with rust and
caked with dirt. A couple of men in tribal police
uniforms lounged in the scant shade offered by the
white truck, with rifles in their hands.

"Is that one of their official duties?" Brass asked,
ducking back behind the cover of an empty house.
"Welcoming committee for a couple of punks who
aren't even on the reservation?"

"Not official," Aguirre said. "But like I told you,

Ruben and Robert Domingo were buds. So I'm not too surprised to see some of Domingo's guys here. I wish they weren't in uniform—that's a little too obvious, isn't it?"

"You could say that."

"How do you want to play this, Jim?"

"Do you know those guys?"

"Sure, I know 'em. Doesn't mean we're friends or anything. If we just walk up to them, they'll sound some kind of alarm, and Ruben and Shep will be gone out the back before we can reach the door. At least we know they're inside, though."

"Then I guess we need to flank them." Brass stepped out of cover long enough to eye the layout of the cul-de-sac. Since they couldn't know what room Solis and Moran were in and because the houses on the curve were set at a slight angle to one another, there was no way to approach from the front without being seen. "I'll hike up into those rocks and come out behind the house. You give me fifteen minutes to get into position, then drive up to the front to distract those cops, and I'll go in the back."

"You sure? Could be a rugged hike."

Brass glanced at his shoes. Polished leather, hard soles. Cop shoes. Not made for mountaineering. But there didn't seem to be a lot of choice. "Well, we don't have a helicopter handy, and I don't see any other way in."

"You want to wait for backup?"

"And stand here while Solis and Moran decide to go somewhere else? I'll make the call on my way, but I don't want to wait."

"It's your call," Aguirre said.

"Then it's a plan. And Richie?"

"Yeah?"

"If you get shot, try to make sure it's loud enough and takes long enough to cover my entrance."

"I'll try to do that. And what are you going to be doing, exactly?"

"I'll be asking Solis and Moran some questions," said Brass.

"Questions? You don't think arresting them might be a good idea?"

"I think it's a great idea. But they're not suspects yet."

"In Domingo's killing. Which is your biggest problem. In the attack on Meoqui Torres's home, they're definitely suspects, and that's my problem."

"True. But they're on my turf now, which gives me first crack. Don't worry, I won't let them go anywhere without releasing them to you."

"Whatever you say, Jim. It's not like I have any jurisdiction here anyway. But if we don't get 'em rattled up, we're never gonna get anything out of 'em on either case."

"Okay," Brass said. "Not a great plan, but it's a plan."

"That's how I look at it." Aguirre raised his chin toward the boulders behind the house that was giving them cover. "Head that way, then circle around," he suggested. "Maybe a quarter-mile, a little less. There probably won't be guards inside. Or not many, at least."

"I just want to talk to them, not get into a gunfight," Brass said. "Maybe you should go in the back door."

"And let you go in the front way? You want to go talk to the guys who we know have guns?"

"What, you don't think they'd welcome me with open arms?"

"I'm more worried about what'll be in their hands. Go ahead, Jim. I'll get back around front and keep them occupied. When you get the drop on Ruben and Shep, get 'em in cuffs and bring 'em outside."

"Got it," Brass said, heading into the rocks. "I'll see you there."

By the time Brass had picked a route between the first boulders, a fine layer of light brown dust had completely coated his shoes and the cuffs of his dark pants. Soon he wished he had left his suit jacket in the Jeep or managed to bring the vehicle's air-conditioning with him. It wasn't a particularly hot day as southern Nevada went, but it wasn't cool, either. Brass took the jacket off and slung it over his shoulder as he worked his way over, around, and between more huge slabs of stone.

He wasn't sure what he would find when he got to the house. But if it was air-conditioned and had a floor, it would be better than this.

When the traffic hemming him in lightened, Ray pressed down on the accelerator pedal and felt the vehicle surge forward. He had been meaning to head for the reservation for hours, certain that Nick and Captain Brass could use another pair of hands there. But one thing after another had come up, stalling him, keeping him otherwise occupied. Now that he was finally on his way, the urge to race there at top speed was almost overwhelming.

He would have to call Nick when he got a little closer. As reservations went, Grey Rock was not a large one, but it still covered a lot of square miles, and he didn't know his way around.

But as he thought about calling Nick, he remembered the last phone call he had received, from Wendy. Domingo, she had said, was killed by a white man with blond hair and blue eyes. Since they didn't have a specific suspect in mind yet, it wasn't necessarily a game changer. But it certainly shifted the emphasis of their search.

As Ray drove, he pondered what else he knew about the case, both things he had learned first-hand from the physical evidence and details he had been told by others. Domingo had been out at a nightclub, where he spent a lot of money and quite a bit of time with a young Paiute woman. He tried to take her home with him, at which point she revealed her true agenda. They argued, and she got out of his Escalade and threw a brick through the passenger window. But she didn't kill him, or so she said. The evidence backed her up on that point.

Domingo continued home. There he lit a cigar and relaxed . . . and then had a visitor. He let the visitor in. They talked. Perhaps they argued. At some point, things got physical. Domingo scratched the visitor, but the visitor whacked him in the head with the heavy gold lighter Domingo had used earlier to light that cigar.

He or she had wiped the lighter clean of fingerprints—or had been wearing gloves the whole time, which seemed unlikely on a pleasant April night— and dropped it into the blood already spreading on the floor. He or she had then written the word "Quantum" on the wall in blood and had taken off. Little physical evidence had been left behind. Some tiny bits of soaptree yucca. A few threads. Orange cat hairs. Footprints had been left behind the house, maybe by the killer but maybe by someone else—perhaps even a witness to the murder.

Footprints, threads, yucca . . . Ray tapped his brakes and searched for the nearest exit. Reaching it, he swung off the highway and pulled to the side of the road to make a quick phone call.

Archie Johnson answered after two rings. "Good, you're still there," Ray said. "Listen, I know this is outside your usual range of duties, but I need some information. I don't know if you'll find it online, but if not, you might have to call the Grey Rock Paiute tribal headquarters. I'm going to give you a name to check on. You ready?"

When the call was finished, he got back on the highway, headed in the opposite direction.

The reservation would have to wait.

A painted sign on a skinny post outside the clinic showed a red cross and the words "Grey Rock Medical Clinic #4." A couple of cars and trucks were parked on the paved lot outside the tiny concrete-block building, a cube painted a kind of sunset rose that made Nick think of diluted blood. Right in front, not in a parking spot but cutting across the entry path, was the white pickup with tribal police markings that Rico Aguirre had sent over. *Guess cops are the same all over,* Nick thought. *They think parking rules apply to everyone but them.*

He was glad to see the vehicle, though, glad that the cop inside had followed orders and come there to guard Torres.

It looked as if the officer was sitting inside the truck, behind the wheel. Nick walked over to check in, to let the cop know he was there before going inside to see how Torres was doing. He crossed the parking lot, hand raised to shield his eyes from the afternoon sun glinting off the truck's windshield.

But when he reached the truck, its driver's-side window was open, and the driver hadn't budged. He was leaning to his right, his head tilted forward, his straw cowboy hat shading his face. Taking a nap, it appeared. "Hey," Nick said, putting some extra volume into it. "Everything okay here?"

The cop didn't respond. Nick went closer, and the smell hit him like a clenched fist.

Nick halted and made a quick scan. Whoever had done the cop didn't seem to be present anymore.

Or, more likely, he had gone inside.

Nick drew a weapon and took a few steps nearer the truck. The guy had been shot through the open window and slumped away from it, but his seatbelt held him in place. The shot had come from a slightly up angle, catching the cop just below his left eye. He had probably been talking to his assailant through the open window when the person outside raised a small-caliber weapon and shot him. The bullet exited out the back of the cop's skull—the truck's passenger side was painted with blood, hair, and brain matter.

Did he know the shooter? Why was he wearing

his seatbelt? Had he been somewhere else and just returned to the clinic? Or was he about to leave?

Another crime, another crime scene. Nick would have to call it into the tribal police headquarters and hope that they had the staffing available to handle one more scene in a day full of them. Or, once again, he would have to work it himself.

Not right away, though. First he had to get into that clinic and make sure that whoever had shot the police officer wasn't doing the same to Meoqui Torres and his friends.

He hurried to the door, which was around the side of the building, under another painted red cross. A concrete ramp led up to it, with an aluminum handrail, and there was a large, square button that a person in a wheelchair could push to open the glass-and-steel door. Nick peered through the glass, seeing a cozy, empty waiting area and a reception counter. The reception area was separated from the waiting area by windows, which would slide open for the person on duty to talk to patients and close for privacy. Behind the counter were racks full of medical file folders. Either it was a quiet day at the clinic, or everyone inside had been chased out.

Pulling the door open, Nick went inside, moving the barrel of his weapon from left to right, covering the space. He couldn't see anybody or hear anything inside. Rather than call out, he covered the tile floor to the reception counter in a few quick steps.

On the floor behind the counter, a young Native American woman in forest-green scrubs lay in a pool of her own blood. The pool was streaked, and now Nick noticed that it had actually begun beyond the edge of the counter. She had fallen past it, then been dragged back behind it to keep her body hidden from the doorway.

Whoever was inside the clinic was racking up a body count.

A heavy wooden door separated the waiting area from the examination rooms. Nick moved to it silently, pressing his ear to it. Hearing nothing, he pushed it open a fraction of an inch, just enough to put his eye to it and look through.

Two crumpled bodies littered the hallway floor. He recognized them as two of the three men who had brought Torres there in the first place.

So the big question facing him now was, where was the third man?

Inside Torres's room?

And if so, was his purpose protection? Or something else?

23

En route to the hospital, paramedics had hooked
Daria up to an IV, putting some needed fluids and
salts back into her body. Once they had arrived, she
was taken swiftly from Greg's sight, off the roofop
helipad and into an elevator. Greg waited for more
than an hour before a nurse told him Daria wanted
to see him, and showed him into her room.

She was sitting up in the bed, still wan but looking better than she had in the desert. "You're the
one who found me?" she asked.

"That's right. Are you feeling better, Daria?"

"They tell me I will be."

"Good. I'm Greg Sanders, with the Las Vegas
Crime Lab. When I found you out there, you were
severely dehydrated."

She managed something resembling a smile.
She was pretty, or she would have been under better circumstances. Her full lips were dried out and

cracked, her eyes bloodshot, her hair a wild tangle, but Greg could see the fine facial structure, high cheekbones and firm jaw, and a narrow, strong nose. She looked like a woman who should be taken seriously.

"I . . . I should be dead," she said. "Thank you for what you did for me."

"I'm just glad I got there in time."

"I . . . I've been so sick."

"You weren't sick," he said. "How much did the doctor tell you?"

"Just that I would be okay, after some treatment. That I was stabilized. Then I said I wanted to see you. I remember you . . . from the helicopter. I woke up once, and saw you sitting beside me." Her face seemed to cloud over. "What do you mean, I wasn't sick?"

"You were being poisoned. Once we stop that, the doctors can get you back on your feet."

"P-poisoned? Really? By who?"

"We don't know yet," Greg said. "Anyway, you shouldn't try to talk. Save your strength."

"I *want* to talk," she said. "I'm worried about my brother. You're with the police, right? Someone needs to check on him."

Greg knew he should stop her there and tell her about what had happened to Troy. But she was in perilous shape and he didn't want to make her any worse. He decided to save the bad news, to let her talk as long as she didn't tax herself too much, and to break it to her when she was better able to receive it. "We will," he said. "You just take it easy."

"Look, I don't know what's going to happen to

me. I mean, I know what you said, and the doctor. But if I don't make it—"

"You will, Daria."

"But if I don't . . . just let me tell you what I found out."

Greg didn't want her to tax herself, but he was afraid that arguing with her would upset her more than simply letting her tell her story.

"Sick or poisoned or whatever . . . I was sure I was dying. I quit my job, stopped going out much, calling friends, all that. Just . . . withdrawing. I've been spending my time in the past . . . looking through old family videos, photo albums. Trying to remember my dad and brother, because I was sure I would be joining them soon. It's just been me and Mom for so long, a family of women, but there was a time that our family included men, too, and it was so much better then."

Greg interrupted her. "Maybe you should wait," he said. "After you're better—"

"No. I want to tell you now. It might be important. You want to sit down?"

"Okay." He parked himself in the visitor's chair. He was torn, because she was right, her story might be important. On the other hand, in her condition she might not know what was important, and she could do further damage to herself if she didn't take it easy.

But she seemed to have held it in for so long that it flowed out of her, like water from a broken spigot that, once turned on, couldn't be easily shut off again.

"When I felt strong enough," she continued, "I

visited some of our old family haunts. Places we went in happier days, with Dad and Troy. Red Rock Canyon, Hoover Dam, the Natural History Museum. We used to have picnics in this park, way at the edge of town, with swing-sets and slides. It was a simple thing, but those are some of my favorite childhood memories. But the park isn't there anymore. Instead there's this homeless city, all these tents and shacks. It's so tragic."

"I know," Greg said. "I've been there."

"Anyway, I went back there again and again, just drawn there because even though the park was gone, there were enough other familiar things that I still felt comfortable there. There was this ice cream parlor, where Daddy used to buy us cones after playing in the park. Even though most of the area has changed, that's still there, and I would sit at a table outside and eat some ice cream and watch people pass by. Just living in the past, I guess. Maybe people do that when they don't have a future anymore."

"You have a future, Daria."

"Maybe so, but I didn't know that at the time. I just knew my mom and I had come down with what seemed like some terrible disease. Even though she's so much older than me—she was in her forties even before Troy and I were born—it seemed like I had it worse. I was so weak, so sick all the time.

"Anyway, next to the ice cream parlor was this music store where Troy and I used to buy cassettes. They sell CDs now, mostly used ones, but when I browsed through the racks I felt like I was right back in those days. The time before we lost Daddy and Troy, when we were a real family.

"So I was sitting there one day, at a table outside the ice cream place, with a double Dutch chocolate sundae. And I saw this homeless guy. He looked like all the rest of them, you know, all dark from sun and dirt, his clothes all turned a shade of almost charcoal gray. But there was something about him, in his eyes maybe. Something familiar."

"And it was Troy," Greg offered.

Her response was so enthusiastic he was afraid she would hurt herself. "Yes! It was Troy. As soon as I realized how familiar he was, I knew it was him. No question, no doubt. Even through all the years and all that's happened to him, I was absolutely convinced.

"He was afraid of me, at first, afraid that I wanted something from him, or would steal what little he had. He didn't know why I could possibly want to talk to him. I had to go back over and over again, persuading him, pleading with him to listen to me. I knew who he was, and I was sure he recognized me, but he didn't trust his own mind. He was defensive, and he had suffered some kind of brain damage, and it took some time to get him to listen to me. He was Troy, but his personality was so different, he had been through something terrible and he couldn't tell me what it was. Or he wouldn't.

"But when he finally listened to me, when he let me show him pictures of the family, or himself, when I told him about things he might remember, and took him to familiar places, he gradually came to believe me. He accepted that he was Troy Cameron, and not—"

"Not Crackers?"

She cracked the first real smile Greg had seen. "That's right, that's what they called him in that place. Crackers. That was the only name he knew. Troy always liked crackers, even when he was a baby. We used to get him saltines, in restaurants, to munch on while we waited for our meals.

"But even though I got him to accept his true identity, he still didn't trust anything else about his old life. I told him who his mother was, and when he found out she had a lot of money, he wouldn't go near her. He was too damaged, too messed up, he said, and if she ever found out about him she would just think he was after her money. I told him that was nonsense, but I couldn't convince him. He wanted to remain a secret. I had to respect that, or risk him withdrawing again, maybe running away. I didn't tell anyone about him, not Mom or anybody else, because I wanted to keep seeing him. I knew that the more I saw him, the more he would trust me, and eventually maybe he would let me convince him to see Mom.

"He didn't remember much of what had happened to him, or to Daddy," she went on. A passing nurse stuck his head in the door. Greg shot him a glance that asked, *Should she be talking?* But the man just shrugged, so Greg let Daria Cameron go on. "But he had these directions he had written out, over and over. He didn't know where they led, just that they were something he'd always had, always rewriting in case some of his older copies got lost. He said it was something very important, he just didn't know what."

"But you had an idea?"

"I had an idea. I figured if it was something that important to him, it might have to do with whatever had happened. How he had gotten this way, what happened to Daddy. I tried to jog his memory, but it wouldn't come back. And he refused to follow the directions with me. He said it was too scary and too sad.

"Anyway, when I started to feel really sick, like I wasn't going to make it, I went back to him. I told him he had to go see Mom—that when I died, he would be all she had, and vice versa. I gave him directions, told him how to get through the gate, and told him what to say when he got there. Then I took a copy of his directions, and went out into the desert. I wanted to find Daddy. I didn't want to die without knowing the truth. I wanted to find out, and then to die with him."

"That took a lot of courage."

She smiled again. Each time she did, her face lit up and Greg could see the woman behind the ravages of poison and exposure. "Courage or stupidity. I started to think it was that. But I kept going, and when I saw the X that Troy had marked on the wall, I knew I was in the right place. Daddy was dead, of course, but I was sure it was him even though I couldn't recognize anything about him. There was no one else it could be."

"I think you're right," Greg said. "That's what I thought when I saw him, too."

"That's right, you were in there! In that little cave." A frightened look washed across her face. "Did . . . did Troy ever get there? To Mom?"

This was the moment Greg had been hoping to avoid. Someone had to tell her, and it looked as if he was elected. He could stall her, maybe for another half hour, an hour at the most. Let her recover more. But for all he knew, her family was waiting outside for him to be finished here. Would it be cruel to leave it for them to tell her?

Family would be the lucky thing. What if some reporter got in here and asked her about it? He didn't know if the media had found out yet, but if they had . . . he didn't want that to happen. Anyway, she had been strong enough to tell her story, so he thought she was strong enough to listen to his. "I'm very sorry, Daria," he said, his voice low and gentle. "There's something I need to tell you. . . ."

24

SAM VEGA DROVE ONTO the Cameron estate just as Catherine was finishing with yet another phone call. She greeted him, and the two of them started toward the house. Dustin Gottlieb opened the door before they reached it. "Does Mr. Coatsworth know you're coming?" he asked, allowing them into the foyer. "He's not here at the moment."

"We just need to see Mrs. Cameron briefly," Sam said.

"Well . . ."

"It's official business, Mr. Gottlieb." Sam gave Gottlieb a look that conveyed both gravity and weariness in equal proportion, the kind of look that young cops had to practice in the mirror because it would serve them so well over the years.

"Fine, I'll fetch her. Wait here."

"You are good," Catherine murmured after Gottlieb left.

"I try."

Catherine had filled Sam in on everything she had learned but only the shorthand version. He eyed her curiously as they waited. "You sure you've got what you need?" he asked.

"I have enough to know what else I need," she replied. "That's the important thing. You brought the warrant, right?"

He touched the inside breast pocket of his suit jacket. Before he could speak again, Drake McCann entered the parlor, followed by Helena Cameron, Craig Stilton, and Dustin Gottlieb. Stilton and McCann got Helena situated on a chair, then turned to Catherine and Sam, who were still standing. Gottlieb leaned against a wall, at some remove from the others.

"Should we ask Marvin Coatsworth to join us?" Stilton asked. "He's just a phone call away."

"That's up to you," Sam said. "For everyone's convenience, we'd like to get this done as quickly as possible."

Helena lifted a weary hand and tapped Stilton's side. "Let it go," she said. "If we need Marvin, we can stop everything until he gets here."

"What can we do for you both, then?" Stilton asked. "You know how hard this whole ordeal has been on Mrs. Cameron."

"Believe me, I know," Catherine assured him. "And we don't mean to make things difficult." She shifted her gaze, addressing Helena directly. "I think you'll feel better after we talk," she said. "I have some of the answers we've been looking for."

Helena looked exhausted, even more so than usual. Her orange-tinged face was drawn, with heavy bags under her bloodshot eyes and a disconcerting quiver to her lower lip. "Answers would be nice," she said in a weak, scratchy voice.

"I'll do what I can," Catherine promised. "First, you should know that we've found Daria." Helena's left hand went to her mouth. "She's alive," Catherine added quickly, before the old woman could misinterpret. "She's at Desert Palm Hospital. A crime scene investigator found her out in the desert and suffering from exposure, as well as the . . . the condition that has affected both of you. But now that the doctors know the real source of that condition, they're confident they'll be able to help her. And you, too, Mrs. Cameron. They should be able to get you back to normal."

"I . . . I don't understand."

"You've been poisoned, Mrs. Cameron. Probably slowly, over a period of time. You're not sick, you and Daria didn't catch the same virus or anything. You're being poisoned, and now that we know what it is, all we have to do is cut off the source and treat it, and you'll be fine."

"That's good news," Stilton said. "If it's true. Although I'm not sure how that could have—"

"It's definitely true, Mr. Stilton," Sam said.

"Oh, thank God," Gottlieb said. He leaned against the wall as if his knees had lost their structural integrity. "Thank you, Supervisor Willows."

"When can I see her? Daria?" Helena asked.

"Very soon, as soon as she's stabilized."

"Was she found at a crime scene?" Stilton asked. "You said she was found by a crime scene investigator."

"She was," Catherine answered. "Not the scene of a recent crime but a crime scene just the same. Our investigator followed some directions found among Troy's possessions, and they led him to a cave out in the desert, walled off with rocks. Inside the cave, he found Daria, alive, and someone else— your husband, Mrs. Cameron. Long dead but almost certainly him."

"He . . . found Bix?"

"That's utterly impossible," Stilton said. "His body would have decomposed after all these years. How could he know?"

"We don't know precisely when he died," Catherine countered. "Only when he disappeared. But in fact, his body was mummified by the dry air and protected by the cave. It's on its way back to our lab to be CT-scanned and DNA-tested. We'll get a positive identification, and I'm sure that will tell us exactly what happened to him."

"That's simply remarkable," Gottlieb said. "You people really are good at your jobs."

"We try to be. There's one more thing, though."

"What now?" Stilton asked. All the news so far hadn't changed his attitude, which was antagonistic. Every word he spat at them was some sort of challenge. "You haven't thrown enough surprises at poor Helena for one day?"

Sam Vega took this one. "Maybe not," he said. "We're pretty sure that when your husband's body is scanned, ma'am, it will turn out that he was shot. Probably with the same weapon that was originally used on your son. Our working theory is that the same person shot them both and left them to die in the desert. But Troy survived, sealed up his father's body with stones in that cave, then made his way back to the city, noting the landmarks along the way. Because of the brain damage he had suffered as a result of that gunshot wound, by the time he reached the city, he didn't remember where the landmarks led, but he never forgot that the destination was an important one. Over all these years, he kept recopying the directions to make sure he never lost them."

"This is all quite remarkable," Stilton said, almost echoing Gottlieb's words and tone but with an undercurrent of impatience. "But if you'll excuse us now, I think Mrs. Cameron could use some time to take this in and process it."

"Now, Craig—" Helena began, but he cut her off with a wave.

"Helena, please, let me take care of you."

"There is one more thing," Sam said, drawing the warrant from his pocket. He pointedly dodged Stilton and handed it to Helena, who then turned it over to Stilton without so much as a glance at it. But at least she had held it in her hand. "That's a warrant to search these premises."

"Searching for what?" Stilton asked.

"Specifically, we'd like to look through Mr. McCann's gun collection."

"Why?" McCann demanded. It was the first word he'd uttered since they had arrived. "You already have the gun I accidentally shot Troy with."

Catherine noted his emphasis on the word *accidentally*. She didn't doubt the basic truth of his story, and the surveillance video backed it up. But his word choice was strange. She didn't think the shooting was an accident, just that he didn't know the victim's identity. Even then, because there was no way McCann could have known, he wasn't being blamed. Not even by the victim's mother, it seemed. Still, he sounded as if someone was accusing him. "We have our reasons, Mr. McCann," she said.

"Very well," Stilton said. "I suppose there's not much we could do to stop you, even if we had something to hide."

"Which we don't," Helena added.

McCann started toward the door. "My suite is this way," he said. "Come with me."

"You wait here, Helena," Stilton said. "Dustin, stay with her. I'm sure we won't be long."

Helena and Gottlieb stayed put, while Catherine and Sam accompanied McCann and Stilton. McCann led them through the house, outside, and then back in through his private entrance in back. Catherine eyed the tennis court and wondered how long it had been since Helena had played. Maybe not since her husband's disappearance or earlier.

McCann's suite was tidy, but it was obviously a bachelor's lair. Electronics dominated the front room—a bank of video monitors, a large plasma TV, a state-of-the-art audio system. A bookcase held only a handful of books but showcased a number of sports trophies proclaiming his achievements in football, baseball, shooting, and track. Car and sports magazines were fanned out on a coffee table. It almost looked posed, a set for a men's fashion spread. Catherine wondered if he had decorated it himself or if Helena had brought a professional in to design the suite somebody thought McCann should have.

"The guns are back here," he said.

A short, wide hallway separated his living area from his bedroom. One wall of the hallway had been fitted out as a gun cabinet—long guns on racks chest high and above, handguns below, and closed cabinets that probably contained supplies and ammunition below that. It wasn't locked, but then he probably rarely had children in there, if ever, and he was no doubt fairly confident about the estate's security.

"That's everything," he said. "If I knew what you were looking for, maybe I could help."

"If it's here, we'll find it," Sam said. "Why don't you two sit down while we look?"

"We'll stay right here," McCann insisted.

"As long as you're out of the way," Sam said.

Catherine had pulled on latex gloves and was already looking at the handguns. McCann must have had thirty of them, of different calibers and ages, and nearly as many rifles and shotguns. "This is quite a collection," she said.

"Some of the pieces I inherited from my father," McCann explained. "He had a large collection, and when he died, it was split between me and my older brothers. Obviously, I don't use the older ones in my work, but I like to keep them around."

Sam pointed at one of the older revolvers, a .45 with a wooden grip. "That's a beauty," he said.

"That's one of my first pistols," McCann said. "I try to get them all out on the range at least once a year, to keep them in working order, and that one has always been a great weapon. Accurate and dependable."

"Smith and Wesson," Sam said.

"That's right."

"What do you think?" Sam asked Catherine.

"Looks like the best bet," she said.

"It's loaded," Sam noted.

"Of course," McCann said. "An unloaded gun is just a lump of steel. But what do you want it for?"

Catherine gingerly took the gun from the rack and deposited it in a plastic evidence bag. "For ballistics testing," she said.

"Testing for what?"

"To see if this is the weapon that killed Bix Cameron and wounded Troy Cameron."

McCann's face flushed. "What?! But . . . I didn't shoot Bix! Or Troy. Bix was like a father to me, after mine passed away."

"Still, we have to check it out," she said. "It's old enough, it's on the premises—"

"Which means nothing," Stilton broke in. "Bix Cameron was shot by some Vegas mobster trying to muscle in on his casinos. Everyone knows that."

"Everyone *theorizes* that," Catherine corrected. "If we *knew* who did it, that would be different."

Sam was still searching the cabinet, opening drawers and doors.

"Now what?" McCann asked. "You already have my forty-five."

"Gun bluing," Catherine said. "Got any?"

"Of course," McCann said. "I take pride in my collection. I take good care of these, and they take care of me. And of the Cameron family."

"Where is it, then?"

McCann pointed at a door on the far right of the cabinet. "In there."

Catherine opened it and found his cleaning supplies and bluing kit. She picked up the bottle of bluing, shook it. "You're almost out," she said.

"I shouldn't be. I just bought it last year."

She unscrewed the plastic cap and looked inside. The bottle was nearly empty. She showed McCann.

"That doesn't make any sense."

"You said you take good care of your guns. It shows. There's nothing I see that needs bluing."

"That's right. I just told you I bought that bottle last year. I used it on a few pieces that had oxidized a little, had a couple of rust spots. But I didn't use that much."

"I'm really not surprised." Catherine capped the bottle again.

"I don't see what you're getting at," Stilton said.

"Are you a shooter, Mr. Stilton?"

"I have shot, on occasion. Drake and I have been hunting, in fact, but not for, what, several years anyway."

"And we used to go out with Bix sometimes," McCann said. "To the Eastern Sierra, mostly. Sometimes Wyoming or Montana."

"So you're familiar with the use of gun bluing."

"It protects the steel from rusting, I believe."

"That's right," Catherine said, inspecting the bottle's label. "And one of the active ingredients in many types of gun bluing, including this brand, is selenium dioxide."

"So?"

"So, Helena and Daria Cameron's condition is the result of selenium poisoning. Probably small doses, administered over a period of time. The selenium could have come from this bottle."

"That's insane!" McCann shouted. "First you accuse me of shooting Bix, then of poisoning Helena and Daria? Isn't it bad enough that I killed Troy without meaning to? Now you're trying to hang everything on me!"

"No one has accused you of anything, Mr. McCann," Sam said.

"We just need to test this bottle, to see if it's where the poison came from."

Stilton pulled a phone from his pocket. "Keep quiet, Drake. I'm calling Marvin," he said. "If you people are going to make rash accusations, he needs to be here."

"Go ahead, call him," Sam said.

"And I'll make sure that on his way over, he calls the mayor and the chief of police. You people are way out of line here."

"We're only looking for the truth, Mr. Stilton," Catherine said.

"I think you're on a witch hunt."

"Not at all."

Stilton pressed a button on his phone, and Coatsworth answered almost immediately. The two had a hurried conversation, after which Stilton brandished the phone like a knife before pocketing it again. "He's on his way. I think we should go back into the house and wait."

"Whatever you like," Sam said.

Catherine put the bluing into another evidence

bag. "Before we rejoin Mrs. Cameron, there's one more thing I'd like to say."

"What's that?" Stilton asked.

"Helena Cameron's finances are in pretty dire shape, I understand."

Stilton raised his head, jutting his chin toward her. "Okay, now you're *really* out of line. I completely resent that. I know exactly what's going on with every dime she has."

"I'm sure you do," Catherine said. "Your financial situation, by contrast, has never looked better. Mr. McCann, did you know that the bank is about to foreclose on this estate and Daria's condo?"

McCann looked stricken. "No . . . I had no idea."

"You're lucky your paychecks aren't bouncing yet. But Mr. Stilton here has been buying up luxury properties around the country, taking advantage of short sales and foreclosure deals. Plus, his stock portfolio is extremely healthy."

"That's all privileged and confidential information," Stilton declared. His face was flushed now, while McCann's had gone pale. "I don't see how you could possibly—"

"Some of it's public record," Catherine said. "Some of it took a warrant. And some we're still checking into. But the general outline of it is correct, isn't it?"

"That can't be true," Helena Cameron said from the doorway. "Is it, Craig?"

25

CRAIG STILTON'S HEAD SWIVELED between Helena and the CSI. He took a step toward Willows, then stumbled and threw a hand out toward the rack, as if to steady himself. Willows reached for him in case he was fainting.

He had often found it advantageous to let people underestimate him. He twisted from her reach, catching himself on the gun rack and coming up with a Glock 9mm in his fist. Loaded, of course—Drake had just confirmed that.

The detective, Vega, was drawing his own weapon as Stilton darted across the room, the Glock aimed at Helena Cameron. He grabbed the elderly woman, wrenching her around in front of him.

"Freeze, Stilton!" Vega ordered.

"I'm sorry, Helena," Stilton said. He pressed the muzzle of his borrowed gun against her temple, holding her so her body was between him and the cops. Helena was as small and frail and weak as a baby bird, fallen from its nest before its time. "I didn't mean for you to get involved in this."

"Craig . . . I don't understand."

"It's simple, Helena. Everything they said is true."

Helena's eyes filled, her mouth hung open, that lower lip quivering like mad now. If Stilton hadn't been holding her up, she would have fallen onto the floor. "No. It can't be."

That was how he had been able to do it, because she trusted him so. Stilton had been skimming from the Cameron accounts for years. A little here, a little there, out of their pockets and into his. Bix Cameron figured it out when he had barely started. He was going to expose Stilton, so he had to die. Just Troy's bad luck that he was with his father at the time.

Of course, he only shot Troy the first time. It took Drake to finish him off ten years later. Stilton had believed Troy was dead; he wouldn't have left him out there to die slowly. He was a thief, but he was no monster.

But it had killed him to see how Bix spent his money. Stilton watched it flowing out for years, trying to get him to stop wasting it on one more hotel, one more casino, one more private apartment for whichever showgirl he was sleeping with behind Helena's back. Stilton knew he could put it to better use. He had worked hard for this family, for decades, and they paid him a reasonable salary. But it wasn't enough. Not nearly. Not when Bix was wasting it thoughtlessly.

Then, of course, the economy fell apart. What Helena had left took a big hit when the markets tanked. When she died, Daria would have been able to look into her finances, and she would have had questions Stilton didn't want to answer. So he'd had to make sure they both went about the same time, in a way that appeared natural. He had done his research, found that although selenium poisoning would show noticeable physical symptoms, it was rare enough that most doctors would run through scores of other tests before they stumbled upon it. And then death would present as congestive heart failure, which could be natural. To slow things down even more, he interfered whenever Dr. Boullet tried to make appointments to diagnose the problem.

"It's true, Helena," Stilton said. "I can't say I'm proud of it, but time was running short. I had to do something."

"It's over now, Stilton," Sam said. "You're not walking out of here without bracelets on."

"Wrong," Stilton argued. "You can't risk shooting Helena, and the two of us are going for a ride."

He didn't believe Helena could survive such a ride. The poisoning had weakened her; that and age and stress had parked her on the edge of a cliff, and at the bottom of the cliff was death. Stilton had dragged her close to the rim, and now he had two hands on her back, ready to give the final shove. None of that mattered, though—all that mattered was that the cops couldn't take a chance on killing her themselves.

Neither of them had a safe shot. Stilton's head was exposed, but he kept bobbing it back behind Helena. Even if they hit him, there was a chance his gun would go off. In her condition, Helena couldn't risk so much as a flesh wound.

"I won't hurt her if you let me walk," Stilton said. "I'll let her go someplace safe, and you'll never see me again."

"You have to know that's not how these things work," Sam told him.

"It's how it's going to work this time. Unless you want to take responsibility for her death. I've got nothing to lose, but she does."

"Think about this, Stilton," Willows said. "Think about what it'll be like out there. On the run, always looking over your shoulder, cringing every time you see a police car. We'll be watching your bank accounts, freeze your credit. Are you sure it's worth it?"

"I have plenty of money," he said. "Tucked away around the world. Sit on a beach somewhere instead of going to jail? Yeah, I think it's worth it." He tugged Helena toward the door. She dragged her feet, and he gave her a rib-crushing jerk. "Come on, Helena. Don't make this diffic—"

The shot rang out in the small space, loud and echoing off the walls, and the bite of acrid smoke reached Catherine's nose while she was still working out what had happened. Stilton's head snapped back, his hands flinging out to the sides, the gun sailing from his open hand and tearing a chunk of plaster from a wall. Blood jetted from the small entry hole in his right temple and gushed from the exit wound opposite. Helena screamed once, then collapsed.

Drake McCann stood there, legs spread, smoke

still wafting from the barrel of the gun in his hand. He looked shell-shocked, eyes wide and jaw slack.

"Drop it!" Sam barked, spinning around and aiming his weapon at McCann.

Blake's expression didn't change, but his fingers went limp and his gun clattered to the floor. "She . . . she never deserved any of this," he said quietly.

Catherine crouched at Helena's side and put her hand to the woman's throat. There was a pulse, weak but steady. Helena drew halting, shallow breaths. Catherine fumbled for a phone to call for an ambulance. Behind her, she heard handcuffs being snapped over McCann's wrists. Dustin Gottlieb came tearing into the suite, demanding to know what had happened, tears spotting his cheeks when he saw.

As she sat waiting for the paramedics, Catherine thought about the two bodies in Doc Robbins's morgue, perhaps side-by-side in drawers. Robert Domingo, a wealthy man from a poor community, and Troy Cameron, a poor man from a rich family. In the greater scheme, she knew, she was one cog in the machinery of state, and whatever inequalities and injustices had affected the lives of the two men, her role, and that of the people she worked with, was to make sure that in death each was treated the same. Nobody took precedence because of personal wealth, no human being was so unimportant that he or she didn't deserve their fullest efforts.

Sam led McCann, in handcuffs, out of the suite. McCann had killed Troy Cameron in the course of his job, protecting the Cameron estate. Now he had killed Craig Stilton while protecting Helena. He would never do time for either killing, and that didn't bother Catherine in the least. This shooting, like the other, would be ruled justifiable. Both were unfortunate; neither was homicide.

Of all of the people with whom Helena had surrounded herself, he might have been the best at his job, the most loyal and honorable.

And he was, it seemed, a very skilled marksman, with just enough of a different angle on Stilton that he'd been able to take the shot. It was still a risky play, but it had paid off.

When Helena Cameron recovered, Catherine would suggest that she give Drake McCann a raise.

26

IF THEY WERE GOING to spot him, Brass figured, it would be now, while he was working his way down off the last boulder and approaching the back door. He couldn't be sure how many people were inside or how vigilant they were, but for all he knew, someone might have been lining up a shot at that very moment from one of the dark windows facing his way.

The backyard had been planted with grass once, but that hadn't lasted long. There were a couple of tufts remaining, and the rest was as dry and dusty as the front. A deck extended from a concrete slab behind the house and wrapped around a covered hot tub, but that was the only feature of note. Instead of a fence, there were the boulders that backstopped the property, some of them as tall as the house itself, jumbled up one atop another as if they'd been shaken out of a can. The scramble up and down and around had been tiring, and Brass's clothing, entirely unsuited to the job, was thrashed.

But he had almost reached his goal.

Seven windows faced him, one small and set high into a wall—a bathroom window, he thought. One, near the far left corner, was floor-to-ceiling, and he could catch glimpses of an empty living room or dining room through that one. A few feet to the right of that was a door with a window inset, which Brass guessed led into a kitchen or utility room. The others were upstairs, more standard-sized and regularly placed, and were probably bedrooms.

He hadn't detected any movement through any of them. For all he could tell, Solis and Moran weren't there after all or had left after Brass and Aguirre split up, and this had all been nothing more than a fairly unpleasant afternoon workout.

Brass stopped in the notch between two boulders he had just climbed down and scanned the back of the house again. All was still. He couldn't hear anything from the house. In the distance, a raven cawed, and muffled conversation from around front sounded as if Aguirre had reached the pair of police officers standing guard. The only smell was the dry tang of desert.

Waiting any longer wouldn't do him any good. He drew his duty weapon and stepped out into the yard. Walking briskly, he made for the back door. No one raised an alarm, and in seconds, he had the doorknob gripped in his left hand. It turned easily. The window was smudged, greasy on the inside, preventing him from seeing through.

Brass took a deep breath and let it out again, willing the hammering of his heart to slow. He had more years on the job than he liked to think about, but no matter how many times he had done it, going through a door blind, into a place he didn't know, where anybody might be waiting, was a nerve-wracking thing. To make it worse, he had to trust that Aguirre was really working on distracting the men out front and not warning them. Ray's friend had speculated that most tribal police would be on Domingo's side. Whether that extended to Aguirre he couldn't know.

He twisted the knob and yanked the door open, inserting his gun into the space first, ready to fire if he needed to.

He was looking into a kitchen, its counters yellow tile, cabinets old, scarred wood. The floor was linoleum, some of the squares peeling up at the corners. A refrigerator and stove, both olive green, had scrapes and rust spots on their doors, and on the side of the refrigerator, Brass could see black mold inching its way up from the floor. More of the same dotted the floor and ceiling. A butcher block stood in the middle of the floor, a few pots and pans hanging from hooks on its sides.

Announce himself? Or not? He didn't have a warrant. But there were people dead and wounded from the assault on Meoqui Torres's home and a potential connection to the murder of Robert Domingo in Las Vegas, and he had probable cause on his side. He had called in for backup and to have search and arrest warrants written up, but, as he had told Aguirre, he didn't want to wait for those to arrive.

He decided not to announce. Surprise would be the best ally he had. He shut the door silently and crossed the kitchen, testing each step to make sure a squeaking floor didn't give him away now that he had come so far. His breathing was shallow, but his heart had started to calm. He was in it now, in the groove. Things would unfold as they unfolded, and the best he could do was to meet events head-on.

From the kitchen, a stub of a hallway led to a carpeted living room. Brass heard someone swallowing liquid, then the clink of a bottle being set down on a hard surface, and finally a soft belch. Two males laughed. "Your mom should have left a TV or something, dude," someone said. "I'll go crazy, we stay here for much longer."

"That won't be a problem, then," Brass said as he swung around the corner.

Two young Native American men faced him, a slender one sitting on an old yellow sofa, so mildewed that it had been left behind, and the other, stocky and as solid as one of the boulders outside, with tattoos all up his arms and wrapped around his neck, cross-legged on the floor. They wore almost identical looks of surprise. An assortment of guns filled most of a low table, including a big .50-caliber automatic rifle and some handguns, with a couple of sweating beer bottles standing amid them. There were more bottles and food wrappers and other trash scattered around the room. Holes at shoulder height looked as if they had been made by someone punching the walls or throwing things into them.

The slender guy snaked an arm toward the table. Brass covered the distance quickly and kicked out, feeling a satisfying crunch under his dusty shoe as the heel smashed into the man's hand. The gun he had been reaching for dropped back onto the table with a heavy *thump*. "I wouldn't try that," Brass said, growling out the words.

"You freakin' hurt me!" the man complained. He held his arm by the wrist, shaking the hand loosely.

"Like you wouldn't have shot me?" Brass kept the gun aimed between the two men, ready to shift it to either side in a heartbeat, and he drew back his blazer to show the badge hanging from his belt. "LVPD," he said. "Just so you don't think I'm trying to jack you or something. Which one of you is Ruben Solis?"

The two men glanced at each other, and then the slender one shrugged and answered, "You must have the wrong house, man."

"There a lot of houses around here with squatters in them?"

"You might be surprised," the slender one said.

"Who says any of us is whatshisname?" the big guy added. "Guy you're looking for."

Brass let his gaze drill into the smaller man. Shep Moran was the one who had done time, and some of the big guy's tats looked like jailhouse ink. "One of you is Ruben, and I'm thinking it's you." He twitched the gun barrel toward the heavier guy. "Which makes you Shep Moran. This is your mom's house, or it was." The big guy turned his gaze toward the floor. "This place has been trashed enough," Brass said. "Let's just go outside and talk."

"Don't make any difference," Moran said. "It ain't her problem anymore."

Brass didn't bother to explain that further damaging the house would only make it harder for this neighborhood ever to get back on its feet. As long as it was mostly empty, the houses occupied by squatters but not by permanent residents, it would be a haven for crime. That would probably suit Shep Moran just fine, but chances were good that his mother wouldn't have felt the same way.

"Outside works for me," Ruben Solis said. His hair was long and straight, his T-shirt baggy and black. The muscles on his arms were toned and firm. Moran strained the seams on his T-shirt, and his pants would have been dangerously droopy on anyone smaller. As it was, Brass thought you could drop a tractor tire through each leg without straining the fabric.

"Let's go, then. On your feet, slow and easy."

The two guys rose, Shep Moran, on the floor, having a harder time of it, using the sofa's arm to brace himself.

They wanted to go outside, Brass knew, because there were more men with guns out there. He hoped Aguirre had them under control.

As he was straightening to his full height, Moran let his right leg snap back into the low table. Guns and bottles went flying. As soon as it happened, Solis took off for the front door at a run. Moran grabbed for one of the guns, and Brass jammed the barrel of his gun against the big man's sweat-soaked neck. "Don't even try," he said. "Try not to be stupid."

Brass pulled out a pair of handcuffs. Now that the two guys were separated, he would have to cuff this one and then go run down Solis. "Hands behind your back."

"Dude, get the gun outta my neck already, okay?"

"I want your hands behind your back, and if you don't do it now, I'll do it for you."

"Okay, okay, whatever. Relax, man." He put his hands behind his back. Brass clicked the cuffs into place over wrists so thick the handcuffs barely closed around them. Now the question was, take him outside and hand him over to Aguirre? Or assume that Aguirre had his hands full with the guards and chain him to something inside while he went after Solis?

Before he had to make up his mind, the front door opened. Brass shielded himself behind Moran and aimed his gun over the man's shoulder. Solis came back inside, his face screwed up with pain and not under his own power. Aguirre shoved him along, twisting Solis's arm behind him.

"You lost one," Aguirre said.

"I was just about to go get him."

"Thought I'd save you a trip."

"I appreciate that."

"This here is Rubin Solis," Aguirre said.

"That's what I figured. Shep Moran and I are already old friends. What happened to the guards out front?"

"I gave them twenty bucks and sent them for beer."

Brass laughed. "Is that how it works around here?"

"You have to know your audience. I happened to know these guys."

Shep Moran spat. "Dudes signed their own death warrants."

"Speaking of warrants," Brass said, "Richie, you want to do the honors?"

"Sure," Aguirre said. "Ruben Solis, Shep Moran, you're under arrest."

"For what?" Solis demanded.

"For being stupid," Aguirre said. "Also, for shooting a bunch of folks at Meoqui's place. So let's see, we've got murder, attempted murder, and assault with a deadly weapon, for starters. Okay with you, Ruben?"

Solis shrugged, as well as he could with Aguirre hanging on to his arm.

"Let's go someplace and talk," Aguirre said. "I think we have a lot to talk about, don't you?"

"We got nothing to say to you."

"Oh, I have a feeling you'll feel differently in a little while. In fact, I'm pretty sure of it."

Aguirre backed out the front door, dragging Solis along with him. Brass prodded Moran, hands cuffed behind his back, head hanging down, along with them.

The two tribal cops hadn't been sent for drinks after all. They were still there in the driveway. But instead of chilling in the shade, they were standing on either side of the pickup's cab, arms stretched inside through open windows, cuffed to each other. The cab's rear window was open, too, probably how Aguirre had cuffed them together. Their weapons were piled in the driveway in front of the truck, well out of reach. The men glared at Aguirre with hatred etched on their faces.

"I thought you sent them to get some beer," Brass said.

Aguirre gave him a big grin. "Yeah, I lied about that. It's a bad habit of mine. But I just didn't think I could trust them with twenty bucks."

27

THE TWO BODIES WERE sprawled on the floor outside an open doorway. Nick stood on the far side of the swinging door for a moment. He didn't know if those men on the floor were alive or dead. He didn't know for sure if Torres was on the other side of that opening. He didn't know how many attackers were inside or if they had finished their work and gone.

But he didn't have much time to find out. Blood was just beginning to flow down the hall, spreading out from the fallen. Nick eased through the swinging door. The smell of gunpowder hung heavy in the air. He hurried down the hall, trying to balance haste with the need to be quiet.

It was unlikely that they'd hear him anyway. Once he was through the door, he heard voices from inside the open room. ". . . whatever you want with me, but leave him alone! If this rez had ten times more like him instead of people like us, it'd be a better place."

"I don't want to hurt any doctors," another voice answered.

"No witnesses," another one insisted. "That's the rule."

Nick knew that when he showed himself in the doorway, he would be exposed to whoever was inside. There would be no cover. But if he didn't move fast, anything could happen in that room. From the sound of things, there were two people alive, but threatened. Quick and definitive action was needed. If only he had a SWAT team or even a gas grenade.

He decided he had to use surprise to take them off guard. Nick covered the last few feet to the doorway in a few steps and swung around inside. "Police!" he shouted in a commanding tone. "Everybody on the floor, now!"

He saw two men standing around Meoqui Torres, who was on his back in a hospital bed, his feet facing the door, and a fourth man, apparently the doctor in question, pressed into a corner on Torres's left, trying hard to make himself one with the wall. One of the men Nick recognized from Torres's house, while the other one, a few years older, wearing expensive Western-style clothes and pointed boots, he didn't know. The smell of alcohol-soaked sweat rolled off him, and both men reeked of tobacco smoke, those odors blotting out the disinfectant and the gunpowder and blood from the hallway. The doctor was Native American, too, his gray hair neatly combed, blue scrubs wrinkled from the day's work, trembling so hard the stethoscope around his neck danced against his chest.

What Nick hadn't seen was the fifth man in the room, back in the corner behind the door. He didn't know that man was there until Torres raised a hand and pointed, and then the familiar *chunk* of a weapon's hammer being drawn back sounded behind him. "Drop that piece, lawman," the man said.

Rookie mistake, Nick thought, angry at himself. *Stupid—so intent on getting the drop on these guys I didn't watch my corners.* Nick took his eyes off the other guys long enough to glance over his shoulder. A Native American man stood there with his right arm extended, the huge muzzle of a .357 Magnum pointed at Nick's head. He, too, was older than Torres.

"I don't think so," Nick said. He froze where he was, keeping his weapon trained on the older of the two men beside Torres.

Nick wasn't a police officer, but he was qualified to use his sidearm, and one of the first rules a cop learned was that you never surrender your weapon. If someone gets the drop on you, you try to talk your way out of it, or you take a bullet. But if you surrender your weapon, the instructors taught, you are going to die, and you'll probably be killed with your own gun. He'd already made one bad mistake; he didn't plan to compound it with another.

"I'm not fooling around here," the man said.

"A doctor and a cop?" Torres said from the bed. His voice was shaky, his face wan. Nick guessed that he hadn't been awake for long before these guys came into the room. There was a tray on a swiveling stand close beside him with a pitcher of water and a plastic cup on it. A few ice cubes floated in the pitcher. "Is that really how you want to spend your day, killing decent men who try to help people?"

"Guys, let's all chill out," Nick said calmly, picking up on Torres's effort. He hadn't moved his gun yet but held absolutely still, not giving the man behind him any reason to worry. "There's no need for anyone else to get hurt here. We've got a standoff here. We could all start shooting, but what'll be left when the smoke clears might not be what we're looking for."

One of the men standing by Torres shifted his guns toward Nick. The other—the one who had been part of Torres's entourage—kept his trained on the man in the bed. It would be easy enough for him to lift the barrel an inch or so, to shoot over Torres and hit the doctor in the corner. "What the hell are you?" one of the older men asked. "You're not a regular cop."

"LVPD Crime Lab," Nick said. "I think I know what you guys are doing here, but I can tell you definitively that Meoqui Torres didn't kill Chairman Domingo." He hoped he had read the situation right, that the two older men were some of Domingo's enforcers, and the younger guy, the one who had been part of Torres's entourage, was secretly in Domingo's pocket.

"You know who did, why ain't you off arresting him?" Torres's supposed friend challenged.

"Let the man speak," the doctor urged.

"How do you know this?" the older man asked. Traces of white flecked his neatly combed black hair. He had a mole under his left eye that made him look as if he was half-squinting. He and Nick had their weapons aimed at each other, but Nick hadn't forgotten the other gun, the one behind him. If shooting started, he would take two rounds. At these ranges, the men weren't likely to miss.

"Because Domingo was killed by a white man with blond hair," Nick said. "We don't know who yet, but we know it wasn't Torres."

"Damn straight," Torres said, flipping his jet-black hair back with his hand.

"You sure about that?" Torres's hanger-on asked. Almost as if reminding the two older men, he added, "Torres took off by himself last night, said he was going for a drive. But he was gone about the same time as Domingo got whacked."

"Oh, I think Torres was there," Nick admitted. "But he didn't kill anyone."

"Then what . . . ?"

"Let's all put down those weapons, and we can talk about it," Nick said.

"I don't know," the second of the older men said. A network of wrinkles bracketed his eyes, and he had a chin as big as a man's fist and a thick stump of a neck. He was the one with liquor oozing out his pores. His voice had a strange kind of calm to it that Nick had heard before in other people—mostly men, mostly hardened murderers. Instead of being upset about his circumstances, the man was as cool and emotionless as if he had been ordering a burger at a take-out window. Nick suspected that this one had done all of the killing, and the other guys were only along for moral—in this case, immoral— support. "We're already in kind of a jam here."

Nick had been hoping they would somehow forget that they had just killed a tribal police officer, a clinic worker, and Torres's two bodyguards. He hadn't expected them to, but expecting and hoping were different things. "Let's not make things worse, then," he said. "Put those weapons on the floor, and slide them to me, and we can take care of this with no one else getting hurt."

The older man's hand was starting to shake a little. Nerves or the booze starting to wear off, Nick wasn't sure which. But the man's gun was twitching, and he tightened his grip on it, and Nick knew that one more involuntary squeeze could jerk the trigger. "Look," he began. "You need to put that—"

The man let his mouth drop open and took a half-step toward Nick. Nick increased the pressure on his own trigger, ready to shoot but knowing that if he did, then lead would fly, and no one would come out unscathed.

But Torres moved first, swatting out with his left arm. The water pitcher flew off its tray into the older man's side. Startled and soaked, the man spun toward Torres.

Nick moved, charging forward. The gun went off behind him, but he was ducking and jumping, and the slug soared past him into the wall, not far from the doctor in the corner. Nick crashed into the older man, driving him back into the wall. The man's gun went off once, pointed toward the floor, and then Nick caught his right wrist and smashed it against the wall while driving his other arm into the man's throat.

At the same time, the younger guy, the one who had been close to Torres, lifted his gun. "I'm sorry,

Meoqui," he said. He turned the gun toward the man in the back corner, who was probably trying to line up a shot at Nick that wouldn't also threaten his friend. "Meoqui's been good to me. I love Domingo, but Meoqui's not the man you think he is. Drop your gun, Luís, so I don't have to cap your ass."

Nick banged his man's hand into the wall a third time, and this time, his fingers went limp, and the gun hit the linoleum floor with a loud *clank*. The man's face was turning purple, so Nick eased off his throat. Still holding the wrist, he sidestepped and twisted the man's arm up behind his back, forcing him to bend forward at the waist, onto Torres's bed. He whipped handcuffs from his belt, wishing he had several more pairs, and snapped them over the man's wrists.

The guy in the corner tossed his gun to the floor. The doctor picked up the gun the older man had dropped and, holding it gingerly between one finger and his thumb, offered it out to Nick. "I hate these things."

"You're not the only one." Nick turned to Torres's once and maybe future friend. "Can you put yours on the floor and then shove yours and his over here?"

The guy didn't look as if he wanted to relinquish his. But the man in the corner was beaten, done, sagging against the wall, and mopping at his face with a tissue. "Sure," the younger man said, and did what Nick asked.

Nick shoved all of the guns into the corner, behind the doctor, well out of reach of anyone else in the room.

It had all gone down better than he had expected, with only two shots fired and no one hurt. These three men had wanted to kill Torres, but maybe all of the killing they had done to get to that point, combined with the news that Torres hadn't done what they thought, had deflated them, taken the wind out of their revenge-driven sails.

"That's better," Nick said. "Now we can all make nice."

"Thank you," the doctor said. "Can I go now? There are people out there who need my help."

"Go on," Nick said. He covered the doctor's hurried retreat with the gun. "And call the tribal police, okay? Stat."

"What makes you think I was at Domingo's house?" Torres asked when the doctor had left. His voice was strained, his face still pale, but he was alert.

"Thanks for that move with the water pitcher," Nick said. "And granted, it's not much to go on, but somebody with feet your size was in Domingo's backyard that night. You were away from your buddies, off on your own. You and Domingo had some kind of feud going. Two and two doesn't always make four, but in this case . . ."

"Lot of people have feet my size," Torres said. "But yeah, okay, I was there."

"You were?" his friend asked.

"Karina Ochoa called me," Torres said. "She had this big argument with Domingo, and she busted one of the windows in his ride. She was afraid he might have her tracked down and hurt or something. I told her I'd go talk to him, try to settle things down. When I got there, his front door was wide open. I thought there was something wrong about that, and so I tried to look in some of the windows. From the back, I could see him in there, and he was dead."

"And you didn't call the police?" Nick asked. He was stalling for time, hoping the doctor would be able to get through to the tribal cops before these killers realized he had no jurisdiction here. The gun in his hand gave him power, for the moment. But there was nothing official backing that up; he possessed no badge that meant anything here.

"Dude, you don't live in my world. If there's a wolf harassing your sheep, do you call in another wolf?"

"I guess not."

"I didn't know who had done him, but I thought maybe I could use his death to spur some dialogue here on the rez. I went in the house, put one of his napkins over my fingers, dipped it in his blood and wrote on his wall."

"You were the one who wrote 'Quantum.' In blood. So you were really writing 'Blood Quantum,'" Nick said. Torres would have to be charged. He had interfered with an investigation, fled the scene of a murder without reporting it. He'd probably get off with a slap on the wrist, make a movie about the experience.

"That's right. As long as Domingo ran things, he had complete control over the tribal rolls. But with him gone, maybe people would get active, take back the tribe from the special interests running it for their own benefit. That's what I was hoping, anyhow."

"Robert ran it for everybody's benefit," the man with the mole said. "This nation has never been better off."

"If by everybody you mean the rich," Torres said. "Or the people who backed him. Not all the people who've been cut from the rolls these last couple of years."

"They're not real Grey Rock."

"Real enough. You can't just wipe away someone's identity and not expect them to be pissed. Anyway, all I was doing was trying to make people talk," Torres insisted. "Not just go along with the same old thing but to consider all the options when it was time to vote for a new chairman."

"Well, between the murder and your little message, you definitely had an impact," Nick said. "Maybe not the one you wanted, though. There have been fights all over the reservation today, people getting beaten, stabbed, shot. It's like a small-scale civil war out there."

Torres covered his face with his hands. "Dammit, that's not what I wanted at all. You gotta believe that. I just wanted conversation. I wanted to get peoples' minds going, make 'em think, not hate."

"People are thinking," Nick said. He let the words hang there for a moment. Was that a siren in the background? "Trouble is, some people are acting, too."

"I never meant anybody to get hurt," Torres said.

"Sometimes what we mean to happen and what really happens are two different things," Nick observed. It was one of those things he had always kind of understood but that Gil Grissom had made clear to him during the time he had run the lab. "Actions have consequences, and you can't always predict what they're going to be."

"So what? Don't ever act?"

"That's not what I'm saying. I'm just saying, be prepared to accept the consequences. Because whether you like it or not, they are what they are."

28

THE SUN WAS EDGING toward the west but still high enough that Lake Mead's ripples caught its light and kicked them out in sharp-edged fragments. *You could cut yourself on that light,* Ray thought, and remembered the last time he had been to the lake at sunset, after a stormy day, when the water was still and bloodred.

That had been a happier occasion, the wedding of a former student and one of his student aides, who had met because of Ray. One of the perks of a university career, he knew. Crime-scene investigators tended to encounter people at their worst, not when they were young and enthusiastic and brimming with life's possibilities but when they were witnesses, victims, or suspects. Funny how one career shift—albeit entirely within his area of expertise—could so dramatically alter the circumstances under which he interacted with his fellow human beings.

He went to the ticket window and bought a ticket for the dinner cruise, then went back outside and stood on the dock, watching waves lap against the pilings, listening to the excited chatter and the echoing *clomp* of people crossing the gangplank to the big steamboat. The air smelled like most lakeside docks he had visited, except those in remote wilderness areas, that fishy undertone trying with only limited success to cut through the oily fumes of boat engines.

Ray was waiting for Keith and Ysabel to show up. He had promised to meet them there if he could, and he had made it with time to spare, before the ship even steamed in from its previous cruise, its paddlewheel carving a wide wake behind it. He had watched the passengers crowding the rails on all three decks, sunburned and tired—the littlest kids fussing, teenagers bored or pretending to be, talking or texting on mobile phones as they neared the landing. Children in between those ages, their parents, and lovers young or old, unencumbered by family responsibilities, seemed to have enjoyed the excursion the most. Gulls wheeled around the ship, looking for last-minute handouts, calling out their plaintive cries.

When the ship was cleared of its passenger load, hands swabbed and wiped and polished, working with practiced efficiency, and in no time it was ready for the next batch. Dollies of food and beverages, paper products, and galley supplies were loaded aboard. Then the crew boarded, the rope was taken down, and passengers were invited aboard.

He saw them as they approached from the parking area, Keith walking slowly, one arm out for Ysabel to hang on to. She wore a long skirt and walked with slow, even steps, so from a distance she seemed to be floating toward the landing. Above the skirt, she had on a blouse and a light leather jacket, and in one hand she carried a canvas bag with a wolf's-head design. Keith, ever the college professor, wore tweed, an Oxford shirt, jeans, and loafers. Ysabel saw Ray first and tugged on Keith's arm, an unself-conscious smile lighting her face. Keith's grin was less committed but appeared just as heartfelt.

"You made it!" he shouted as they neared.

"I said I'd try," Ray replied. "I'm glad I got here before she shoved off."

"We have to pick up our tickets," Ysabel said.

"I'll do that," Keith offered. "Why don't you wait here with Ray? You have yours yet, Ray?"

Ray showed his ticket. "I'm good."

Keith turned Ysabel over to him, and she took Ray's arm instead of her husband's. She barely needed the support; either that, or she weighed less than Ray had thought. She had definitely lost a lot of weight, and it was more apparent there than it had been when she was sitting in her bed. She seemed shorter, less solid—less present, somehow. Her gaze flitted about from one spot to another, as if afraid she might miss something.

"I love it here," she said. She swept her free hand across the landscape. Ray looked out at the hills ringing the blue, blue water: dun-colored, brown, gray, and purple at the farther reaches. "It's so different, isn't it? Like someone turned on a hose one day and decided to fill a desert valley with water."

"That's not far from the truth," Ray reminded her. "Except it was the Hoover Dam, not a hose, that filled it."

"I know, it's unnatural. It doesn't belong here. But water is life, and so much of it in one place . . . I can't help it, it just makes me smile."

"That makes me smile," Ray said. "Here comes Keith."

He started toward the gangplank, walking at her pace. Keith joined them. "We're all set," he said. Something about his enthusiasm for the journey seemed forced. "Let's see if we can stake out a good spot on the deck."

The boat launched a few minutes later, the two men flanking Ysabel as it went. Her grip on the deck rail was firm, Ray noted, and Keith kept a hand on her the whole time they stood there watching the landing recede. Ysabel enjoyed the gentle rocking motion of the boat, the smell of the water, the sight of desert mountains slipping into shadow as the sun sank farther.

After a while, they took her inside the main cabin to their reserved table. "I'm going to get a drink," Keith said. "You sit here, Ysabel." She sat down, and he wandered off toward the bar. From her bag she took a partially completed basket and her basket-making kit. She loosened the ties and unrolled it on the red tablecloth, revealing her weaving tools. "Will you sit with me, Ray?" she asked.

"I will, in a few minutes," he said. "First I'm going to talk to Keith a little. But let me ask you— that kit you have? What's that made of?"

"Oh, the tools? They're bone and antler and—"

"No," he interrupted gently. "I mean the outside, the part that holds everything in."

"Oh, that's just plain yucca. It's pretty old, but it does the job."

"Thanks, Ysabel. I'll be right back, okay?"

"I'll be here," she said. Her voice was as cheerful as ever, with the singsong quality that everybody who knew her came to love.

Ray reluctantly left her and started toward the bar. He encountered Keith on his way back to the table, caught his friend's arm, and nodded toward the exit. "Can we go out on deck for a few minutes?" he asked.

Keith tensed, but only for a moment. "Sure," he said. He freed his arm from Ray's grip and went out the hatch. They stood together at the rail, Keith taking occasional sips from his drink. Water *shush*ed past the bow, relatively smooth until it caught the paddlewheel's choppy wake.

"You've had silver hair as long as I've known you," Ray said.

"It turned early. I started going gray while I was still in college."

"To be fair, you spent a long time in college."

Keith laughed once, in a startled way. "I never wanted to get out. I guess I never did. From student to teacher is a short trip. I guess I've never not been part of academia."

"It isn't a bad life," Ray admitted. "Constant intellectual stimulation. A lot of politics to deal with, but what workplace doesn't have that? Decent salary, good benefits."

"Administration is where the real money is,"

Keith said. "You know that. In these days of budget cuts, education cuts, we mere professors are an endangered species. Not only were there no raises the last couple of years, but fully a quarter of the department's faculty was phased out. Class sizes are getting insane, and—" He stopped, took a sip, looked at Ray. "You didn't bring me out here to get the same old lecture about university life, did you?"

"I've seen pictures of you from when you were younger," Ray told him. "Your hair was light then. Blond, right?"

"Yeah, I was always pretty sandy-haired. I guess that's why I didn't mind the gray so much—it didn't seem like that much of a change."

A breeze blew up from nowhere, fluttering Keith's silver hair, wafting the smell of bourbon from his cup.

"And your eyes," Ray said. He waved his hand at the water. "Always been as blue as Lake Mead."

The sun had dropped more, streaking the sky with salmon and orange, colors repeated in the rippling lake surface. "Not so blue right now."

"The lake, no. Your eyes, yes."

"I'm glad you admire my physical perfection so much, Ray," Keith said. "Is this leading up to something?"

"I'm afraid so," Ray said. "Can you take your jacket off? Roll up your shirtsleeves?"

Keith held his gaze. "It's getting a little cool out here. Maybe we should go back in."

"I guess you don't have to. Not yet, anyway. If there's some reason you don't want to show me your arms . . ."

"It's just—"

Ray didn't want his friend to have to lie to him. "You probably had a perfectly good excuse," he said. "Not that murder is ever justified, but if it was self-defense, something like that . . ."

Keith looked away at that, toward the water, and drained the rest of his cup.

"Ysabel's basket-making stuff is wrapped in old yucca," Ray said. "There were bits of yucca on Domingo's body. He scratched his killer, probably in a struggle, and the DNA tells us that the killer was a white man, with blond hair and blue eyes. If you can show me your arms, and they're not scratched, if you can tell me where you were when Domingo died . . . Keith, I'm asking you to let yourself off the hook here. Help me out."

Keith drew back his left sleeve far enough to show Ray deep gouges on the back of his arm, just past the wrist. He shrugged, then released the sleeve again. "He ruined everything." His eyes brimmed, but he wiped them with his right hand and continued. "I'm getting pressure from the university to take early retirement. I could do it, but the deal's not as good as it would have been even last year. Their pension fund took a big hit, and so did my 401(k). Her medical bills. Sharing in proceeds from the new casino would have been a big help, but Domingo screwed us there. Ysabel's dad was Apache, and her grandmother on her mother's side was Pyramid Lake Paiute. Under Domingo's new blood-quantum rules, she's not Grey Rock enough. They cut her off."

"I know. I had one of our people check with

tribal police, and they told me she was dropped. I'm sorry."

Keith snapped, anger replacing sorrow for the moment. "Yeah, me, too. It's like they say, Domingo was trying to keep as much tribal wealth as he could for himself and his friends, no matter what it cost other people."

He paused, turning the empty cup in his hands, then continued. "And think how Ysabel felt about it. All her life, she's considered herself Grey Rock Paiute. To suddenly be told that she's not—it crushed her. I have no doubt it weakened her resistance, allowed the cancer to get a stronger grip. That's why she's in the shape she's in now."

"That's got to be hard," Ray said.

"It's not just about money, Ray," Keith insisted. "Not at all. That cancer? Ysabel started smoking in the first place as a young woman. Back then, the smoke shop was the tribe's main profit center, and most members smoked. It was a way of giving back to the community, if you had anything to give. It turned into a lifetime habit for her. She wanted to support the community, and what she got out of it was lung cancer. She finally quit after she was diagnosed, but it was hard on her. On both of us."

"So, like I said, you had good reason."

"I was so *pissed*. Furious. Domingo kept the smoke shop going all these years, even knowing he was selling poison to his own people and anyone else who stopped in. The other businesses were doing well; he could have afforded to close that one. But he was a greedy sonofabitch, wanted every dime he could scrape together, so he could have his fancy house in the city, the lifestyle, the nightclubs and women and trips.

"I went to see him, to try to reason with him. I thought if I just talked to him, I could make him understand, get him to change his mind, to relax the blood-quantum standards. But he wouldn't listen, wouldn't engage. Just stood there puffing on that big cigar and looking at me like I was an ant, barely worth his notice.

"I got mad. I pushed him. He started to fall—he had been drinking, and he was unsteady on his feet—but he caught my arm, scratching me. When he was upright again, he laughed at me and told me to get the hell out of his house. He turned his back on me, that's how little I meant to him. I lost it then, picked up that heavy lighter, and smashed his skull in. Tried to, anyway. I'm not much of a fighter, I guess."

"It did the trick," Ray said.

"I wiped it off on my shirt and dropped it. I ran out of there so fast . . . I'm surprised I'm not one of those guys who leaves his wallet at the scene, I was so scared."

"You did a good job, all things considered," Ray said. "Didn't leave us much to work with."

"Enough, though."

Ray nodded. "Enough, that's true. We didn't have a match for the DNA, but if you'll submit to a swab test—"

"Is that necessary?" Keith said. "If I confess?"

"Probably not, but it won't hurt to have it for backup. Will you turn yourself in?"

The sun had reached the western hills, and the

water had turned into a pool of glittering, molten gold. "When we get back," Keith said. "Right now, I'd like to go be with my wife. She wanted to watch the sunset."

"That'll be fine, Keith. You watch the sunset with Ysabel."

Ray went with him, and together they took Ysabel's arms and walked her out on deck. The sway of the ship affected her balance, and she stumbled a couple of times, but the two men kept her going and held her at the rail. The sun stained her beaming face with gold.

"It's so pretty," Ysabel said.

"It sure is," Keith agreed. But he was not watching the sunset, he was watching his wife, seeing the delight and wonder she took in the simplest of natural processes, the way the earth's rotation made its surface slide past the sun, bringing darkness to the day and then brightness to the dark.

Ray Langston watched them both, old friends, still desperately in love with each other after so many years. He knew this would not be Ysabel's last sunset, but it would probably be her last sunset on the water, certainly her last one with her husband at her side, and Ray held on to her warm, fragile hand, cupping it against the ship's rail, and he wanted to live in that moment, skimming across the lake's surface with Ysabel and Keith, for as long as he could.

About the Author

JEFF MARIOTTE IS THE award-winning author of more than forty novels, including *CSI: Crime Scene Investigation—Brass in Pocket*; *CSI: Miami—Right to Die*; horror trilogy *Missing White Girl*, *River Runs Red*, and *Cold Black Hearts* (all as Jeffrey J. Mariotte); *The Slab*; the *Witch Season* teen horror quartet; and others, as well as dozens of comic books, notably *Desperadoes* and *Zombie Cop*. He's a co-owner of the specialty bookstore Mysterious Galaxy in San Diego and lives in southeastern Arizona on the Flying M Ranch. For more information, please visit www.jeffmariotte.com.

Not sure what to read next?

Visit Pocket Books online at

www.simonandschuster.com

Reading suggestions for
you and your reading group
New release news
Author appearances
Online chats with your favorite writers
Special offers
Order books online
And much, much more!